THIS BOOK
BELONGS TO

VINTAGE CLASSICS

Janusz Korczak

KING MATT THE FIRST

Translated by Richard Lourie

VINTAGE BOOKS
London

3 5 7 9 10 8 6 4

Vintage
20 Vauxhall Bridge Road,
London SW1V 2SA

Vintage Children's Classics is part of the Penguin Random House group of companies whose addresses can be found at global.penguinrandomhouse.com.

First published in Great Britain in 2005 by Vintage
First published in Polish with the title *Król Maciuś Pierwszy* in 1923
Published in the US by Farrar, Straus and Giroux, Inc. in 1986

www.vintage-books.co.uk

A CIP catalogue record for this book is available from the British Library

ISBN 9781784870539

Typeset in India by Thomson Digital Pvt Ltd, Noida, Delhi

Printed and bound by Clays Ltd, Elcograf S.p.A.

Penguin Random House is committed to a sustainable future for our business, our readers and our planet. This book is made from Forest Stewardship Council® certified paper.

WHEN I was the little boy you see in the photograph, I wanted to do all the things that are in this book. But I forgot to, and now I'm old. I no longer have the time or the strength to go to war or travel to the land of the cannibals. I have included this photograph because it's important what I looked like when I truly wanted to be a king, and not when I was writing about King Matt. I think it's better to show pictures of what kings, travelers, and writers looked like before they grew up, or grew old, because otherwise it might seem that they knew everything from the start and were never young themselves. And then children will think they can't be statesmen, travelers, and writers, which wouldn't be true.

Grownups should not read my novel, because some of the chapters are not very nice. They'll misunderstand them and make fun of them. But if they really want to read my book, they should give it a try. After all, you can't tell grownups not to do something—they won't listen to you, and you can't make them obey.

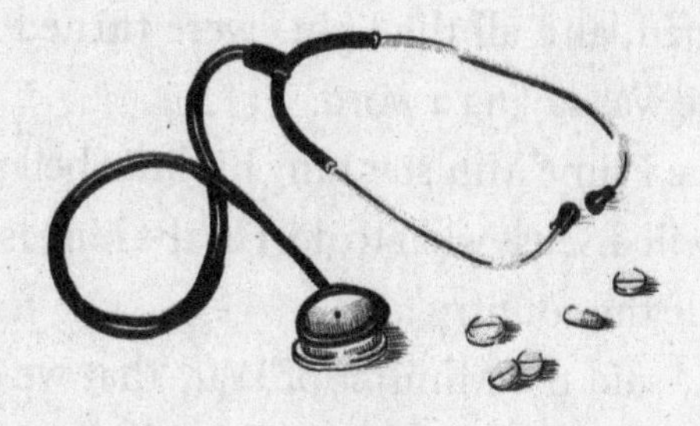

AND so this is what happened.

The doctor said it would be very bad if the king didn't get better in three days.

The doctor's exact words were: 'The king is seriously ill and it'll be bad if he doesn't get better in three days.'

Everyone was very worried. The Prime Minister put on his glasses and asked: 'So then what will happen if the king doesn't get better?'

The doctor did not wish to give a definite answer, but everyone understood that the king would die.

The Prime Minister was very worried and called a meeting of the ministers.

The ministers assembled in the great hall and sat on comfortable armchairs at a long table. On the table in front of each minister was a sheet of paper and two pencils: one was an ordinary pencil, but the other was blue on one end and red on the other. There was also a little bell in front of the Prime Minister.

The ministers had locked the door, so they wouldn't be disturbed, and all the lights were turned on now. But no one was saying a word.

Then the Prime Minister rang his little bell and said: 'Now we will discuss what to do. For the king is sick and cannot rule the country.'

'I think,' said the Minister of War, 'that we ought to summon the doctor. And he will have to state clearly whether he can cure the king or not.'

All the ministers were very afraid of the Minister of War because he always carried a saber and a revolver, and so they did what he said.

'Fine, let's summon the doctor.'

They sent for the doctor at once, but the doctor could not come, because he was just putting twenty-four cupping glasses on the king.

'Too bad, we'll have to wait,' said the Prime Minister. 'But meanwhile let's discuss what to do if the king dies.'

'I know,' replied the Minister of Justice. 'According to the law, after the death of the king his eldest son inherits the throne. That's why he is called the successor to the throne. If the king dies, his eldest son takes the throne.'

'But the king has only one son.'

'That's all he needs.'

'All right, but the king's son is little Matt. What kind of king could he be?'

'Matt doesn't even know how to write yet.'

'That is a problem,' replied the Minister of Justice. 'Nothing like this has ever happened before in our country, but in Spain, Belgium, and other countries, kings have died and left little sons. And that little child had to be the king.'

'Yes, yes,' said the Minister of Mail and Telegraphs, 'I have seen postage stamps with pictures of little kings like that.'

'But, gentlemen,' said the Minister of Education, 'how is it possible to have a king who does not know how to write or count, who does not know geography or grammar?'

'Here's what I think,' said the Minister of Finance. 'How will the king be able to do his accounts, how will he be able to figure out how much new money is to be printed if he doesn't know his multiplication tables?'

'Gentlemen,' said the Minister of War, 'the worst thing of all is that none of my men will be afraid of such a little child. How will he deal with soldiers and generals?'

'It's not only a question of the military,' said the Minister of Internal Affairs. 'No one will be afraid of such a little child. We'll have constant strikes. I won't be able to guarantee public order if you make Matt king.'

'I don't know what will happen,' said the Minister of Justice, red with anger, 'but I know one thing—the law says that after the death of a king his son inherits his throne.'

'But Matt is too little,' shouted all the ministers.

A terrible quarrel would have surely broken out, but at that moment the door opened and a foreign ambassador walked into the hall.

It may seem strange that a foreign ambassador walked in on a meeting of the ministers when the door was locked. So I must tell you that when they sent for the doctor they forgot to lock the door. Later on, some people even said that it was treason, that the Minister of Justice had left the door open on purpose because he knew that the ambassador was coming.

'Good evening,' said the ambassador. 'I am here on behalf of my king to demand that your next king be Matt the First. And if he's not, there will be war.'

The Prime Minister was very afraid, but he pretended that he was not in the least concerned. With the blue end of his pencil, he wrote 'Fine, let there be war' on a sheet of paper and handed it to the foreign ambassador.

The ambassador took the paper, bowed, and said: 'All right, I will inform my government of this.'

At that moment the doctor came into the hall, and all the ministers began pleading with him to save the king, for there could be trouble or even war if the king died.

'I have already given the king all the medicines I know. I have put cupping glasses on him, and there is nothing more I can do. But we could call in other doctors.'

The ministers took his advice. They summoned famous doctors to come consult on how to save the king and sent all the royal automobiles to the city to fetch them. Then they asked the royal cook for dinner because they were very hungry. They hadn't known the meeting would last so long and so they didn't eat dinner at home.

The cook set out the silver dishes and poured the best wine into the carafes, because he wanted to stay at court even after the death of the old king.

And so the ministers began eating and drinking and even began to grow merry. Meanwhile, the doctors had gathered in the hall.

'I think,' said one old doctor with a beard, 'that we must operate on the king.'

'But I think,' said another doctor, 'that we should put hot compresses on the king and he should gargle.'

'The king must take powders,' said a famous professor.

'Drops would be better, of course,' said another doctor.

Each of the doctors had brought a thick book with him and each pointed out that his book said to treat the illness a different way.

It was already late and the ministers very much wanted to go to sleep, but they had to wait to hear what all the doctors said. There was so much noise in the royal palace that the little heir to the throne, Matt, the king's son, had already woken up twice.

I ought to see what's going on, thought Matt. He rose from his bed, dressed quickly, and went out to the corridor.

He stood outside the door to the dining room, not to eavesdrop, but because in the royal palace the door handles were so high that little Matt couldn't open the door himself.

'The king has good wine,' shouted the Minister of Finance. 'Let's have some more, gentlemen. If Matt becomes king, he won't need the wine, because children aren't allowed to drink wine.'

'Children aren't allowed to smoke cigars, either. So we can each take a few cigars home,' cried the Minister of Commerce loudly.

'And if there's a war, gentlemen, I assure you that nothing will be left of this palace, because Matt won't be able to defend us.'

Everyone started laughing and shouting: 'Let's drink to the health of our defender, the great king, Matt the First.'

Matt didn't really understand what they were saying; he knew that his father was sick and that the ministers often held meetings, but why were they laughing at him, Matt, and why were they calling him the king, and what kind of war could there be? Matt did not understand at all.

A little sleepy and a little scared, he went farther down the hall, and outside the door to the council room, he heard another conversation.

'And I'm telling you that the king will die. You can give him all the powders and pills you want, nothing will do any good.'

'I bet my life the king won't last a week.'

Matt stopped listening. He dashed down the corridor, past two other royal chambers, until, breathless, he reached the king's bedroom.

The king was lying in bed. It was hard for him to breathe, and he was very pale. The same good doctor who treated Matt when he was sick was sitting by the king's bed.

'Daddy, Daddy,' cried Matt with tears in his eyes. 'I don't want you to die.'

The king opened his eyes and looked sadly at his son.

'I don't want to die either,' said the king softly. 'I don't want to leave you all alone in the world, my son.'

The doctor put Matt on his lap, and no one said any more.

Matt remembered that he had already done something like this once before. That time it was his father who had put him on his lap and it was his mother in the bed, pale and breathing with difficulty. Daddy will die like Mommy did, thought Matt.

A terrible sadness tugged at his heart, and he felt a great anger and resentment for the ministers who were laughing at him, Matt, and at his daddy's death.

I'll pay them back when I'm the king, thought Matt.

THERE was a great procession at the king's funeral. Black crepe was wound around the streetlights and all the bells were rung. The band played a funeral march. Cannons and soldiers went by. Special trains brought in flowers from the warmer countries. Everyone was very sad. The newspapers said that the whole nation wept for the loss of its beloved king.

Matt was sitting in his room. He was sad, too, for even though he was to become king, he had lost his father and was now all alone in the world.

Matt thought of his mother. It was she who had given him the name Matt. Although his mother had been the queen, she had not been distant and haughty at all: she played games and blocks with him, told him fairy tales, and explained the pictures in his books to him. Matt had not seen very much of his father, because the king was often with the army or with his guests, entertaining other kings. And he always had meetings and consultations.

But whenever the king could find a free moment for Matt he would play ninepins or go out riding with him down the long tree-lined paths of the royal gardens, the king on a horse, Matt on a pony.

But what would happen now? He'd be stuck with his boring foreign tutor, who always looked as if he had just drunk a glass of vinegar.

And was it really so much fun to be a king? It probably wasn't. If there really was a war, you could at least fight. But what does a king do in peacetime?

Matt was sad when he was alone in his room, and he was sad when he looked through the gate of the royal gardens at the servants' children playing happily in the palace courtyard.

Seven boys were playing war, their usual game. They were always led into attack, drilled, and commanded by a small and very jolly boy. His name was Felek. That's what the other boys called him.

Many times Matt had wanted to call him over and even talk with him a little through the gate, but he did not know if he was allowed to and what would happen if he did, and he did not know what to say to start a conversation.

Meanwhile, proclamations had been posted on every wall saying that Matt was now the king, that he sent greetings to his subjects, and that all the ministers would stay on and help the young king in his work.

All the stores were full of photographs of Matt. Matt on a pony. Matt in a sailor suit. Matt in an army uniform. Matt reviewing the troops. The theaters showed newsreels about Matt. All the illustrated magazines in the country and abroad were full of Matt.

To tell the truth, everyone loved Matt. The old people pitied him because he had lost both parents so young. The boys were happy that now there was a boy whom everyone had to obey; even generals had to stand at attention and grownup soldiers present arms when Matt was there. The girls liked the little king on his handsome pony. But the orphans loved him most of all.

When the queen was still alive, she always sent candy to the orphanages on the holidays. After she died, the king had ordered that the candy continue to be sent. And though Matt knew nothing about it for a long time, candy and toys were being sent in his name to the orphans. Only much later did Matt learn that an entry in the budget could make people very happy without his even knowing about it. Six months after Matt had succeeded to the throne, he chanced to acquire great popularity. That means that everyone was talking about him, not just because he was the king, but because he had done something that people liked.

I'll tell you what happened. For a long time Matt begged his doctor for permission to take walks around the city or at least to be brought once a week to the park where the children played.

'I know the royal gardens are beautiful, but it's boring to be alone even in the most beautiful gardens.'

Finally, the doctor promised, and he applied through the marshal of the court to the palace administration; at the council of ministers, the king's guardian obtained permission for King Matt to take three walks every two weeks.

It might seem strange that it was so difficult for a king to go out for an ordinary walk. But the marshal of the court only agreed out of gratitude to the doctor, who had recently cured him when he had eaten a fish that was none too fresh. And the palace administration only gave its agreement because it hoped that now it would be given money to build a new stable, and the Minister of Internal Affairs (who was head of the police) only agreed to get even with the Minister of Finance. Every time the king went out for a walk, the police would receive three thousand ducats and the sanitation division a barrel of eau de cologne and a thousand gold ducats. Before King Matt left for his walk, two hundred workers and one hundred cleaning women would clean the park thoroughly. Before each walk, they would rake the park and repaint the benches. All the paths would be sprinkled with eau de cologne, the dust wiped from the trees and leaves. The doctors made sure that everything was clean and free of dust, because dirt and dust are unhealthy. The police made sure that there were no bad boys in the park who would throw stones, punch and shove, fight and shout, when the king was out walking.

King Matt had a wonderful time. He wore regular clothes so no one would recognize him. And it never even entered anyone's mind that the king would come to an ordinary park. King Matt walked all around the park twice and then asked if he could sit on a bench by the square where the children were playing. He had only been sitting there a little while when a girl came up to him and asked: 'Do you want to play?'

She took Matt by the hand and they started playing together. The girls were singing songs and going around in a circle. Then, while they were waiting to start a new game, the girl started talking to Matt.

'Do you have a little sister?'

'No, I don't.'

'What does your daddy do?'

'My daddy is dead. He was the king.'

The little girl must have thought Matt was joking, because she broke out laughing and said: 'If my father was the king, he would have to buy me a doll that reached up to the ceiling.'

She told him that her father was a captain in the fire department, that her name was Irenka, and that she loved the firemen, who sometimes let her ride on their horses.

Matt would gladly have stayed longer, but he only had permission to stay until forty-three seconds past four-twenty.

Matt waited impatiently for his next walk, but it rained, and they were too worried about his health to let him go out.

The next time, Matt was playing ring-around-the-rosy with the girls when a few boys walked over and one of them shouted: 'Look, a boy playing with girls.'

They started laughing.

King Matt noticed that he really was the only boy playing ring-around-the-rosy.

'You should come play with us,' said the boy.

Matt looked at him closely. It was Felek! The same boy Matt had wanted to meet so long ago.

Felek looked closely at Matt, then shouted at the top of his lungs: 'This kid looks just like King Matt!'

Matt felt terribly embarrassed because everyone had started looking at him. He began running away as fast as possible toward the adjutant who had brought him to the park and who was also disguised in regular clothes. But, either from haste or from embarrassment, he fell and scraped his knee.

At the council of ministers it was decided that the king could no longer be allowed to go out for walks. They would do everything the king wanted, but he could not go to regular parks because there were naughty children who would pick fights with him and laugh at him. The council of ministers could not allow the king to be laughed at; it was an insult to his royal honor.

Matt was very upset, and for a long time he thought about his two days of happy games in the park. Then he remembered Irenka's wish: She wants a doll that reaches up to the ceiling.

Soon that was all he could think about.

I am the king, after all, and I have the right to give orders. And everybody has to obey them. I'm learning to read and write just like all the other children. The multiplication tables are the same for kings as they are for everyone else. Why be a king if you can't do what you want?

So Matt rebelled, and during an audience he demanded very loudly that the Prime Minister buy the biggest doll in the world and send it to Irenka.

'Your Royal Highness deigns to remark ...' the Prime Minister began to say.

Matt knew what would happen—that unbearable person would talk for a long time and say a lot of things that didn't mean anything at all, and in the end, nothing would happen with the doll. Then Matt remembered how once that same minister had started to explain something to his father in the very same way. The king had stamped his foot and said, 'That is my absolute wish.'

And so Matt stamped his foot just like his father used to, and said very loudly: 'Mr Prime Minister, that is my absolute wish.'

The Prime Minister looked at Matt in surprise, then wrote something down in his notebook and mumbled: 'I will present your Royal Highness's wish at the next council of ministers.'

No one knows what was said at the next council of ministers, because their meeting was held behind closed doors. However, they did decide to buy the doll, and the Minister of Commerce ran around to all the stores for two days inspecting all the largest dolls. But a doll as big as the one Matt wanted was nowhere to be found. Then the Minister of Commerce summoned all the doll manufacturers to a meeting, and one manufacturer agreed to make the doll in four weeks at his factory, for a very high price. And when the doll was ready, he displayed it in the window of his store with a sign: *The Purveyor to His Royal Majesty's Court has produced this doll for Irenka, the daughter of a captain in the fire department.*

Right away, the newspapers began featuring photographs of the fire department fighting fires, as well as pictures of Irenka and her doll. People said that King Matt loved to watch the fire trucks go by and to watch fires. Someone wrote a letter to the newspaper saying he was ready to burn his own house down if their beloved King Matt loved fires. Many girls wrote letters to King Matt saying they, too, wanted dolls badly, but the secretary of the court never read those letters to Matt, because he had been strictly forbidden to by the Prime Minister, who was very angry about the entire affair.

Crowds of people stood in front of the store for three days looking at the king's present, and it was only on the fourth day that, by order of the prefect of police, the doll was taken off display so that the crowds would not block the trolleys and cars. For a long time, people talked about the doll and about Matt, who had given Irenka such a beautiful present.

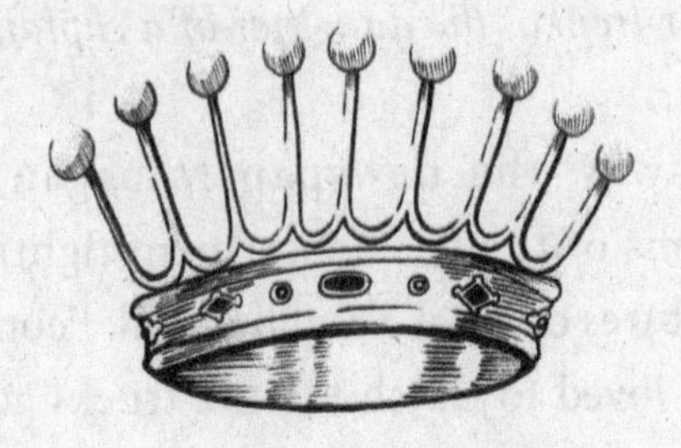

EVERY day, Matt would get up at seven o'clock in the morning, wash and dress, shine his boots himself, and make his bed. This custom had been established by his great-grandfather, the valiant king Paul the Conqueror. After washing and getting dressed, Matt would drink a glass of cod-liver oil and sit down to breakfast, which could not last more than sixteen minutes thirty-five seconds. That was because Matt's grandfather, the good king Julius the Virtuous, had always taken that amount of time for his breakfast. Then Matt would go to the throne room, which was always very cold, and receive the ministers. There was no heat in the throne room because Matt's great-grandmother, the wise Anna the Pious, had nearly been asphyxiated by a faulty stove when she was a little girl, and in memory of her lucky escape, she had decreed that the throne room not be heated for five hundred years.

Matt would sit on the throne, his teeth chattering from the cold, while his ministers told him what was happening throughout the country. This was very unpleasant because, for some reason, the news was always bad.

The Minister of Foreign Affairs would tell him who was angry at them and who wanted to be their friend. Usually, Matt could not make heads or tails of any of it.

The Minister of War would list how many fortresses were damaged, how many cannons were out of commission, and how many soldiers were sick.

The Minister of the Railroads would say that they had to buy new locomotives.

The Minister of Education would complain that the children weren't studying, were late to school, that the boys were sneaking out to smoke cigarettes and were also tearing pages out of their workbooks. The girls were calling each other names and arguing, the boys were fighting, throwing stones, and breaking windows.

The Minister of Finance was always angry that there was no money, and he didn't want to buy new cannons or new machines because they cost too much.

Then Matt would go to the royal gardens. For an hour he could run and play, but it wasn't very much fun to play alone.

So he was always ready enough to go back to his lessons. Matt was a good student, because he knew it was hard to be a king if you didn't know anything. He quickly learned how to sign his name with a grand flourish. He had to learn French and all sorts of other languages so he could speak with other kings when he went to visit them.

Matt would have been a better and more willing student if he had been able to ask all the questions that came to his mind.

For example, Matt had been wondering for a long time whether it was possible to invent a magnifying glass which could make gunpowder catch on fire from far away. If Matt could invent a magnifying glass like that, he would declare war against all the other kings, and on the day before the battle, he would blow up all his enemies' ammunition. He would win the war because he would be the only one left with ammunition, and then he would be a great king, even though he was so little. But his teacher shrugged his shoulders, made a face, and wouldn't even answer Matt's question.

Another time, Matt asked if it was possible for a father to pass his intelligence on to his son when he was dying.

Matt's father, Stephen the Wise, had been very intelligent. And now here was Matt sitting on the same throne and wearing the same crown, but he had to learn everything from the very beginning. Would he ever know as much as his father had? But what if, along with the crown and the throne, he could have inherited his great-grandfather Paul the Conqueror's courage, his great-grandmother's piety, and all his father's knowledge?

But that question did not meet with a friendly response, either.

For a long time, a very long time, Matt wondered if it was possible to get a hold of a Cap of Invisibility. Wouldn't that be dandy—Matt would put on the cap, go wherever he liked, and no one would be able to see him. He would say that he had a headache. They would let him spend the day in bed so he could rest. Then at night he would put on the Cap of Invisibility and go into town, walk around his capital, look in all the store windows, and go to the theater.

Matt had been to the theater only once, to attend a gala performance when his mother and father were still alive; he remembered practically nothing about it because he had been very little then, but he knew that it had been very beautiful.

If Matt had a Cap of Invisibility, he would go from the gardens to the palace courtyard and make friends with

Felek. And he could go everywhere in the palace, to the kitchen for a peek at how the food was prepared, to the stables to see the horses, and to all the other buildings he was not allowed to enter.

It may seem strange that so many things were forbidden to the king. And so I must explain that there is a very strict etiquette at royal courts. Etiquette tells how kings have always acted. A new king cannot do otherwise without losing his honor and without everyone ceasing to fear and respect him for not respecting his father the king, or his grandfather the king, or his great-grandfather the king. If the king wants to do something differently, then he must inquire of the master of ceremonies, who watches over court etiquette and knows what kings have always done.

I have already said that King Matt's breakfast lasted sixteen minutes thirty-five seconds because that's how long it took his grandfather and that there was no heat in the throne room because that's what his great-grandmother, who had died a long time ago, had wanted and there was no way of asking her if the room could be heated now.

Once in a while a king could make little changes, but then there would be long meetings, as there had been when Matt wanted to take walks. And it was no fun to ask for something and then have to wait and wait.

King Matt was in a worse position than other kings because etiquette had been established for grownup kings and Matt was a child. And so there had to be certain little changes. Instead of tasty wine, Matt had to drink two glasses of cod-liver oil, which he didn't like at all, and instead of reading the newspapers, he only looked at the pictures, because he still could not read very well.

Everything would have been different if Matt had had his father the king's intelligence and a magical Cap of Invisibility. Then he would have really been a king, but now, as things stood, he often thought it might have been better to have been born an ordinary boy, to go to school, tear pages from his workbooks, and throw stones. One day Matt got an idea: when he learned how to write, he would write a letter to Felek, and maybe Felek would write back, and that would be almost like talking with Felek.

From that time on, King Matt worked hard at learning to write. He wrote for days on end, copying stories and poems from books. He would even have given up his time in the royal gardens and would have just written from morning to night, but this he could not do, because etiquette and court ceremony demanded that the king go straight from the throne to the gardens. And there were twenty footmen ready to open the doors which led from the hall to the gardens. If Matt had not gone to the gardens, those twenty footmen would not have had any work to do and would have been very bored.

Some people might say that opening doors is not really work. But those would be people who do not know court etiquette. So I must explain that these footmen had already worked five whole hours. Every morning they took a cold bath, then the barber combed out their hair and trimmed their mustaches and beards. Their clothes had to be extra-clean, without even a single speck of dust on them, because once, three hundred years ago, when Henryk the Hasty had been king, a flea had hopped from one of his footmen onto the king's scepter. This had cost that careless man his head, and the marshal of the court barely escaped death. From then on, the overseer checked the cleanliness of the footmen, who bathed, dressed, and groomed themselves and then had to stand waiting in the corridor from seven minutes past eleven until seventeen past one to be inspected by the master of ceremonies himself. They had to be very careful, because the punishment for a button not buttoned was six years in prison; for poorly combed hair, four years at hard labor; for an insufficiently nimble bow, two months in jail on bread and water.

Matt knew a little about all these complications. He was worried that they might start rummaging through history and find some king who never left the palace. Then, of course, they'd say that this applied to Matt, too. And so why learn to write if he couldn't pass Felek his letters through the garden gate?

Matt was intelligent and he had a strong will. He said: 'I will write my first letter to Felek in a month.'

And, in spite of all the obstacles, he worked so hard that after one month, with no help from anyone, he wrote a letter to Felek.

> DEAR FELEK, For a long time I have been watching you have fun playing in the courtyard. I want to play, too, a lot. But I am the king and so I can't. But I like you very much. Write and tell me about yourself because I want to get to know you. If your father is a soldier, maybe they will let you come to the royal gardens sometime.
>
> KING MATT

Matt's heart was beating hard when he called to Felek through the gate and gave him the letter.

And his heart was beating very hard the next day when Felek handed him his reply through the gate.

> DEAR KING, My dad is the platoon leader of the palace guard and he is a soldier and I would very

much like to come to the royal gardens. I am loyal to you, my King, and ready to follow you through fire and water to defend you to the last drop of my blood. Anytime you need help, just whistle and I will come at your first call.

FELEK

Matt put this letter at the very bottom of his drawer, under his books, and then gave all his energy to teaching himself to whistle. Matt was careful. He did not want to give himself away. If he demanded that Felek be allowed in the gardens, that would immediately cause lots of meetings. They would ask why, how he had learned Felek's name, and how they had made friends. Felek was just a platoon leader's son. If only his father were a lieutenant …

'I better wait a while,' decided Matt. 'In the meantime, I'll teach myself to whistle.'

It's not easy to learn to whistle if there's no one to show you how. But Matt had a strong will and he worked at it.

He started whistling.

One day, Matt whistled to test out his ability and see if he really could. How astonished he was when, a moment later, Felek was standing in front of him, stiff as a ramrod.

'How did you get in here?'

'I climbed over the fence.'

There were thick raspberry bushes in the royal gardens. So King Matt and his friend hid there to talk things over.

'LISTEN, Felek, I am a very unhappy king. Since I learned to write, I have been signing all the papers, and they say that I am ruling the whole country. But all I'm really doing is what they tell me to. And they tell me to do the most boring things, and they forbid me to do anything that's fun.'

'And who is forbidding Your Royal Highness and giving you orders?'

'The ministers,' said Matt. 'When my dad was alive, I did what he told me, too.'

'Of course, back then you were a royal prince and the heir to the throne and your dad was the Royal Highness, the king. But now—'

'But now it's a hundred times worse. There's no end to these ministers.'

'Are they soldiers or civilians?'

'Only one is a soldier, the Minister of War.'

'And the rest are civilians?'

'I don't know what "civilians" means.'

'Civilians are people who don't wear uniforms or carry swords.'

'Yes, they're civilians.'

Felek put a handful of raspberries into his mouth and began thinking seriously. Then he asked slowly and with a certain hesitation: 'Are there any cherry trees in the royal gardens?'

This question surprised Matt, but he trusted Felek, and so he told him that there were cherry trees and pear trees in the royal gardens. Matt promised that he would give Felek cherries and pears through the fence whenever he wanted them.

'All right, then,' said Felek, 'we can't see each other too often, because they might find out about it. We'll pretend we don't know each other at all. We'll write each other letters. We can hide the letters on the fence and use cherries to mark the spot. When Your Royal Highness leaves me a secret message, you can whistle and I'll come get it.'

'And when you write back to me, you whistle, too,' said Matt happily.

'A person doesn't whistle at a king,' said Felek passionately. 'I'll make a sound like a cuckoo. I'll stand far away and make the sound.'

'Good,' agreed King Matt. 'But when will you come again?'

Felek thought for a long minute and finally answered: 'I can't come here without permission. My father is a platoon leader and he has very sharp eyes. My father won't even let me go near the fence around the royal gardens. He told me many times: "Felek, I'm warning you, don't get any ideas about climbing up the cherry tree in the royal gardens. And remember, as your own born father I'm telling you—if you're ever caught over there, I'll skin you alive." '

Matt was worried.

That would be terrible. It had been so hard to find a friend. And it would be Matt's fault if his friend was skinned alive. No, that really was too dangerous.

'And so how will you get back home now?' asked Matt anxiously.

'Your Royal Highness should go first. I'll figure something out.'

Realizing that this was good advice, Matt slipped out of the bushes. Just in time, too, for Matt's foreign tutor, worried by the king's absence, was searching for him in the royal gardens.

Now Matt and Felek were a team, even though they were separated by the fence. Matt sighed frequently in the presence of the doctor, who weighed and measured him every week to be sure that the little king was growing. Matt complained of loneliness and once even mentioned to the Minister of War that he would very much like to learn military drill.

'Perhaps, Mr Minister, you know some platoon leader who would be able to give me lessons.'

'Of course, Your Royal Majesty's desire to acquire military knowledge is praiseworthy. But why does it have to be a platoon leader?'

'Perhaps it could even be the son of a platoon leader,' said Matt in good spirits.

The Minister of War frowned and made a note of the king's desire.

Matt sighed; he already knew what the answer would be: 'I will bring Your Royal Majesty's request to the very next session of the council of ministers.'

Nothing would come of it; they'd probably send him some old general.

Things, however, took a different turn.

At the next session of the council of ministers, there was only one subject under discussion.

Three countries had declared war on King Matt all at the same time.

War!

Matt was the great-grandson of the brave Paul the Conqueror, and his blood was up.

Oh, if only he had a magnifying glass to blow up the enemy's ammunition from far away, and a Cap of Invisibility, too.

Matt waited until evening; the next day, he waited until noon. Not a word. It had been Felek who told him about the war. Before then, Felek had only made the cuckoo sound three times, but that day he must have made it a hundred times. Matt realized Felek's letter would contain unusual news. But he had no idea just how unusual that news would be. There had not been a war for a long time, because Stephen the Wise had somehow been able to get along with his neighbors. And so, even though there was no great friendship among them, they always managed to avoid war.

It was clear that Matt's enemies were taking advantage of his youth and inexperience. But this only strengthened Matt's resolve to show them they were mistaken, and that, though he was little, King Matt was able to defend his country.

Felek's letter read: 'Three countries have declared war on Your Royal Highness. My father always promised that if war broke out he would get drunk from joy. I am waiting for that to happen because we must see each other.'

Matt was waiting, too: he thought he would be summoned to a special session of the council that very day, and that now he, Matt, the lawful king, would begin to run the government. There was a meeting that night, but Matt was not summoned.

The next day his foreign tutor gave him his lesson as usual.

Matt knew court etiquette and was aware that the king was not allowed to pout, be stubborn, or get angry, and especially at a moment like this, he did not want to lower his dignity or royal honor in any way. He just kept frowning and furrowing his brow, and when, during his lesson, he'd glance in the mirror, he'd think to himself: I almost look like Henryk the Hasty.

Matt was waiting for the hour of the audience.

But when the master of ceremonies announced that the audience had been called off, Matt, calm but very pale, said decisively: 'It is my absolute wish that the Minister of War be summoned to the throne room.'

Matt said the word 'war' with such emphasis that the master of ceremonies realized at once that Matt already knew about everything.

'The Minister of War is in a meeting.'

'Then I will attend that meeting, too,' responded King Matt, and started to leave the room.

'If Your Royal Highness would deign to wait just one moment. Have pity on me, Your Royal Highness. I am not allowed to bring you there. I will be held responsible if I do.'

And the old man began weeping out loud.

Matt felt sorry for the old man, who knew precisely what the king could do and what would not be suitable. They had often sat together on long evenings by the fireplace, and Matt had enjoyed hearing the old man's interesting stories about his father the king and his mother the queen, court etiquette, foreign balls, gala performances in the theaters, and the military maneuvers in which the king had taken part.

Matt's conscience was bothering him. Writing letters to the son of a platoon leader had been a great blunder, and stealing cherries and raspberries for Felek tormented Matt most of all. In fact, the gardens belonged to him; in fact, he had not stolen the fruit for himself but as a gift; but he had done it sneakily, and who knows, perhaps he had stained the knightly honor of his great ancestors.

Besides, it was no accident that Matt was the great-grandson of saintly Anna the Pious. Matt had a good heart, and he had been moved by the old man's tears. Then Matt almost committed another mistake by letting his feelings show, but he caught himself in time and only furrowed his brow deeply and said coldly: 'I will wait ten minutes.'

The master of ceremonies ran out. The royal palace was in an uproar.

'How did Matt find out?' cried the Minister of Internal Affairs, who was quite vexed.

'What does that snot-nosed kid have in mind?' the Prime Minister shouted in excitement.

Finally, the Minister of Justice called him to order: 'Mr Prime Minister, the law forbids the king to be spoken of in such fashion at official meetings. In private you can say what you like, but this is an official meeting. And you are only free to think, not to speak.'

'This meeting's been interrupted,' said the Prime Minister, who was frightened and trying to defend himself.

'There has to be an announcement that you are breaking off the meeting. You, however, did not do that.'

'Please excuse me, I forgot.'

The Minister of War glanced at his watch. 'Gentlemen, the king has given us ten minutes. Four minutes have passed, so let's not quarrel ... I am a soldier and I must obey the king's express command.'

The poor Prime Minister had reason to be afraid; on the table was the sheet of paper on which he had clearly written with the blue end of his pencil: 'Fine, let there be war.'

Back then, it had been easy to pretend to be brave, but now it would be hard to answer for those careless words. Besides, what would he say when the king asked why he had written that? And of course it had all started when they didn't want to elect Matt after the death of the old king.

All the ministers knew this and were even a little glad about it. They did not like the Prime Minister, because he gave too many orders and acted too important.

No one wanted to offer advice. All they cared about was avoiding the king's wrath for hiding such important information.

'One minute left,' said the Minister of War. He buttoned his jacket, straightened his medals, twirled his mustache, took his revolver from the table, and a minute later was standing at attention in front of the king.

'So it's war?' asked Matt softly.

'It is, Your Highness.'

That was a load off Matt's shoulders, for I must add that Matt, too, had spent those ten minutes in great anxiety, wondering if Felek had only made the whole thing up. Maybe it wasn't true? Maybe Felek had just been joking?

Those two little words, 'It is,' relieved all Matt's doubts. It was war, and a big one, too. The ministers had wanted to deal with it without him, but Matt had discovered their secret.

An hour later the newsboys were yelling at the top of their lungs: 'Extra, extra, read all about it! Crisis in the ministry!'

That meant the ministers were quarreling.

THE crisis was that the Prime Minister pretended that his feelings were hurt and that he no longer wished to be in charge. The Minister of the Railroads said that he could not transport the troops because he didn't have enough locomotives. The Minister of Education said that naturally the teachers would go to war, and more windows would be broken and desks destroyed in the schools, and he was resigning.

A special conference was called for four o'clock.

Taking advantage of the confusion, King Matt slipped out to the royal gardens and whistled nervously. Then he whistled again, but Felek did not appear.

'Who can I talk to at such an important time?' Matt felt a great responsibility weighing on him, but he could not figure out what to do.

Suddenly Matt remembered that anything of importance should begin with a prayer. That was what his good mother had taught him.

Striding decisively, Matt went deep into the gardens where no one could see him, and then he prayed fervently to God.

'I am a little boy,' prayed Matt. 'I cannot manage without your help, oh God. It was your will that I wear the royal crown, and so now help me, because I am in great trouble.'

Matt prayed to God for help for a long time, hot tears running down his face. Even a king is not ashamed to let God see him cry.

King Matt prayed and cried, cried and prayed, until he fell asleep leaning against the stump of a birch tree.

Matt dreamed that his father was sitting on the throne and all the ministers were standing at attention in front of him. Suddenly the throne room's great clock, which had last been wound four hundred years ago, began to chime like a church bell. The master of ceremonies walked into the hall, followed by twenty servants carrying a golden coffin. Then Matt's father, the king, stepped down from the throne and lay down in the coffin. The master of ceremonies took the crown from Matt's father's head and placed it on Matt's. Matt was about to sit on the throne, but then he saw that his father was sitting there again. But now his father wore no crown and seemed somehow strange, as if he were only a ghost. His father said: 'Matt, the master of ceremonies has given you my crown, and now I will give you my intelligence.'

The ghost of the king took off his own head and held it in his hands. Matt's heart was pounding as he wondered what would happen next.

But then somebody shook Matt awake. 'Your Royal Majesty, it's nearly four o'clock.'

Matt rose from the grass where he had been sleeping a moment before, and for some reason he felt more refreshed than after a night in bed. At that moment Matt had no idea that soon he would be spending many a night on the grass under the open sky and that he would be saying farewell to his royal bed for a long time.

And, just as he had dreamed, the master of ceremonies handed Matt the crown. At four o'clock on the dot, Matt rang his bell in the conference hall and said: 'Gentlemen, let us begin our discussion.'

'I request the floor,' said the Prime Minister.

The Prime Minister began a long speech. He said he could not work any more and he was sad to leave the king alone at such a difficult hour, but he had to, because he was sick.

Four other ministers said the same thing.

Matt was not the least bit scared, and just answered: 'That's all fine and dandy, but it's war now and no time to be sick or tired. You, Mr Prime Minister, know everything, and so you must stay on. We'll talk again when I win the war.'

'But the newspapers said that I'm resigning.'

'So now they'll write you're staying on, for that is my—request.'

King Matt had been about to say: 'That is my order.' But the ghost of his father seemed to advise Matt that it was better to say 'request' than 'order' at such an important moment.

'Gentlemen, we must defend the country, we must defend our honor.'

'And so Your Royal Highness will fight all three countries?' asked the Minister of War.

'And would you have me beg them for peace, Mr Minister? I am the great-grandson of Paul the Conqueror. God will help us.'

The ministers liked Matt's speech, and the Prime Minister was satisfied because the king had requested him to stay. He played stubborn for a little while, but then he agreed.

The meeting went on for a long time, and when it was over, the newsboys on the street shouted: 'Extra, extra, read all about it! Crisis resolved.'

That meant that the ministers had made friends again.

Matt was a little surprised that nothing had yet been said about his making a speech to the people and riding a white horse at the head of his valiant troops. The ministers and the newspapers talked about railroads, money, bread, boots for the soldiers, and about hay, oats, oxen, and pigs, as if they weren't talking about a war but about something completely different.

Matt had heard a lot about the ancient wars, but he knew nothing about modern war. He was only just now learning what bread and boots had to do with war.

Matt's anxiety grew when the next day his foreign tutor appeared for his lesson at the usual time.

The lesson was scarcely half over when Matt was summoned to the throne room.

'The ambassadors from the countries which have declared war on us are here and ready to leave.'

'But where are they going?' asked Matt.

'Back to their homes.'

It seemed strange to Matt that they were allowed to leave in peace; he would have preferred to have them impaled or tortured.

'But why have they come here?'

'To bid farewell to Your Royal Highness.'

'Should I act offended?' asked Matt softly, so that the servants would not hear, for he was afraid they would lose respect for him.

'No, Your Royal Highness should bid them farewell politely. Besides, they'll do the same.'

The ambassadors were neither tied up nor bound in chains hand and foot.

'We have come to say farewell to Your Royal Highness. We are very sorry that there has to be a war. We did everything to prevent a war. A pity we failed. We are forced to return the medals we received from Your Royal Highness, for it would not be fitting for us to wear the medals of a country with which our governments are at war.'

The master of ceremonies took back their medals.

'We thank Your Royal Highness for our stay in your beautiful capital, of which we bear the fondest memories. And we have no doubt that this petty quarrel will soon be over and our old cordial friendship will once again unite our governments.'

Matt rose and responded in a calm voice: 'Tell your governments that I am truly happy that war has broken out. I will try to defeat you as quickly as possible, but my conditions for peace will be lenient. That is what my ancestors always did.'

One of the ambassadors smiled slightly and then bowed deeply. The master of ceremonies struck the floor three times with his silver staff and said: 'The audience is now concluded.'

King Matt's words were quoted by all the magazines and were greatly admired.

An enormous crowd formed in front of the palace and wouldn't stop cheering.

Three days passed. King Matt waited in vain to be summoned. For, after all, what kind of a war is it if the king is studying grammar, doing dictations, and solving arithmetic problems?

Matt was walking around the gardens in low spirits when he heard the signal, the cuckoo sound.

A second later, he was holding a precious letter from Felek.

> I'm leaving for the front. My father got drunk just as he promised he would and instead of going to bed he began packing his bags. He couldn't find his canteen, jackknife, and cartridge belt. He thought I took them so he gave me a good thrashing. I'm running away from home tonight or tomorrow night. I was at the railroad station. The soldiers promised to take me with them. If Your Royal

Highness wishes to give me any orders, I will be waiting at seven o'clock. The best dried kielbasa, a canteen full of vodka, and a little tobacco would come in handy for the road.

It's a sad thing when a king has to sneak out of his palace like a pickpocket. It's even worse when his sneaking out is preceded by an equally secret expedition to the royal pantry, where a bottle of cognac, a tin of caviar, and a large piece of salmon all disappear at the same time.

But it's war! thought Matt. And in war you're even allowed to kill people.

Matt was very sad, but Felek was beaming.

'Cognac is even better than vodka. It doesn't matter that there's no tobacco.' Felek had dried some leaves and later on he would receive the usual soldier's tobacco ration. 'Things are going pretty good. The only problem is that the commander in chief is a boob.'

'A boob! Who is he?'

Matt's blood was boiling. The ministers had deceived him again. It turned out that the army had been on the march for a week, and two not very successful battles had already occurred. The troops were being led by an old general; even Felek's father had once called him a dolt, though of course he had been a little tipsy at the time. Matt might be allowed to observe a battle, but only from a safe distance. Matt would study, and the people would defend him. When the wounded men were brought to the capital, Matt would visit them in the hospital, and when a general was killed, Matt would attend his funeral.

'How could that be? So it's not me who'll defend the people, but the people who'll defend me. What does that say about my royal honor, and what will Irenka think?' Was King Matt only a king who studied grammar and gave girls dolls which reached to the ceiling? No, and if that's what the ministers thought, then they didn't know Matt.

Felek was just eating a handful of raspberries when Matt grabbed him by the arm and said: 'Felek!'

'Yes, Your Royal Highness?'

'Do you want to be my friend?'

'Yes, Your Royal Highness.'

'Felek, what I'm going to tell you now is a secret. Remember that, so you won't betray me.'

'Yes, Your Royal Highness.'

'I'm going to run away with you to the front tonight.'

'Yes, Your Royal Highness.'

'Let's kiss each other.'

'Yes, Your Royal Highness.'

'And don't call me Your Royal Highness.'

'Yes, Your Royal Highness.'

'I'm not the king any more. Now I'm—wait a second, what should my name be? Now I'm Tomek. I'll call you Felek and you'll call me Tomek.'

'Yes,' said Felek, hastily swallowing a bite of salmon.

The plan was that Matt would be by the gate at two o'clock that morning.

'Listen, Tomek, if there's going to be two of us, we'll need more provisions.'

'All right,' answered Matt reluctantly, for it seemed indecent to think about your stomach at such an important moment.

The foreign tutor frowned when he noticed the streak of raspberry juice on Matt's cheek left from his exchange of kisses with Felek, but did not say anything about it because the war had the palace in such confusion.

It was unheard of—someone had stolen a bottle of cognac, some excellent caviar, and half a salmon from the royal pantry; that was special food which the foreign teacher had ordered ahead of time when he had taken on his post as tutor to the heir to the throne while the old king was still alive. And now, for the first time, he was to be deprived of his special foods. Even though the cook would replace the loss, new requisitions had to be made out and stamped by the palace administration and signed by the palace steward; and another bottle of cognac could only be supplied by order of the master of the wine cellar. And if a person was insistent and wanted permission before the investigation of the theft was completed, he could forget about his cognac for a month or more.

The tutor angrily poured the king a glass of cod-liver oil and, five seconds earlier than the regulations required, he gave Matt a sign that it was time for recess.

'IS that you, Tomek?'

'It's me. Is that you, Felek?'

'Yes. Damn it, it's dark, we might run into the guards.'

It cost Matt a lot of trouble to shinny up the tree, climb from the tree to the fence, and then hop from the fence to the ground.

'He may be the king, but he's as clumsy as an old woman,' Felek muttered to himself as Matt tumbled down from the fence, which was quite high. Then the voice of the palace sentry rang out: 'Who's there?'

'Don't answer,' whispered Felek.

When he fell to the ground, Matt had scraped the skin on his right hand and arm—his first wound in the war.

Then they slipped across the road to a ditch where, crawling on their bellies, they passed right under the guards' noses and reached a path lined with poplar trees which led to the barracks. They went around the right side of the barracks, guided by a large searchlight on the barracks' prison; then they crossed a little bridge and went straight down a smooth road to the central military railroad station.

What Matt now saw reminded him of the stories he had heard about the old days. Yes, it was a military camp. Wherever your eye looked, there were campfires burning, with soldiers sitting around them making tea, talking, or sleeping.

Matt was not surprised that Felek knew the quickest way to the station. Matt thought that all boys who weren't kings were like that. But Felek was an exceptionally able boy. It would not have been the least bit difficult to get lost in that crowd where every hour another train arrived with troops, where whole divisions were constantly on the move, either pushing toward the tracks or looking for the most comfortable spots to wait. Even Felek stopped a few times, uncertain which way to go. He had been there in the daytime, but a lot had changed since then. A few hours before, there had been cannons there, but now they had been taken away by train. Meanwhile, a field hospital had arrived. Now the military engineers were near the tracks, and there were telegraph operators where they'd been before. Part of the camp was illuminated by large searchlights, and part of it was sunk in darkness. As bad luck would have it, rain had begun to fall, and since the grass had been trampled, their feet started sticking in the mud.

Matt did not dare stop, for fear of losing Felek, but he was out of breath because Felek was running rather than walking, jostling the soldiers passing him and being jostled in return.

'I think it should be right here,' said Felek all of a sudden, looking around with narrowed eyes. Then his glance fell on Matt. 'You didn't bring an overcoat?'

'No, my overcoat is in the royal cloakroom.'

'You didn't bring a knapsack either? Only a chump would set out for war like that,' blurted Felek.

'Or a hero,' answered Matt, his feelings hurt.

Felek bit his tongue: he had forgotten that, no matter what, Matt was still the king. But he had been overcome by anger—because it was raining, because he couldn't find the soldiers who had promised to hide him in their part of the train, and because he had brought Matt along without telling him just what he ought to take for the road. Felek had been beaten by his father, but at least he had a canteen, a jackknife, and a cartridge belt, the basic things any smart soldier took when setting off to war. And Matt—good God!—was wearing patent-leather shoes and a green cravat which, tied in haste and now smeared with mud, made his face look so pitiful that

Felek would have burst out laughing were it not for all the troubling thoughts that had occurred to him a bit too late.

Suddenly, a cry rang out: 'Felek, Felek!' A big boy, another volunteer, wearing a soldier's raincoat and looking almost like a real soldier, walked over to them. 'I've been waiting for you. The other soldiers are in the station already. We'll be boarding in an hour. Quick.'

Oh, no, not quick again! thought King Matt.

'Who's the kid with you?' asked the big boy, pointing at Matt.

'Well, you see, I'll tell you later. It's a long story, I had to take him.'

'Oh, yeah, well I don't believe it. If it hadn't been for me, they wouldn't have taken you. And now you come with this little puppy.'

'Pipe down,' answered Felek angrily. 'Thanks to him, I've got a flask of cognac,' he added in a whisper, so Matt wouldn't hear.

'Give me a taste.'

'We'll see.'

The three volunteers walked for a long time without saying a word. The big boy was angry that Felek did not give him any cognac, Felek was worried that he had gotten himself into big trouble, and Matt was suffering from a case of hurt feelings; if he didn't have to keep his lip buttoned, he would have shown the new boy how kings respond to such insults.

'Listen, Felek,' said the big boy, stopping suddenly. 'If you won't give me any cognac, you're on your own. I got you a place, and you promised to do what I told you to. What's going to happen later on if you start disobeying now?'

A quarrel broke out, and they might even have started fighting if a box of flares hadn't suddenly exploded. Someone had been careless and the box had caught on fire. Two artillery horses bolted in fear, confusion broke out, a howl split the air. After another moment of panic, they saw the big boy lying in a puddle of blood, his leg broken. Felek and Matt didn't know what to do. They were ready for death, blood, and wounds, but later, on the field of battle, not now.

'What's going on here, what are these kids doing here?' grumbled a man who was obviously a doctor, pushing Matt and Felek out of the way. 'I should have known, a volunteer. You should be home sucking a nipple, you little brat,' he muttered, cutting open the big boy's pants leg with a pair of scissors he had taken from his knapsack.

'Let's get out of here, Tomek,' cried Felek suddenly, spotting two field policemen in the distance, walking beside the stretcher the medics were carrying over for the unlucky volunteer.

'But can we leave him behind?' asked Matt timidly.

'What else can we do? He'll go to the hospital. He's no good for war now.'

They hid in the shadow of a tent. A minute later, the area was deserted again, except for the wounded boy's boot and raincoat, which the medics had thrown away when putting him on the stretcher. There was blood on the ground.

'The raincoat'll come in handy,' said Felek. 'I'll give it back to him when he's better,' he added in justification. 'Come on, let's get to the train. We've already lost ten minutes.'

Their division was just being checked in when they elbowed their way onto the platform.

'Do not disperse,' ordered a young lieutenant. 'I will return immediately.'

Felek told the soldiers what had happened to the volunteer and, rather worried, introduced Matt.

What will they say? Matt wondered.

'The lieutenant will throw him off the train at the first station. They've already told him about you and he made a face.'

'Hey, soldier, how old are you?'

'Ten.'

'Nothing'll come of it. He can get on the train if he wants. But the lieutenant'll throw him off, and naturally we'll get an earful.'

'If the lieutenant throws me off the train, I'll walk to the front line,' shouted Matt rebelliously.

Matt was choking on his tears. How could this be? He was the king and should have ridden a white horse down the flower-strewn streets of his capital, leading his legions to war. But instead he had to slip away like a thief in the night to be able to do his sacred duty of defending his country and his subjects. And now he was being pelted with one insult after another!

But the sight of the cognac and salmon quickly changed the expressions on the soldiers' faces.

'Royal cognac, royal salmon,' said the soldiers in praise.

It gave Matt pleasure to watch the soldiers drink his tutor's cognac.

'All right, then, little buddy, have a drink of this, we'll see if you know how to fight.'

At last, Matt was drinking what kings drink.

'Down with tyrants, tutors, and cod-liver oil!' cried Matt.

'Ha-ha, he's a revolutionary,' said a young corporal. 'But who are you calling a tyrant? Not King Matt? Better be careful, sonny. One of those "Down withs" might get you a bullet.'

'King Matt is not a tyrant,' objected Matt excitedly.

'He's still young yet. Nobody knows what he'll grow up to be.'

Matt was about to say something else, but Felek changed the subject skillfully. 'I'll tell you what happened to us. There were three of us on the way here. Then there was this big explosion. I thought it was a bomb from an airplane. But it was only a box of flares. It looked like stars falling out of the sky.'

'What the devil do they need flares for in a war?'

'To light up the road when there are no searchlights.'

'There was heavy artillery over to one side. The horses were frightened and rushed at us. Me and Tomek hopped off to one side, but the other volunteer didn't have time.'

'Was he hurt bad?'

'There was a lot of blood. They took him right to the hospital.'

'That's war,' sighed one of the soldiers. 'Drink a little more cognac. Where is that train?'

Just then, the train pulled up, hissing steam. Noise, confusion, commotion.

'Don't board yet,' cried the lieutenant, running toward them from a distance.

But his voice was lost in the uproar.

The soldiers threw Matt and Felek onto the train like two pieces of luggage. Farther down, two horses who didn't want to board the train were kicking up a fuss. Some of the cars had to be uncoupled; the train started moving, but then there was a loud clank and the train returned to the station.

Someone came into their car holding a lantern and called out the soldiers' names. Then the soldiers grabbed their mess kits and ran for their soup.

Matt saw and heard a little of what was going on, but his eyelids were getting heavy. He was asleep when the train got going at last, and when he awoke, the even beat of the wheels on the rails told him that the train was racing full steam ahead.

I'm on my way, thought King Matt, and fell asleep again.

THE train was made up of thirty freight cars full of soldiers, a few open platform cars carrying trucks and machine guns, and one special car for the officers.

Matt woke up with a slight headache. His leg, back, and eyes hurt. His hands were sticky and dirty, and worst of all, they were unbearably itchy.

'Get up, you dopes, or your soup'll get cold.'

Matt wasn't used to army food and could barely swallow two spoonfuls.

'Eat it, brother, because that's all you're getting,' said Felek to encourage Matt, but it didn't help.

'I have a headache,' said Matt.

'Listen, Tomek, don't even think about getting sick,' whispered Felek in a dejected voice. 'You're allowed to get wounded in a war, but not sick.'

Suddenly, Felek began scratching himself. 'The old guy's right—they're crawling all over us. Are they biting you?'

'Who?' asked Matt.

'Who? The fleas. Or maybe something worse. The old guy told me that in a war bullets are less of a problem than those little buggers.'

Matt knew the story of the unfortunate royal footman, and he wondered what the insect that made the king so angry looked like.

But there was no time to wonder, for suddenly the corporal shouted: 'Hide, the lieutenant's coming!' Matt and Felek were shoved into one corner of the freight car.

There was a uniform check, and it turned out that some of the soldiers lacked proper uniforms, but it also turned out that there was one soldier in their car who was a tailor and loved to work. The tailor was bored, and so he was glad to make army uniforms for the volunteers.

Boots were more of a problem.

'Listen, are you boys really thinking of fighting in the war?'

'That's right.'

'All right, fighting's one thing, but marching is tough, too. Next to his rifle, a soldier's best friend is his boots.

You're a soldier as long as your legs are strong, but when they give out, you're finished. A dead dog. Good for nothing.'

They traveled slowly, chatting away the time. There were long stops. Sometimes they halted at stations for an hour or more. Sometimes they were put on a sidetrack to let more important trains pass. Sometimes they had to return to a station that they had already passed. And sometimes they stopped a mile or so before the station because there was another train on the track.

The soldiers sang songs: somebody was playing an accordion in the next car. At some of the stops, the soldiers even danced. But to Matt and Felek the trip seemed to be taking forever, because they were not allowed out of the car.

'Don't you even poke your head out, or the lieutenant will see you.'

Matt was as tired as if he had been through not one but five great battles. He wanted to go to sleep, but he couldn't because the fleas made him too itchy; he wanted to go out but was not allowed to, and it was stuffy in the freight car.

'You know why we're staying here so long?' said one of the soldiers, cheerful and high-spirited, who had brought the latest news; he was always worming out information and bringing back news.

'Why? The enemy probably blew up a bridge or damaged the tracks.'

'No, our soldiers are keeping a close eye on the bridges.'

'So they must have run out of coal, the railroad couldn't have known they'd need so much extra for all the trains.'

'Did a spy damage the engine?'

'Not that, either. All transports have been stopped because the king's train will be passing by.'

'But who's going to be riding on it? It couldn't be King Matt.'

'What good can he do here?' said one soldier.

'That doesn't matter. He's the king, and that's that,' said another.

'Nowadays, kings don't go to war.'

'Other kings might not, but Matt would,' interrupted Matt, even though Felek was pulling at his sleeve.

'All kings are the same. In the old days, it might have been different.'

'What do we know about the old days? Maybe back then the kings just lay around on their feather beds and now they tell us lies about them since there's nobody around who can remember.'

'Why should they lie?'

'All right, but you tell me how many kings get killed in a war and how many soldiers.'

'That's because there's one king and a lot of soldiers.'

'And maybe you'd like more than one king? We're in enough of a mess with the one we've got.'

Matt could not believe his own ears. He had always been told how much the people loved their king, especially the soldiers. Just the day before, he had thought that he better disguise himself so that people would not crush him with love, but now he saw that if he revealed who he was, it would not cause any enthusiasm at all.

It was strange—the soldiers were going off to fight for a king they didn't like.

Matt was afraid they would say something bad about his father, but they didn't. They even praised him: 'The old king didn't like war. He didn't want to fight himself, and he didn't force his people into war.'

That remark brought some relief to Matt's aching heart.

'And what would a king do in a war, anyway? If he slept on the grass, he'd catch a cold right away. And he wouldn't be able to sleep anyway, because of the fleas. The smell of a soldier's clothes would give him a headache. Kings have delicate skin and delicate noses.'

Matt was fair. He had to admit they were right.

Yesterday he had slept on the grass, and now he really did have a cold. He had a headache, and he itched unbearably all over.

'Well, you guys, forget it, there's nothing we can do about it. Better if we sing some happy songs,' said one soldier.

'There goes the train!' someone shouted.

And in fact the train had begun to pull away quite quickly. Strange as it may seem, every time someone said that it was going to be a long stop, the train would suddenly pull away and the soldiers would have to jump up and run after it. Some of them weren't quick enough and were left behind.

'They're teaching us to stay alert while we're traveling, that's why,' somebody guessed.

They pulled into a large station. It turned out that some great, important person was to go past. There were flags, honor guards, ladies dressed in white, and two children holding beautiful bouquets.

'The Minister of War himself is going to the front in the king's train.'

Again their train was shunted to a sidetrack, where they spent the whole night. Matt slept like a log. Hungry, tired, and sad, Matt didn't have a single dream.

At daybreak, the cars were cleaned and washed. The lieutenant ran around and inspected everything himself.

'We have to hide you boys, because there's going to be an inspection,' said the corporal.

Felek and Matt were taken to a poor little hut that belonged to the switchman. His kindhearted wife liked to take care of soldiers. She was curious, too, and thought the young ones might tell her something.

'Oh, children, children,' she lamented, 'why did this happen to you? Isn't school better than war? Have you been fighting a long time? Where have you been, and where are you going?'

'My dear lady,' said Felek somberly. 'Our father is a platoon leader. And this is what he told us when we were leaving—a good soldier has legs for marching, hands for holding his rifle, eyes for seeing, ears for listening, but he should keep his mouth shut and only open it for a spoonful of soldiers' soup. A soldier defends himself with his rifle. But one loose tongue can destroy a whole unit. Where we've been and where we're going is a military secret. We don't know anything, and we won't say anything.'

Now the good-hearted woman's mouth was hanging wide open. 'Who would ever have expected it—a little boy, but he talks like a grownup. And you're right, too, because many spies have slipped in among the soldiers. They wear uniforms and ask questions and find out everything and then off they go to tell the enemy.'

Out of her great respect for the boys, she not only gave them tea but sausage as well.

Matt found the breakfast very tasty, especially since he had washed up and was now nice and clean.

'The royal train, the royal train,' a cry rang out.

Felek and Matt climbed the ladder that was leaning against the switchman's cow shed.

'Here it comes.'

A beautiful private train with large windows was pulling into the station. A band played the national anthem. The Minister of War was standing by the window.

For an instant, the minister's eyes met Matt's.

Matt shuddered and bent over quickly—what if the minister had recognized him?

The minister could not have recognized Matt, first, because his mind was occupied with very important affairs, and second, because the Prime Minister had not told a soul about Matt's disappearance. The Minister of War had been seen off by Matt, but not the real Matt. But I'll tell you more about that later.

The Minister of Foreign Affairs had ordered the Minister of War to prepare to wage war against one king, but now they had to fight against three.

And so now the Minister of War had plenty on his mind: It's easy to say go and fight when three armies are attacking. But what if you beat one or two and then the third one beats you?

They might have enough soldiers, but they didn't have as many rifles, cannons, or uniforms as they needed. The minister was working on a plan: Attack suddenly, smash the first enemy, take all his supplies and equipment, and only then attack the second.

Matt was a little sad as he watched the troops standing at attention, the minister being given flowers, the band playing on and on.

I should be doing all that, he thought.

But, because he was fair, Matt said to himself: Yes, it's easy to walk around and salute, listen to music, and accept bouquets. But how would I know where to send my armies when I still don't know geography?

For what did Matt really know? He knew a few rivers and mountains and islands, he knew the earth was round and rotated on its axis, but a minister had to know all the fortresses, all the roads, and every forest path. Matt's great-great-grandfather had won a major battle because he hid in the forest when the enemy attacked; he waited until the enemy was deep in the forest, and then, using the forest's paths, he came up from behind and smashed him. The enemy thought he would meet Matt's great-great-grandfather head-on, but he had struck unexpectedly from the rear and driven him into the swamps.

But did Matt know his own forests and swamps?

He was learning them now. If he had stayed in the capital, all he would know was his royal gardens. But now he was seeing his whole kingdom.

The soldiers were right to laugh at Matt. Matt was still a very little and ignorant king. Maybe it was bad that war had broken out so soon. If only he had had another two years, or even one.

NOW I must tell you what happened in the palace when they noticed that the king was gone.

The head footman went into Matt's bedroom in the morning and could not believe his eyes—the window was open, the bed looked slept in, but there was no trace of Matt.

The royal footman was a wise man: he locked the bedroom, ran to the master of ceremonies, who was still sleeping, woke him up, and whispered in his ear: 'Your lordship, the king is missing.'

In utmost secrecy, the master of ceremonies telephoned the Prime Minister.

Ten minutes had not passed before three cars squealed up to the palace. The Prime Minister stepped from one car, the Minister of Internal Affairs from another, and the prefect of police from the third.

'They've kidnapped the king.'

It was perfectly clear. The enemy must have thought it a good idea to kidnap the king. Matt's army would find out there was no king, lose their will to fight, and then the enemy could take the capital without a battle.

'Who knows the king is missing?'

'No one knows.'

'That's good.'

'We have to find out whether Matt was just kidnapped, or killed, too. I am asking you, Mr Prefect of Police, to look into this. I want an answer in an hour.'

There was a pond in the royal gardens. Maybe they had drowned him. A diver's suit was brought from the naval ministry. The helmet of the diver's suit was an iron globe with little windows; air was pumped in through a hose. The prefect of police put the iron globe on his head and went down to the bottom of the pond, where he walked around searching for the king.

The sailors pumped him air from up above. But he did not find Matt.

The doctor and the Minister of Commerce were summoned to the palace. Everything was done in the utmost secrecy, but people had to be told something. After all, the servants knew that something had happened, because the ministers had been running around like lunatics since early that morning. So they said Matt was ill and the doctor had prescribed crayfish for breakfast, which was why the prefect of police had gone down into the pond.

The foreign tutor was told that Matt would have no lessons that day because he was sick in bed. Everyone believed that this was the truth because the doctor was there.

'All right, fine, we don't have to worry today,' said the Minister of Internal Affairs. 'But what will we do tomorrow?'

'I am the Prime Minister and my head isn't just a decoration. You'll see soon enough.'

The Minister of Commerce arrived.

'Do you remember the doll that Matt ordered for Irenka?'

'I remember it perfectly well. The Minister of Finance gave me some trouble because he thought I was spending money foolishly.'

'So, go right this minute to that same doll manufacturer and tell him that by tomorrow a doll must be made from Matt's photograph so that no one, absolutely no one, can tell the difference; so that everyone will think they're seeing the real Matt, in the flesh.'

The prefect of police came out of the pond, and to avoid suspicion, he brought out ten crayfish, which were immediately dispatched with much ado to the royal kitchen.

The doctor dictated his prescription:

Rx. Crayfish soup
Disp. 10 crayfish dosis una
Sig: A spoonful every two hours

When the doll manufacturer, who now called himself Purveyor to the King, heard that the Minister of Commerce himself was awaiting him in his office, he rubbed his hands with joy.

King Matt must have come up with a new idea.

The manufacturer needed business because, since the outbreak of the war, practically all the fathers and uncles had gone away, and no one was buying dolls.

'Mr Manufacturer, this is a rush order. The doll must be ready tomorrow.'

'That will be difficult. Almost all my workers have gone off to war, and I only have women and sick people working for me now. Besides, I am up to my ears in work because practically every father who's going off to war is buying his children dolls so they won't cry and won't miss him and be naughty.'

The manufacturer was lying through his teeth. None of his workers had gone off to war, because he paid them so poorly that they were all weak from hunger and unfit for military service. And he had no orders whatsoever.

He only said that because he wanted a lot of money for the doll.

His eyes lit up when he learned that it was to be a doll of Matt.

'Just think,' said the minister, 'the king has to appear in public often. He will have to go around the city in an open car so people won't think he's hiding because he's afraid of the war. But why should a young child ride around so much? It might rain and he could catch cold. It's especially important now to safeguard the king's health.'

The manufacturer was too smart not to guess that something was being covered up. 'So it has to be ready tomorrow?'

'Tomorrow, by nine o'clock.'

The manufacturer picked his pen up and pretended to make some calculations—after all, Matt would have to be made of the best porcelain, and he didn't know if he had enough. Yes, it was going to be extremely expensive. And the workers would have to be paid extra for keeping it a secret. And his best doll-making machine had just broken down, and it would cost a pretty penny to fix! And, of course, he would have to delay all his other orders. He spent a long, long time going over his figures.

'Mr Minister of Commerce, if there were no war—and I do understand that right now great sums of money are being spent on troops and cannons—if there were no war, you would have to pay twice this amount. But, with things as they are, the best price I can give you is ...'

The minister groaned when he heard the price.

'But that's highway robbery.'

'You are insulting a national industry, Mr Minister.'

The Minister of Commerce telephoned the Prime Minister because he was afraid to spend so much money himself. But, afraid that somebody might be listening in on their conversation, he said 'cannon' instead of 'doll.'

'They're asking an awful lot of money for that cannon.'

The Prime Minister guessed immediately what was going on, and so he said: 'Don't haggle, just tell them that the cannon must have a pull string so it can salute.'

The telephone operator, who was listening in, was very surprised to hear about newfangled cannons that were supposed to salute.

The manufacturer began to grow very excited: 'That's not part of the order. That's not our business. You should talk to the royal mechanic or a watchmaker. I'm a serious manufacturer, not a magician. Matt will open and close his eyes, but he won't salute, and that's that. And I won't lower my price by a single cent.'

But finally the doll maker agreed to make a doll that saluted.

Hungry and tired, the Minister of Commerce returned home.

Hungry and tired, the prefect of police returned to the palace. 'Now I know how they kidnapped Matt. I have examined everything thoroughly. This is what happened: while Matt was sleeping, they threw a sack over his head and carried him out to the royal gardens near the raspberry bushes. I saw some trampled spots there. Matt passed out. So they gave him raspberries and cherries to bring him back to consciousness. There were six cherry stones there. When they were lifting Matt over the fence, he must have struggled, because there are traces of blue blood on one of the trees. Then they seated him on a cow so people would think he was a peasant boy.'

The prefect had seen the hoofprints himself. The trail had led to the forest, where a sack was found. Then, of course, they had hidden Matt somewhere, but the prefect did not know where, because he had not had enough time, and he could not question anyone, because that would mean betraying the secret. They should keep an eye on the foreign tutor, who was acting very suspiciously—he kept asking if he could see Matt. And then the prefect of police showed the Prime Minister the cherry pits and the sack.

The Prime Minister placed the sack and the pits in a chest, padlocked it, and sealed it with red wax on which he wrote in Latin: *Corpus delicti.*

It is customary to write in Latin when a person doesn't know what he's talking about and doesn't want others to find out.

The next day the Minister of War made a farewell report to Matt the doll, who did not say a word but only saluted.

On every street corner, announcements were posted that the people of the capital could go calmly about their business, because King Matt would be touring the city every day in an open car.

THE Minister of War's plan succeeded brilliantly. Matt's three enemies had thought that Matt's troops would attack all of them at once. But meanwhile the Minister of War had assembled his soldiers in one place, attacked one of the enemy armies with all his might, and smashed it to pieces. He took a great deal of booty and distributed rifles, boots, and knapsacks to those who were short of them.

Matt arrived at the front just when the spoils were being divvied up.

'What kind of soldiers might these two be?' marveled the chief of supply, who issued food and clothing to the soldiers.

'We're the same as all the rest,' said Felek. 'Just a little smaller.'

Everyone chose a pair of boots, a revolver, a rifle, and a knapsack. Now Felek regretted that he had taken his father's cartridge belt and jackknife—he could have been spared the beating if he'd only waited. But who can ever foresee the surprises that war brings?

It was no accident that people said the commander in chief was none too smart. Instead of collecting the booty, pulling back, and digging in, he continued on the attack. He took another five or six more cities, none of which he needed. And only then did he order ramparts to be built. But it was too late, for by then the other two enemy armies were on their way to help the one he had defeated.

That's what people said later on, but at the time Matt's division knew nothing, because in war everything is kept a secret.

An order came to go here, then there, an order came to do this, then that. Go where you're told, do what you're told, ask no questions, and keep your lips sealed.

Matt liked everything he saw in the foreign town they had conquered. People slept in large, comfortable rooms; though they did sleep on the floor, it was still better than a cramped hut or an open field.

Matt was longing for his first taste of battle, because so far he had seen and heard many interesting things, but he had not seen any real war. What a shame that they had been too late.

They only stayed in that city one night; the next day they were on their way again.

'Halt. Dig in.'

Matt knew absolutely nothing about modern war. He thought that soldiers just fought, stole horses, and rode onward, trampling the foe. But he never dreamed that soldiers dug trenches, drove in posts connected by barbed wire in front of those trenches, and then sat in those trenches for weeks on end. He was in no great hurry to set to work. He was tired and weak, all his bones ached; it was a king's task to fight, but digging trenches—anybody could do that better than Matt.

But orders kept coming to hurry because the enemy was approaching. Now cannon fire could be heard in the distance.

A colonel of the engineers came by in an automobile; he shouted, clenched his fists, and threatened to shoot anyone who didn't do a good job of digging.

'There's going to be a battle tomorrow and they're doing nothing! And why are those two here?' he shouted in a fury, pointing at Matt and Felek. 'Who are these two giants?'

All the colonel's anger might have come down on the two volunteers, but fortunately, just then, an enemy airplane began to roar overhead.

The colonel looked up at the sky through his binoculars, then turned quickly, got into his car, and slipped away. And then—boom, boom, boom—three bombs fell one after the other. No one was actually wounded, but everyone scrambled into the trenches for cover.

Bombs and cannon shells are constructed to contain lots of shot and shrapnel. When a shell explodes, everything inside it flies out in all directions, wounding and killing. But if you're down low, in a trench, everything flies over your head. That is, unless the shell falls right into the trench. But that's rare, because cannon shells travel over a mile and it is difficult to aim them precisely from such a distance.

Those three bombs taught Matt a great deal. He no longer sulked and rebelled, he just picked up his shovel and worked so long that his exhausted hands dropped all by themselves, and overcome with fatigue, he fell deeply asleep, right at the bottom of the trench. The soldiers did not wake him up even though they kept working all through the night by the light of the flares. And with the dawn came the enemy's first attack.

Four enemy horsemen appeared. They had been sent out to look for Matt's army, which then opened fire on them; one fell dead from his horse, the other three fled.

'The battle will start any minute,' shouted the lieutenant.

'Stay in your trenches, show your rifles, and wait,' sounded the order.

And indeed, the enemy's troops appeared a minute later. Both sides opened fire. But Matt's division was concealed in trenches and the enemy was crossing an open field. The enemy's bullets flew, buzzing and whistling, over the trenches and over the heads of the crouching soldiers. But the enemy was suffering heavy losses.

Now Matt understood that the colonel of the engineers had been right to be angry yesterday, and that in war every order must be carried out quickly and without any unnecessary gab.

Yes, a civilian could do what he wanted, hesitate, and waste time talking, but a soldier knows only one thing: an order must be carried out without delay, every command fulfilled to the letter.

If it's forward, it's forward; if it's back, it's back; and if it's dig, then you dig.

The battle lasted an entire day. Finally, the enemy realized that there was no point in continuing, because they were just losing men, and they could not even reach Matt's army because of the barbed wire. So they retreated and began digging in. But it's one thing to dig trenches calmly when no one's hampering you and quite another when bullets are flying from all sides.

That night, flares were set off every few minutes and lit up the sky, and though there was less shooting because the weary soldiers took turns shooting and sleeping, the battle still continued.

'We're holding the line,' said the soldiers, pleased.

'We're holding the line,' the lieutenant telephoned headquarters, for they had already laid the telephone wire.

And so they were very surprised and angry the next day when they received the order to retreat.

'What for? We dug trenches, we held the enemy, we can defend ourselves.'

Had Matt been the lieutenant, he probably would not have obeyed the order. It must be some mistake. The colonel should come and see how well they were fighting. So many enemy soldiers dead, but they had only one man wounded: he'd been firing from the trench when an enemy bullet grazed his hand. How could the colonel see what was happening from so far away?

There was a moment when Matt had been ready to shout at the top of his lungs: 'I am King Matt. Let the colonel give all the orders he wants, but I will not allow a retreat. A king is higher than a colonel.'

He did not do it, because he wasn't sure they would believe him, and then they might make fun of him.

And for the second time Matt was to learn that in war you don't have to understand, but you do have to obey orders without delay.

They were sorry to abandon those trenches dug with such sweat and effort and to leave behind part of their supplies—their bread, sugar, and lard. They were sorry to return through the village where the villagers asked in surprise: 'Why are you running away?'

While they were on the march, a messenger on horseback overtook them with a note saying to march quickly and take no rest.

'Take no rest'—that's easy to say, but after two nights without sleep, one night digging trenches, the other fighting, it was impossible to march without resting. Besides, the soldiers had little food and were angry and upset, too. Soldiers like to advance, they get their second wind and speed up, but they don't like to retreat and quickly run out of strength.

They marched and they marched and then they marched some more, when suddenly shots began ringing out left and right.

'I see,' cried the lieutenant. 'We advanced too far, and the enemy has come up from the rear. The colonel was right when he ordered us to flee quickly. They would have taken us prisoner.'

‘A fine kettle of fish,’ said one soldier. ‘Now we’ll have to fight our way out.’

And that was no easy thing. Now the enemy was in the trenches, firing from both sides, and it was Matt’s army’s turn to take flight.

NOW Matt understood why boots, oats for the horses, and bread were discussed by the council of ministers.

If it weren't for the bread in their knapsacks, they would have died of hunger, because for three days they had nothing but that bread to eat. They took turns sleeping, only a couple of hours each. And by now their feet were in such bad shape that blood was gurgling in their boots.

Quiet as shadows, they fled through the forests; the lieutenant kept looking at his map to find ravines or thickets for them to hide in.

Enemy riders kept appearing again and again to see where Matt's army was fleeing and tell the pursuit party which direction to take.

Matt looked entirely different now. He became thin as a rail, stooped, smaller than ever. Many soldiers threw down their rifles, but Matt held on to his, his fingers numb.

How could a person live through so much in just a few days!

Daddy, Daddy, thought Matt. Oh, how hard it is to be a king and fight a war. It was easy to say: 'Why should we be afraid—I will conquer you just like my mighty great-grandfather.' Easier said than done. Oh, what a foolhardy child I was. All I thought about was leaving the capital on a white horse while the people threw flowers at me. But I wasn't thinking how many people would be killed.

Many people had been felled by bullets, and perhaps Matt had been spared only because he was so small.

How happy they were when they finally met up with their own troops and saw trenches already dug.

Now they're going to laugh at us, thought Matt.

But he was soon to learn that even in war there is justice.

The fresh troops occupied the trenches and opened fire, while they marched another three miles to the rear and halted in a little town.

The colonel of the engineers met them there on the square and now was not the least bit angry. He only said, 'All right, lads, now do you understand what trenches are for?'

Did they ever!

Then the soldiers who had thrown away their rifles were separated from those who had returned with theirs. And to those who still had their rifles, the general made the following speech: 'Hats off to you for keeping your weapons. True heroes show themselves in adversity.'

'Look,' cried the colonel of the engineers. 'Those two little boys are here. Long live the two brave brothers!'

While resting up, the soldiers heard that the Minister of War had had a terrible argument with the commander in chief and only King Matt had been able to get them to make up.

Matt knew nothing about the doll that had replaced him in the capital and was very surprised to hear people talking about him as if he were still home. Matt was still a very young king and did not know what diplomacy was. Diplomacy means lying all the time, so that your enemy has no idea of what you're really doing.

And so they rested up, ate their fill, and settled down in the trenches. Then the trench war began. This means that both Matt's army and the enemy fired at each other but the bullets flew over their heads because all the soldiers were below ground level.

Every once in a while, when they were bored, one side would attack and move a mile or so forward, and the other a mile or so back.

The soldiers walked back and forth in the trenches, played music, sang, played cards, while Matt tried diligently to keep studying.

Matt was given lessons by the lieutenant, who was bored, too. In the morning he would post a guard to watch out for an enemy attack, then he would telephone headquarters that everything was in order and have nothing to do for the whole rest of the day.

And so he was glad to teach little Matt. Matt would sit in the trench and study geography, the skylarks would be singing, and once in a great while a shot would ring out. It was quiet and pleasant.

Then suddenly it sounded like dogs were whining.

It was starting!

Small field artillery.

And then—boom, boom. A big cannon was barking.

It was starting. The rifles were croaking like frogs, bullets were whistling, hissing, droning. And it never let up for a second.

It went on like that for half an hour, or an hour. Sometimes a cannon shell would land in a trench and explode, killing a couple of people and crippling a few more. But the men, already used to it, did not make much of their lost friends.

Too bad, he was a good guy.

Some would say 'May he rest in peace,' and make the sign of the cross.

The doctor would examine the wounded and send them to the field hospital at night.

That's war.

Even Matt did not escape being wounded. He was sad to go to the hospital. It was such a little wound, the bone hadn't even been touched. But the doctor insisted and sent him off to the hospital.

Matt was in a bed for the first time in four months. What happiness! A mattress, a pillow, a quilt, a white sheet, a linen towel, a white table by the bed, a cup, a plate, a spoon a little like those he had used in the royal palace.

His wound healed quickly, the nurses and the doctors were very nice, and Matt would have felt perfectly fine if it weren't for one awful problem.

'Come see how much he looks like King Matt,' a colonel's wife said one time.

'It's true! He looked familiar somehow, but I couldn't place him.'

They wanted to take his picture for the newspaper.

Not for anything in the world.

They told him that King Matt might send him a medal when he came across a picture of such a young soldier in the newspaper, but Matt refused.

'You can send your father the picture, you silly boy, it will make him happy.'

'No, no, no!'

Matt had had enough of having his picture taken, and besides, he was really scared. What if they recognized him and figured everything out?

'Leave him alone if he doesn't want to. Maybe he's right. It might even hurt King Matt's feelings and make him sad that he's driving around the capital while other boys his own age are being wounded.'

Who the hell was this Matt they were always talking about?

Matt used the word 'hell' because he had forgotten about etiquette and had picked up soldiers' slang.

It's a good thing I ran away, and that I'm at the front now, thought King Matt.

They did not want to release Matt from the hospital. They even pleaded with him to stay—they'd give him extra tea in the morning, he could help out in the kitchen.

Matt grew indignant. 'No, not for anything in the world!'

Let that make-believe Matt in the capital hand out presents in hospitals and go to officers' funerals. He, the real King Matt, was going back to the trenches.

Which is just what he did.

'WHERE'S Felek?'

'He's gone.'

Felek had grown bored with life in the trenches. He was a restless boy and could never sit still for a minute. And he had to sit in the trenches for weeks on end and never stick out his head, because the enemy would start shooting at once and the lieutenant would grow furious.

'Get your stupid head down!' the lieutenant would shout. 'They'll shoot the fool, and then we'll have to take him to the hospital to be bandaged up. We've got enough trouble as it is, without you causing any more.'

The first two times the lieutenant only shouted, but the third time he sent Felek to the brig for three days with nothing but bread and water for food.

And here's what happened.

The troops in the enemy's trenches were being relieved. One division was going for a rest, replaced by fresh troops during the night. The trenches were now so close that one side could hear what the other side shouted. And so they began to insult each other.

'Your king is a snot-nose,' shouted the enemy.

'And yours is a good-for-nothing beggar.'

'You're the beggars. You've got holes in your boots.'

'And you're hungry dog-faces. You get slops instead of coffee.'

'Come on over here and try it. When we take your soldiers prisoner, they're hungry as wolves.'

'And yours are ragged and starving.'

'It's a good thing you ran away from us.'

'But we'll beat you in the end.'

'You don't know how to shoot. You couldn't hit the broad side of a barn.'

'And you know how to shoot?'

'Sure we do.'

Felek grew furious, jumped up out of the trench, turned his back to the enemy, bent over, pulled up his coat, and shouted: 'Come on, shoot!'

Four shots rang out, but all four missed.

Great marksmen!

The soldiers laughed, but the lieutenant was very angry and sent Felek to the brig.

The brig was a deep underground pit covered by boards. The soldiers took boards from ruined huts and made walkways, floors, and even little awnings to keep the rain off them down in the trenches.

Felek only spent two days in the wooden underground cell, because the lieutenant forgave him. But even those two days were too much for him.

'I don't want to serve in the infantry.'

'But where will you go?'

'To the air force.'

At that time there was a shortage of gasoline in Matt's kingdom, and that made it difficult for airplanes to carry heavy loads. And so an order went out that only light soldiers were to fly in the airplanes.

'Not guys like you, you big sausage,' said the soldiers, laughing at one fat soldier.

After much discussion, they let Felek go. Because who could be lighter than a twelve-year-old boy? The pilot would fly the plane and Felek would drop the bombs.

Matt was a little sad that Felek was gone, but he was a little happy, too.

Felek was the only one who knew that Matt was the king. True, Matt had asked him to call him Tomek. But it wasn't right for Felek to treat him as an equal. And he didn't even do that. Matt was younger, and so Felek was disrespectful to him. Felek drank vodka and smoked cigarettes, but whenever someone wanted to treat Matt to some, Felek would say right away: 'Don't give him any, he's too little.'

Matt didn't like drinking or smoking, but he wanted to say no, thank you, himself, and not have Felek answer for him.

Felek would always talk the soldiers into taking him on night reconnaissance missions.

'Don't take Tomek. What good'll he be to you?'

Reconnaissance was dangerous and difficult. You had to crawl silently on your belly right up to the enemy's barbed wire and cut it with clippers while keeping an eye out for the enemy's sentries, who would be hiding. Sometimes you had to lie still for an hour, because if they heard the slightest sound, they would set off flares immediately and start shooting at the daredevil reconnaissance team. So the soldiers took pity on Matt because he was smaller and more delicate, and usually took Felek. This made Matt sad.

But now Felek was gone and Matt was able to perform great services for his unit: he brought cartridges to the sentries, he crawled under the barbed wire to the enemy's trenches, twice stealing over to their side in disguise.

Dressed like a shepherd, Matt slipped under the barbed wire, walked more than a mile, then sat down in front of a ruined hut and pretended to cry.

'Why are you crying?' said a soldier who spotted him.

'Why shouldn't I cry? Our hut's been burned down and I can't find my mother.'

The soldiers took Matt to headquarters and gave him coffee. Now Matt felt bad.

These are good people, he thought. They gave him food, they even gave him an old jacket because he was shivering from the cold; Matt had put on some miserable old rags for his disguise. These were good people, and he was deceiving them; he had come there to spy.

Then Matt decided that he wasn't going to tell his own officers anything. Let them say that he was stupid and didn't know anything and not send him out any more. He didn't want to be a spy. But then he was called in to see the staff officer.

'What's your name, little boy?'

'My name is Tomek.'

'All right, listen, Tomek, you can stay with our soldiers if you want, until your mother comes back. You'll get clothes, a mess kit, soup, and money. But you have to slip over to the other side and see where their ammunition dump is.'

'What's an ammunition dump?' asked Matt, pretending not to know.

So they took him to theirs and showed him the cannon-balls, bombs, grenades, gunpowder, and cartridges.

'Understand now?'

'Now I do.'

'All right, then, go over there and see where they keep theirs, then come back here and tell us.'

'All right,' agreed Matt.

The enemy officer was so pleased with himself that he gave Matt a whole bar of chocolate.

So that's how it works, thought Matt with relief. Well, if I have to be a spy, I'd rather do it for our side.

They brought him back to the trenches, then sent him on his way. So that no one would hear him moving, they shot a few times, but only up in the air.

On his way back, Matt felt happy and started nibbling on the chocolate, crawling on his belly some of the time and on his hands and knees the rest of the time.

Then, suddenly—bang, bang—his own men were shooting at him. They could even have killed him, because they had caught sight of someone stealing up on them and didn't know who it was.

'Set off three flares over there,' shouted the lieutenant.

He looked through his binoculars and began to tremble with fear. 'Don't shoot. It looks like Tomek coming back.'

Matt made it the rest of the way without any more problems and then told the lieutenant about everything he had seen. The lieutenant immediately telephoned the artillery. They didn't waste a second and began firing on the enemy's ammunition dump right away. The first twelve shots missed, but there was no question about the thirteenth. The ammunition kept exploding until the whole sky was red, and there was so much smoke you couldn't breathe.

Pandemonium broke out in the enemy's trenches. The lieutenant lifted Matt up in the air and said three times: 'What a kid, what a kid, what a kid!'

Now the soldiers loved him even more, because the division was awarded a whole keg of vodka. And because the enemy now had no powder, they could sleep for three days in peace. And now the lieutenant said they could even leave the trenches for a short while and stretch a little. Meanwhile, the enemy had to stay in their trenches, and they were furious, because they couldn't do anything.

Then everything went back to normal. In the daytime, Matt studied with the lieutenant. Sometimes he would do some digging, because the rain was constantly ruining the trenches, or he might be put on guard duty or even fire at the enemy. Many times Matt thought: How strange. I wanted to invent a magnifying glass to blow up the enemy's ammunition dump. And my wish came true, in a way.

And so fall came to an end and winter began.

Snow fell. They were brought warm clothing. Everything was white and still.

AGAIN Matt was to learn something new and important. After all, the troops couldn't just sit there in the trenches. What would be the point of that? How would the war end that way?

It was quiet in the trenches at the front, but there was an enormous amount of work going on in the capital. Everything had to be prepared so that Matt's army could be concentrated in one spot to strike the enemy full force and break through his lines. Then the enemy would have to flee, because Matt's army would pour through the breach and start firing on them from behind.

After the winter, the lieutenant was promoted to captain, and Matt was given a medal. That made him very happy. And his unit had already been commended twice for valor.

A general came to their trench and read the order: 'In the name of King Matt, I thank this unit for blowing up the enemy's ammunition dump and for valiant service in defense of our country and our countrymen. And now I will give you a secret order—you are to break through the enemy's front line as soon as the weather becomes warm.'

That was a great honor.

Secret preparations were begun at once. Many cannons and shells were brought up to the front. The cavalry came up from the rear and waited.

Every day the soldiers looked up at the sun to see if it was getting any warmer. By now they were terribly bored.

So the poor soldiers kept waiting and working. But they didn't know how much they were going to have to suffer. The captain had invented a new military strategy—rather than send in all their forces on the first day, only part of their troops would attack. They would only pretend to advance but then would retreat right away. The enemy would think that they were weak. Only on the second day would they hurl all their forces into battle and break through the enemy line.

They tried the new plan.

They sent half the troops in to attack. Before the attack, the captain ordered the artillery to fire long and hard at the enemy's barbed wire to rip it apart and make a clear path for the infantry.

'Charge!'

How wonderful to run out of those unbearable wet trenches, run as fast as you could and shout 'Hurrah! Charge! Forward!' Terrified by the sight of them rushing forward with bayonets fixed, the enemy fired only a few shots, and poor ones at that. Matt's troops had already reached the barbed wire, which had been torn apart in places, when the captain gave the signal to withdraw.

But Matt and a few other soldiers either didn't hear the command or had already gone a little too far; they were surrounded by the enemy's sentries and taken prisoner.

'Aha, your men got frightened,' the soldiers teased them. 'They came running full speed ahead, shouting and hollering, but as soon as they got near us, they turned tail and ran. Weren't all that many of you, either.'

The enemy soldiers said those things because they were ashamed of themselves for acting like cowards and even forgetting to shoot.

For a second time, Matt was brought to their headquarters. The first time he had been a military spy in disguise, but now he was a prisoner of war in a soldier's coat.

‘We know you, my little bird,’ shouted the enemy officer, who was enraged. ‘You were here during the winter, and our ammunition dump was blown up because of you. Oho, this time you won’t give us the slip the way you did before. Take the other soldiers to the prisoner-of-war camp, and the little one is to be hanged for spying.’

‘But I’m a soldier!’ cried Matt. ‘You have the right to shoot me, but not to hang me.’

‘You think you’re so smart,’ shouted the officer. ‘Now look what he wants. Maybe now you’re a soldier, but back then you were Tomek and you betrayed us. And we are going to hang you.’

‘You can’t hang me,’ Matt insisted, ‘because I was a soldier then, too. I came here in disguise and I sat down in front of the burned house on purpose.’

‘Enough talk. Put him under heavy guard and take him to prison. Tomorrow a military tribunal will examine the case. If you were really a soldier back then, too, then maybe you’ll win yourself a firing squad, but I’d rather see you hang.’

The next day the field court met.

‘I accuse this boy,’ said the officer to the court, ‘of spying on us last winter, finding out where our ammunition dump was located, and reporting that information to enemy artillery. They fired twelve times without a hit, but the thirteenth shot was a direct hit.'

'Is that true? Do you admit you are guilty?' asked one judge, a gray-haired general.

'It wasn't like that. I didn't sneak around. That officer took me there, showed me everything, and then ordered me to find out where our ammunition dump was and tell him. And he gave me a chocolate bar. Isn't that so?'

The officer turned very red, because he had made a bad mistake—a soldier is never supposed to tell anyone where his ammunition is stored.

'I was a soldier and I was sent out on a reconnaissance mission, but your officer wanted to make a spy out of me,' Matt continued boldly.

'How was I to know?' said the officer, trying to explain himself.

But the general did not allow him to finish. 'Shame on you for being tricked by such a little boy. You made a bad mistake and you will be punished for it. But this little boy cannot be forgiven either. What do you think?' said the general to the lawyer.

The lawyer began defending Matt to the judges. 'Your honors, the defendant, known as Tomek, is not guilty. He was a soldier and he had to obey orders. He went out on reconnaissance because he had been sent out. And

I think he should be sent to the prisoner-of-war camp along with the others.'

This made the general a little happier, because he was feeling sorry for the little boy. But he didn't say anything, because a soldier does not have the right to show he's feeling sorry for anybody, especially an enemy soldier.

And so he only bent over the book that listed all the rules of war, to see what it said about military spies.

'Oh, here it is,' he said finally. 'Civilian spies who betray us for money are to be hanged at once; military spies can be shot at once, but if the lawyer appeals, all the papers must be sent to a higher court and the firing squad put off for a little while.'

'And so I demand,' said the lawyer, 'that this case be sent to a higher court.'

'Fine,' agreed the general and all the other judges.

Matt was taken back to prison.

Matt's prison was just an ordinary country hut. There are no big stone buildings with bars on the windows out on the battlefield. The front is not like a city. And so Matt was escorted back to his hut, but now there were two soldiers with loaded rifles and revolvers by the windows and two more by the door.

Matt sat down and began thinking about his fate. But somehow or other, he still hadn't lost all hope … They were going to hang me, but they didn't. And I might even get out of the firing squad, too. So many bullets have missed me already.

He ate his dinner hungrily. It tasted good because people who are sentenced to death are fed well, that's even a rule. And Matt was being treated like a man sentenced to death.

Matt sat by the window and looked out at the sky, where airplanes were darting past. Are those ours or the enemy's? he wondered.

Then three bombs exploded, all of them right by Matt's prison.

Matt didn't remember what happened next, because another hailstorm of bombs fell. One hit the hut, and everything heaved up in the air. There were groans, shouts, roars. Matt felt someone picking him up but couldn't lift his head to see who it was. He was dizzy, so dizzy. And when he finally came to again, he was in a great big bed in a room full of beautiful furniture.

'AND how does Your Royal Majesty feel?' asked the same general who had pinned a medal on Matt last winter for helping blow up the ammunition dump. The general was saluting.

'I am Tomek, an ordinary soldier, General, sir,' cried Matt, tearing off his covers.

'I see,' said the general, bursting into laughter. 'We'll check that right now. Call Felek in here.'

In came Felek, wearing an aviator's uniform.

'Tell me, Felek, who is that?'

'That is His Royal Highness, King Matt the First.'

Matt could not deny it any more. Now there was no need to hide anything. On the contrary, the situation demanded that all the troops and the whole country hear the message loud and clear—King Matt was alive and had been fighting at the front.

'Is Your Royal Highness now able to take part in consultations?'

'I am,' answered Matt.

And so the general told Matt that a doll had been made to take his place, that every day the doll had been driven about the capital city in a car, that the Prime Minister had even placed the doll on the throne during audiences, and that the doll nodded its head and saluted when a string was pulled.

The newspapers said that the king was carried to his open car because he had given his word that his foot would not touch the ground again until all their territory was free of every last enemy soldier.

The trick had worked for a long time; people believed it, even though they thought it was strange that King Matt always sat in the same position on his throne and in his open car, never smiling, never saying anything, only nodding his head from time to time and saluting.

At first, a few people here and there were suspicious, but as time went by, quite a few people learned about the disappearance of King Matt. Informed by their spies, the enemy had some idea but pretended not to know anything, because what difference did it make—it was winter, and in winter all you could do was sit in your trenches.

Only when they found out that Matt's troops intended to break through their front line did they begin to snoop around seriously. And then they found out the whole secret.

And so, on the day before the attack, they hired a bad boy, who threw a stone with all his might at the doll of King Matt.

The doll broke. The porcelain went flying to pieces; only one arm was left, saluting the air because the head was gone. Some people fell into despair; some grew angry that they had been tricked, and threatened to start a revolution; but others just laughed.

On the day after the first attack, when King Matt had been taken prisoner and the general attack was supposed to begin, airplanes suddenly appeared over Matt's army, but instead of dropping bombs, they dropped little printed leaflets. These were proclamations.

'Soldiers!' said the leaflets. 'Your generals and ministers are deceiving you. King Matt is no more. Since the beginning of the war, all you've been seeing was a porcelain doll, which today was broken by a stone thrown by a bad boy. Stop fighting and go home.'

It had been very hard to convince the soldiers to wait a little while longer, that it all might be a lie. But now they had lost all desire to attack.

Then Felek had confessed everything.

The generals were happy. They telephoned the captain and ordered him to send Matt to headquarters immediately. But they were horrified when they found out that Matt had been taken prisoner during the first attack.

What to do?

They couldn't tell the rebellious soldiers that Matt had been taken prisoner; they'd been tricked once and wouldn't believe it. At a special meeting, they decided to attack the enemy with airplanes and snatch Matt back during the panic and confusion.

The airplanes were divided into four squads. One was to attack the prisoner-of-war camp, one Matt's prison, one the new ammunition dump, and one the officers' headquarters.

And that is precisely what they did. They bombed the building where all the officers were, and so there was nobody left to give orders. They also bombed what they thought was the ammunition dump, but they had no luck this time. The third squadron attacked the prisoner-of-war camp in search of Matt, but they didn't find him. It was the fourth squadron which snatched Matt away. He was unconscious when they found him, and it hadn't been easy to bring Matt back around.

'You acquitted yourselves valiantly, gentlemen,' he said. 'But how many airplanes did we lose?'

'We sent out thirty-four, and fifteen returned.'

'How long did the attack last?' asked Matt.

'From takeoff to landing, forty minutes.'

'All right, then,' said Matt, 'tomorrow we begin the general attack.'

The officers clapped their hands in joy.

What a surprise! Wonderful! The soldiers all along the front would hear that very night that King Matt was alive and with them and that he would lead them in the attack. That would make them very happy and they would fight like lions.

Immediately the telephone and telegraph lines between the army and the capital began to buzz.

That night, all the newspapers put out special supplements.

King Matt wrote two proclamations, one to the soldiers, one to the people. Nobody was thinking about a revolution any more; only a few young people and some children stood outside the Prime Minister's palace booing and hissing.

The council of ministers assembled at once and issued their own proclamation, saying that everything had been done on purpose to trick the enemy.

The soldiers were so excited that they couldn't wait for morning to come, and kept asking what time it was.

Then the attack began.

Three kings were making war on Matt. Matt's forces smashed the first army head-on and took their king prisoner, and they beat the second king so badly he couldn't fight again for three months because he had lost almost all his cannons and more than half his troops. So there was the one king left who had stayed in reserve.

When the battle was over, Matt met with his ministers again to make further plans. Both the commander in chief and the Prime Minister, who had arrived on an express train from the capital city, attended the meeting.

'Should we pursue the enemy or not?'

'Pursue him!' cried the commander. 'If we did so well against two armies, we'll do even better against the one that's left.'

'I say no,' said the Prime Minister. 'We already had one good lesson when we pursued the enemy farther than we should have.'

'That was a different story,' said the commander in chief.

Everyone was waiting to hear what Matt would say.

Matt desperately wanted to pursue the defeated enemy who had wanted to hang him. Besides, it was usually the cavalry who did the pursuing, and Matt hadn't been on a horse even once during the whole war. He had heard a lot about kings conquering on horseback, but all he had done was crawl on his belly and sit hunched over in a trench, and so he wanted to ride a horse even if only for a little while.

But Matt remembered what he'd seen at the beginning of the war—they had advanced too far and almost been defeated. Matt also remembered that people had said that the commander in chief was a boob. And last, Matt remembered that he had promised the departing ambassadors that he would try to conquer them quickly and make lenient peace terms.

For a long time Matt did not say a single word, everyone waiting in silence.

'Where is our royal prisoner of war?' he asked all of a sudden.

'Not far from here.'

'Please bring him here.'

The enemy king was brought in in chains.

'Off with his chains!' cried Matt.

His order was carried out at once. A guard stood by the prisoner to keep him from escaping.

'Defeated king,' said Matt, 'I know what being a prisoner means. I give you your freedom. You have been beaten, and so I ask you to remove the rest of your soldiers from my country.'

The defeated king was then taken by car to the front line, and from there went on foot back to his own men.

THE next day, a paper arrived signed by all three enemy kings.

'King Matt,' they wrote, 'you are brave, wise, and noble. Why should we fight? We want to be friends with you. We're returning to our own countries. Do you agree?'

King Matt agreed.

Peace was concluded.

All the soldiers were happy, and so were their wives, mothers, and children. Only those who had been robbing and stealing during the war may have been dissatisfied, but there weren't too many of them.

And so Matt was greeted with joy when his royal train returned to the capital.

He ordered the train to halt at one station while he went to see the switchman's good wife.

'I've come to have a cup of coffee with you,' said Matt with a smile.

The switchman's wife was so overjoyed she didn't know what to do. 'I'm so happy, so happy,' she kept saying, the tears trickling from her eyes.

There was a car waiting for him in the capital, but Matt demanded a white horse.

The master of ceremonies was so happy that he jumped for joy. 'Oh, that Matt is so smart. Of course a king should come riding back from war on a horse and not in some jalopy.'

And Matt rode his horse slowly through all the streets, and there were people, mostly children, waving from every window.

The children threw the most flowers and shouted the loudest: 'Hurray, long live King Matt! Vivat, vivat, vivat!'

Matt held himself up straight, but he was very tired. The attack, being taken prisoner, the meeting, the other battles, the trip, and now this terrific shouting had all so tired Matt that sometimes he heard a roaring in his ears and thought he was seeing stars.

And then some idiot threw his cap up in the air and it landed right on the head of Matt's horse. A thoroughbred from the royal stables and very sensitive, the horse bolted and Matt fell off.

Matt was immediately carried to a horse-drawn carriage, and brought to the palace at a full gallop. Matt hadn't hurt himself or passed out, he was just sound asleep. He slept and slept and slept, all through the night and the next morning and on till noon.

'Gimme some food, damn it!' Matt bellowed. His terrified footmen turned white as ghosts.

One minute later, there were a hundred dishes with food and dainty tidbits on his bed, beside his bed, and even under his bed.

'Take these foreign fricassees away this minute,' roared Matt. 'I want kielbasa, cabbage, and beer.'

But, good Lord, there wasn't a single piece of kielbasa in the entire royal pantry. Fortunately, the corporal of the palace guard lent them some.

'Oh, you mama's boys, you sissies, you pantywaists, you dimwits, you jerks, you nincompoops,' shouted Matt, using all the new words he had learned as a soldier. 'Now you're going to get it from me!'

While stuffing himself with kielbasa, Matt thought: Now they will know I'm a real king, one they have to obey.

Matt had a premonition that now, after winning the war, he would have to fight even harder with his own ministers.

While Matt was at the front, word had reached his ear that the Minister of Finance was all in a fury.

'A fine victory,' said the Minister of Finance. 'Why didn't Matt demand that our enemies pay us reparations? In the past, the loser always had to pay. Yes, he's very noble; so let him run the economy himself now that the treasury's empty. Let him pay the manufacturers for the cannons, the shoemakers for the boots, the merchants for the oats, peas, and kasha. They all waited while the war was on, but now the war's over and it's time to pay up. And we don't have a penny!'

The Minister of Foreign Affairs was furious, too.

Never in all history had peace been concluded without the Minister of Foreign Affairs.

'What am I, just a decoration?' said the Minister of Foreign Affairs. 'The other officials are laughing at me.'

The doll manufacturer kept pestering the Minister of Commerce. 'Pay me,' he said, 'for the porcelain doll.'

The Prime Minister's conscience was bothering him, and the prefect of police was worried that he had not done a very good job of covering up Matt's disappearance.

Matt knew a little, and he guessed the rest. He decided to put them all in their places.

The ministers had ruled long enough. Either they obey him or out they go. Then he wouldn't need the Prime Minister's permission to take a day off.

Matt licked his lips after the kielbasa, spat on the carpet, and ordered a bucket of cold water to be poured over him.

'That's how a soldier takes a shower,' he said with satisfaction.

He put his crown on his head and went into the conference room. The Minister of War was the only one there.

'But where are the others?'

'They didn't know that Your Royal Highness wanted to confer with them.'

'Perhaps they thought I would come back from the war and settle down to my lessons with my foreign tutor, while they do whatever they damn please … Well, they are sadly mistaken! Mr Minister, I am calling a conference for two o'clock. When we assemble in the meeting room, a platoon of soldiers is to form up in the corridor without making a sound. The platoon leader is to stand by the door and listen—when I clap my hands, he is to come into the room with his soldiers. I'll tell you the truth: if the ministers want to do everything the old way, the way it was before the war—I'll have them arrested, it'll hit them like a hundred thousand bombs. But that's a secret.'

'Yes, Your Royal Highness,' said the minister, bowing.

Matt took off his crown and went out to the palace gardens. He hadn't been there for a long time.

‘Oh, right,’ he exclaimed. ‘I completely forgot about Felek.’

He whistled and heard the cuckoo sound answer him.

‘Come here, Felek. Don’t be scared. Now I’m a real king, and I don’t need to explain anything to anyone.’

‘All right, but what will my father say?’

‘Tell your father that you are the king’s favorite and I forbid him to even lay a finger on you.’

‘If only Your Royal Highness would put that in writing.’

‘I’d be glad to. Come to my office.’

Felek didn’t have to be asked twice.

‘Mr Secretary of the Court, I would like you to write a paper stating that Felek has been named my favorite.’

‘But, Your Royal Majesty, there has never been such a position at court.’

‘Maybe there hasn’t, but there is now, for that is my royal desire.’

‘Perhaps Your Royal Highness would prefer to postpone writing the paper until the meeting of the ministers. That would not be much of a delay, and it would make it all a bit more official.’

Matt was ready to yield, but Felek tugged softly at his sleeve.

‘I demand that the paper be written immediately, damn it!’ roared Matt.

The secretary scratched his head and then wrote two papers. One said:

> I, King Matt, absolutely demand that a paper be written without delay and then be given me for signature. When that paper has been sealed, Felek will be the official Royal Court Favorite. If my will and royal command are not fulfilled at once, those guilty of the delay will be given the most severe and ruthless punishment. This I make known to the Secretary of the Court and confirm with my own signature, written in my own hand.

The secretary explained that only after Matt signed the first paper would he have the right to issue the second one.

King Matt signed the first paper and then the secretary gave him the stamped paper naming Felek the favorite.

Matt and Felek went to the royal playroom and played with toys and read books. They talked about their adventures during the war, and then they ate lunch together.

After lunch, they went out to the gardens. Felek called over some other boys their age from the courtyard, and they all had great fun playing until it was time for the conference of ministers.

'I have to go,' said Matt sadly.

'If I were king, I'd never *have to* do anything.'

'You don't understand, Felek, even us kings can't always do what we want.'

Felek shrugged his shoulders, which meant that he had a different opinion, and then started reluctantly for home; even though he had a paper signed by the king himself, he would still have to meet his father's stern gaze and the familiar question: 'Where've you been, you mongrel? Come on, out with it.'

Felek knew what usually came after that question, but this time it was going to be different.

THE ministers were moaning and groaning.

The Minister of Finance said that there was no money. The Minister of Commerce said that the merchants had lost a lot of money because of the war and could not pay their taxes. The Minister of the Railroads said that many of the trains that had been sent to the front had been badly damaged and would have to be repaired at great expense. The Minister of Education said that the children had run wild during the war because their fathers weren't at home and their mothers couldn't control them. And so the teachers were demanding an increase in pay and the replacement of all broken windows. The fields had not been planted because of the war. The stores were nearly empty. And on and on it went for a whole hour.

The Prime Minister drank a glass of water, which he always did when he was going to speak for a long time.

Matt hated to see the Prime Minister drink a glass of water.

'Gentlemen, this is a strange meeting. Anyone who heard us talking like this would think we had been beaten and lost the war. But we are the victors, after all. Until now, the loser always had to pay a lot of money to the winner. And that was fair. Because the winning country was the one that didn't stint on cannons, powder, and food for its soldiers. We spent the most money and we won the war. Our heroic King Matt could judge for himself that our troops had everything they could need. But why should we pay more money now? They attacked us, they started it, we have forgiven them, which shows our generosity and our goodness. But why shouldn't they pay us what we spent on the war? We don't want anything of theirs, but give us what we've got coming. Heroic King Matt was carried away by nobility and made peace with the enemy, a deed as wise as it was beautiful, but that free peace has created unprecedented financial difficulties. We can deal with this because we have experience, because we have read many wise books, because we are cautious and skillful, and if King Matt honors us with the same confidence we enjoyed before the war, if our council is willing to accept—'

'Mr Prime Minister,' interrupted Matt, 'enough of all this hot air. That's not the point. The point is you want to run the country and I'm supposed to act like a porcelain doll. And so I say, blast it with a hundred thousand bombs! I won't have it.'

'Your Royal Highness—'

'Enough. I won't have it, and that's that. I am the king, and I'm going to stay the king.'

'I would like the floor,' said the Minister of Justice.

'Fine, just keep it short.'

'According to the law, supplement 5 to paragraph 777,555, book XII, volume 814 of the book of laws and regulations, on page 5, paragraph 14, we find: "If the successor to the throne has not completed his twentieth year—" '

'Mr Minister of Justice, I don't care about that.'

'I see. Your Royal Highness wishes to violate the law. I am prepared to cite you the laws which deal with such violations. Numbers 105 and 486.'

'Mr Minister of Justice, I don't care about that.'

'And there's a law for that, too. "If the king treats the law lightly, paragraphs number—" '

'Will you stop plaguing me, you pest!'

'There's a law for that, too. "In case of an outbreak of plague or cholera—" '

His patience exhausted, Matt clapped his hands. The soldiers entered the room.

'I am arresting you, gentlemen,' shouted Matt. 'Take them to prison.'

'There's a law for that, too,' cried the Minister of Justice, rejoicing. 'It's called martial law. Hey, this is really getting illegal now,' he cried, when a soldier poked him in the ribs with his rifle butt.

Their faces white as chalk, the ministers were taken off to prison. The Minister of War was the only one to remain free. He made a military bow and left the room.

Now the conference room was as silent as the grave. Matt was all by himself. He clasped his hands behind him and walked back and forth for quite a long time. And every time he passed the mirror, he glanced over at it and thought: I look a little like Napoleon.

But what was he supposed to do now?

The ministers had left stacks of papers on the table. Should he sign some, or all of them? What did they say? Why had some been marked 'Approve,' and others, 'Postpone' or 'Forbid'?

Maybe he shouldn't have arrested all the ministers.

Maybe he shouldn't have done it at all. What would happen now?

Just why had he done it? What harm had they done? To tell the truth, Matt had acted stupidly. Why had he made peace in such a hurry? He could have summoned his ministers; the Minister of Finance would certainly have told him about reparations.

Who could have known there was such a thing as reparations? What's right is right. Why should the winner have to pay? And besides, they'd started it themselves.

Perhaps he should write to the kings. Since there were three of them, that would make it easier—each one could pay a third.

But just how did you write such letters? What had that minister said—volume 814. How many of those books were there? And all Matt had ever read was two books of stories and a biography of Napoleon. That was awfully little.

Matt's thoughts were becoming even gloomier, when suddenly he heard the cuckoo signal through the open window.

At last he wasn't alone any more.

'Felek, tell me, what would you do in my place?'

'In Your Royal Highness's place, I'd just play in the park and not go to any of their meetings. I'd do whatever I felt like doing, and I'd let them do what they wanted, too.'

Matt thought that Felek was a very simple boy and did not understand that, after all, a king's duty was to make his people happy, and not just play tag and ball. But that wasn't the problem, and so he didn't say anything about it to Felek.

'It's a tough spot, Felek. The ministers are in prison.'

'Let them stay there if that is Your Royal Highness's desire.'

'But look how many papers have to be signed. And if I don't sign them, there won't be railroads, factories, or anything.'

'So then you have to sign those papers.'

'But you see, the thing is that I don't know what to do without the ministers. Even old kings need their ministers.'

'So let them out of prison.'

Matt almost threw himself on Felek with joy. It was such a simple solution, but it hadn't occurred to him. Nothing really terrible had happened. He could set them free any time. But he would make certain conditions. They wouldn't be so free to give orders, they would have to obey him. From now on, the king would not have to steal food for his friends from the pantry or the gardens, or stare in envy through the gate at the other boys playing. He wanted to play, too. He wanted the good captain under whom he had served during the war to be his teacher now. What was so bad about all that—he wanted to be like all the other boys, so they wouldn't tease him.

Felek could not stay long because he had some important business in the city; he had only come to borrow a little money, not a lot, just enough for his trolley fare and maybe for some cigarettes and chocolate.

'My pleasure. Here, Felek.'

And then Matt was alone again.

The master of ceremonies was avoiding Matt, his tutor was hiding somewhere, and the footmen were being as quiet as shadows.

Then suddenly Matt realized that everyone might be thinking that he had turned into a tyrant.

He was seized by fear.

That would be horrible. After all, he *was* a direct descendant of Henryk the Hasty, who killed people like flies.

What to do now, what to do?

If only Felek were there, or someone.

Then Matt's old doctor came quietly into the room. This made Matt very happy.

'I have some important business,' began the doctor timidly, 'but I'm afraid Your Royal Highness will refuse.'

'Why, do you think I'm a tyrant or something?' asked Matt, looking the doctor right in the eye.

'What kind of tyrant could you be? But I've come on a delicate matter.'

'What is it?'

'I want to ask you to grant the prisoners a few small requests.'

'Speak freely, Doctor. I agree to everything in advance. I'm not the least bit angry with them, and I'm going to release them from prison. They just have to promise me that they won't give too many orders.'

'Oh, spoken like a true king,' cried the doctor, overjoyed. Now he felt free to list the prisoners' requests. 'The Prime Minister requests a pillow, a mattress, and a quilt. He can't sleep on a straw mat because it makes his bones ache.'

'But I've slept on the ground,' interjected Matt.

'The Minister of Health requests a toothbrush and tooth powder. The Minister of Commerce requests white bread because he cannot eat black prison bread. The Minister of Education requests books to read. The Minister of Internal Affairs requests pills because worry is causing him headaches.'

'How about the Minister of Justice?'

'He is not requesting anything, because he read in volume 425 of the law that ministers who are imprisoned only have the right to ask favors of their Royal Majesty after three days of imprisonment, and they have been in prison only three hours.'

Matt ordered that all the ministers immediately be sent bedding and a royal lunch from the palace and, in the evening, a dinner with wine. And he also ordered that the Minister of Justice be brought to him under guard.

When the Minister of Justice arrived, Matt ordered him to please be seated, and then asked: 'Would it be legal if I let all of you out of jail tomorrow?'

'Not entirely, Your Majesty. But if we call it a martial-law summary procedure, then everything will be formally correct.'

'But, Mr Minister, if I let them out, can they put me in jail?'

'They do not have the right to. But, on the other hand, volume 949 does mention that there can be a legal coup d'état.'

'I don't understand,' admitted King Matt. 'How much time does it take to understand all this?'

'A good fifty years,' answered the minister.

Matt sighed. The crown had never seemed light to him, but now it felt as heavy as a cannonball.

THE chains were taken off the ministers. Then they were brought to the prison dining hall, where they were met by the Minister of Justice, who was now a free man. The guards took their places, their sabers bared. The meeting began.

This is the plan Matt had devised during the night.

'You will be in charge of the grownups, I will be king of the little children. When I am twelve years old, I will rule the children up to twelve. When I am fifteen, the children up to fifteen. As the king, I can do whatever I wish. Everything else will stay the same. Since I'm young, I know what young people need.'

'We were young once, too,' said the Prime Minister.

'Fine, but how old are you now?'

'Forty-three,' said the Prime Minister.

'But you rule over people who are older than you. The Minister of Railroads is young, but the trains carry old people, too.'

The ministers said: 'That's true.'

'So, what do you say to all this, Mr Minister of Justice? Is this legal?'

'Absolutely not,' said the Minister of Justice. 'According to the law (volume 1349), children belong to their parents. There is only one possibility.'

'What is it?' asked everyone curiously.

'King Matt must be called King Matt the First, the Reformer (volume 1764, page 377).'

'What does that mean?'

'That means he is a king who changes the law. If the king says: "I want to make such and such a law," I say: "You cannot, because there is already another law." But if the king says: "I want to introduce such and such a reform," then I say: "Fine."'

Everyone agreed. But the biggest problem was Felek.

'He cannot be the favorite.'

'Why not?'

'Because court etiquette won't allow it.'

The master of ceremonies was not at the meeting, and the ministers could not provide Matt with a good explanation of court etiquette. They knew only one thing for sure: a reformer king could not have favorites in his own lifetime. That didn't mean that, God forbid, King Matt had to die, but that paper had to be gotten back from Felek at any cost.

'That is not a legal document,' confirmed the Minister of Justice. 'Felek can come see the king, he can be his best friend, but that can't be written down on paper and sealed.'

'All right, then,' said Matt to test them, 'but what if I won't agree and make you stay in prison?'

'That is a completely different story,' said the Minister of Justice. 'Kings can do anything.'

Matt was surprised that for something so silly, a piece of paper, so many people would be willing to stay in jail.

'Your Highness,' said the Minister of Justice, 'please do not be offended, but laws have been made about this, too. The subject of favorites is discussed in volume 235. A king can appoint favorites during his lifetime, but then he cannot be called a reformer.'

'So then what can he be called?' asked Matt nervously, because he had already begun to guess what it was.

'He must be called the Tyrant King.'

Matt rose, the prison guards brandished their sabers, the room became perfectly silent. All the ministers turned pale with fright while waiting to hear what Matt would say. Even the prison flies stopped buzzing.

Then Matt said loudly and slowly: 'From this day on, I will be called King Matt the Reformer. You gentlemen are free.'

The warden at once took the chains back to the cells because they were no longer needed, the guards sheathed their sabers, and the guard with the key ring opened the heavy iron door. The ministers rubbed their hands in happiness.

'One moment, gentlemen. I want to make a reform. Tomorrow every schoolchild is to be given a pound of chocolate.'

'Too much,' said the Minister of Health. 'A quarter of a pound, at the very most.'

'All right then, a quarter of a pound,' said Matt.

'We have five million schoolchildren in the country,' said the Minister of Education. 'If the bad boys and the lazy boys get chocolate—'

'All of them!' cried Matt. 'All of them, and no exceptions.'

'Our factories will need ten days to make that much chocolate.'

'And it will take a week to deliver it all through the country by train.'

'As Your Royal Highness can see, it will take no less than three weeks to carry out your command.'

'Too bad,' said Matt, but he thought to himself: How good it is that I have such experienced assistants. Without them, I wouldn't even have known how much chocolate was needed and who would make it. And I forgot that it would have to be delivered throughout the whole country.

But Matt said none of this aloud. He even pretended that he was a little unhappy.

'And so, if you please, I would like this reform to be announced in tomorrow's newspapers,' added Matt.

'I'm very sorry,' said the Minister of Justice. 'All this is very nice, but it is not a reform. It's only a present from the king to the schoolchildren. If King Matt were to issue a law that every schoolchild is to be given chocolate every day at state expense, that would be another story. That would be a law. But this is only a treat, a present, a surprise.'

'So let it be a treat, then,' agreed King Matt, because he was tired and afraid they would never stop talking.

'The meeting is closed. Goodbye, gentlemen.'

Matt went by royal automobile to his palace, ran straight to the gardens, and whistled for Felek.

'You see, Felek, now I am a real king. Now everything's fine.'

'For Your Royal Highness, but not for me.'

‘Why not?’ asked Matt in surprise.

‘Because when I showed my father the paper, he beat me so hard I saw stars.’

‘He really beat you?’ said Matt in surprise.

‘That’s right. “It’s the king’s right,” he says, “to grant you his favor, but it’s my right as a father to count your bones with my fist, you mongrel. In the palace you belong to the king, but here you’re mine. And a father’s hand can be relied on more than a king’s favor.” ’

Matt had learned to be cautious. Now he knew that you should never act too hastily. In life, as in war, if you wanted to win, you had to prepare your attack well. He had been in too much of a hurry with that paper, and so he made a mess of things. He had made trouble for himself and caused Felek pain. And now his royal honor had been stained. He, the king, gives Felek a document, and then some platoon leader beats Felek because of that royal paper.

‘Listen, Felek, we were in too much of a hurry. Remember, I even wanted to wait a little. There’s something else I have to tell you.’

Matt told him what had happened with the chocolate. ‘Kings cannot do everything they want,’ he said.

‘All right, Your Royal Highness—’

‘Listen, Felek, call me Tomek. After all, we fought in the war together and you helped rescue me.’

Matt and Felek decided that they would talk the way they used to when they were alone together.

'All right, Felek?'

'All right, Tomek.'

Now it was easier for Matt to take back the unfortunate document from Felek.

'I'll trade you some skates, two rubber balls, a stamp album, a magnifying glass, and a magnet for that piece of paper.'

'But my old man will beat me again.'

'That's true, Felek, but be patient. You can see for yourself that kings can't do things all at once. Kings have to obey the law.'

'What is the law?'

'I still really don't know myself. A bunch of books or something.'

'All right,' said Felek sadly, 'since you're always at meetings, you're learning everything little by little, but I ...'

'Good old Felek, don't worry, you'll see, everything will work out fine. If I can give five million children chocolate, then I can do you some good, too. It just has to be done right. You have no idea how long it takes me to fall asleep at night. I lie in bed and I keep thinking and thinking. And I'm killing myself trying to figure out how to do something that will be good for everyone. What can I do for the grownups? I can give them cigarettes, but they've got money and can buy them themselves. If I gave them vodka, they'd get drunk and what would happen then?'

'I don't know,' said Felek. 'You're trying too hard to look out for everybody. I'd just order a seesaw for the park, a merry-go-round, the kind that plays music—'

'You see, Felek, you're not the king, so you don't understand. Fine, let there be a merry-go-round, but not just one. First thing at the next meeting, I'll order seesaws and merry-go-rounds installed in all the schools.'

'And bowling alleys. And rifle ranges.'

'See what I mean …'

AS soon as the ministers were released from prison, they went straight to a café for coffee and cream cake. They were none too merry, even though they had regained their freedom.

'First of all, we must borrow some money.'

'Can't we print some new money?'

'We can't right now, because we printed too much during the war. We'll have to wait a little bit.'

'But how can we wait when there are so many bills to be paid?'

'I say we must borrow from the foreign kings.'

They each ate four cream cakes, drank their coffee, and went home.

The next day, the Prime Minister went to the king for an audience and said that it would be necessary to borrow money from the richer kings. That would be difficult, because they would have to write very precise documents to the foreign kings, and for that reason there would be two meetings a day every day.

'Fine,' said Matt. 'You hold your meetings, but I'm starting my lessons with the captain today.'

The Minister of War arrived with the captain. Matt greeted him warmly and even wanted to promote him to major, but the captain had just been promoted from lieutenant and so had not served long enough yet to qualify for major.

'You will teach me all my classes, and my foreign tutor will only teach me languages.'

And Matt began to study so avidly that he even forgot about going out to play. Because the captain lived far away, Matt suggested that he and his family move into the palace. The captain had a son, Stash, and a daughter, Helenka. So they all studied together and played together. Sometimes Felek came to their classes, but he missed a lot of them. He didn't like school.

Matt went to the council meetings very seldom now.

'It's not worth the time,' he'd say. 'It's boring, and I don't understand much of it anyway.'

Children were glad to come to the royal gardens. Felek's father, who was a carpenter before he joined the army, made them a seesaw. And so they played on the seesaw, they played tag, ball games, and firemen, they rowed on the royal pond and went fishing. This made the royal gardener a little angry, and he went to complain to the palace administration. Two windows had already been broken through carelessness. But nobody could say anything, because Matt was now the Reformer King and he made his own arrangements.

A stove had been ordered for the throne room, because Matt had announced that there was no sense in freezing during an audience.

When it rained, they played indoors. The footmen were a little angry because the kids tracked up the floors, which then had to be cleaned and waxed. But now the footmen paid less attention to buttoning all their buttons, and so they had more time to work. Anyway, the palace had made them sad before, when it had been as quiet as a tomb. Now it was full of children laughing, running, and shouting. Sometimes the jolly captain joined in their games, even the old doctor would pep up and start dancing or skipping rope with them once in a while. And that was really funny.

After building the seesaw, Felek's father knocked together a little cart for them. The cart only had three wheels and kept tipping over, but that was no problem. It was even more fun like that.

Here is how the chocolate was given out to the children who lived in the capital city: after all the schoolchildren were lined up in two rows along the streets, soldiers came by in trucks and handed out the chocolate. When the soldiers were finished, Matt drove through all the streets of the city. The children ate their chocolate, laughed, and shouted: 'Long live King Matt!'

Matt kept standing up, blowing them kisses, and waving his hat and handkerchief; he wiggled, smiled, and kept moving his arms and head on purpose, so that the children would not think they were being tricked again by some porcelain doll.

No chance of that. Everyone saw that this, of course, was the real King Matt. The children's fathers and mothers were with them on the streets, and they were happy, too, because now the children would do better in school, knowing that the king loved them and cared about them.

The Minister of Education added his own surprise to the festivities by inviting all the diligent, well-behaved students to the theater that evening. And so that night Matt, the captain, Felek, Helenka, and Stash sat in the royal box in a theater full of children.

As Matt entered his box, the orchestra struck up the national anthem. Everyone rose, and Matt stood at attention, as etiquette required. Now the children could see their king for the entire evening, but they were a little upset that he was not wearing his crown, even though he was in military uniform.

The ministers were not at the performance, because they were just finishing up the document concerning loans from abroad and so had no time. But the Minister of Education dropped by the royal box for a couple of minutes and said, sounding pleased: 'This at least makes sense. The students who really deserved it are getting their reward.'

Matt thanked him politely, and the day ended very nicely.

But, to make up for it, the next day Matt had difficult duties to perform.

All the ministers and all the foreign ambassadors would be there, and he would hand them the paper about the foreign loan with much ceremony.

Matt had to sit and listen to what they had been writing for three months. This was harder than ever for Matt, since he had lost the habit of going to meetings, and especially right after such a pleasant day.

The document was divided into four parts.

In the first part, the ministers had written in Matt's name how often Matt's great ancestors had helped the foreign kings by lending them money when they needed it. That was the historical section of the loan document.

Then came a very long geographical section. It contained a list of how much land belonged to Matt, how many cities, how many forests and factories, how many coal and salt mines, how much oil, how many people lived in his kingdom, and how much grain, potatoes, and sugar Matt's kingdom grew each year. That was the geographical section.

The third part of the document was the economic section. Here the ministers boasted that Matt's country was rich and had lots of money, that taxes flowed into the treasury every year and, of course, he would repay the loan, they shouldn't be the least bit afraid.

If Matt wanted to borrow, it was only to make his economy even stronger and richer.

In the fourth section, they wrote about the new railroads, cities, houses, and factories that would be built in Matt's kingdom.

It might even have been interesting, but there were so many numbers—a million of this, ten million of that; the ambassadors kept checking their watches, and Matt had begun to yawn.

When at last the reading was over, the ambassadors said: 'We will send this document to our governments; our kings very much want to live in friendship with Matt and of course will agree to lend him the money.'

Then Matt was given a gold pen inlaid with precious stones, and he added:

> YOUR ROYAL MAJESTIES, I defeated you and demanded no reparations. Now I am asking you to lend me money. So don't be piggy about it, lend me the money.
>
> KING MATT THE FIRST
> THE REFORMER

MATT was invited to visit the foreign kings and to bring the captain, the doctor, Stash, and Helenka.

'King Matt can be certain he will not regret it. We will do everything in our power to make sure that he has a good time and gets everything he wants.'

Matt was terribly happy. Matt had only been in one foreign city, and that was during the war. Now he was to become acquainted with three capitals, three foreign palaces, and three royal gardens, and he was very curious to see if they were different. One capital was supposed to have a beautiful zoo with animals from all over the world. Another was supposed to have a building so high that, as Felek said, it almost reached the sky. The third capital had stores with such beautiful displays that you could look at them for a whole year and never be bored.

The ministers were very angry that they had not been invited, but there was nothing they could do about it. The Minister of Finance just pleaded with Matt not to accept any money from the other kings or sign anything, because they would trick him.

'You don't have to worry about that,' said Matt. 'I didn't let them trick me before, and I won't now, either.'

'Your Majesty, they'll pretend to be your friends just as they did after the war, but they'll always be trying to have everything their own way.'

'As if I didn't know that,' said Matt, but deep down he was glad to have been warned, and he decided not to sign any papers while he was outside the country. And it really did seem strange to him that none of his ministers had been invited.

'I'll keep an eye out,' added Matt.

Everyone envied Matt the journey that would take him far and wide. The trunks were packed, the tailors delivered new clothes, and the shoemakers new boots. The master of ceremonies kept dashing around the palace to make sure nothing was forgotten. Helenka and Stash were bursting with happiness.

At last, one day, two cars drove up to the palace. Matt and the captain got in one, the doctor, Helenka, and Stash in the other; and then they drove through the cheering town to the station, where the royal train and all the ministers were awaiting them.

Matt had already ridden in the royal train once, on his way back from the war, but he had been very tired then and hadn't been able to have a good look at everything. This time was different. Now he was traveling for pleasure, and so he didn't have to worry about anything at all.

After such a difficult war and so much work, he deserved a rest. Laughing with happiness, Matt told his companions how he had hidden under a blanket from the lieutenant, who was now his teacher. He told them about the soup, the flea bites, and about seeing the Minister of War while standing on a ladder against a cow shed and looking at the train he was riding in now.

'We once spent a whole day there,' said Matt. 'And we left for home from this station, too!'

The royal train was composed of six cars. The first car was a sleeper. Everyone had his own compartment with a comfortable bed, a washstand, and a little table and chair. The second car was the dining car, which had a table, chairs, a beautiful carpet on the floor, and flowers everywhere. The third car was the library car, which, besides books, contained the king's best toys. The fourth car was the kitchen car; the fifth carried the palace servants, the cook and the footmen; and the sixth was the baggage car, where all their jam-packed trunks were stored.

The children liked to look out the windows when they weren't playing.

The train stopped twice when the locomotive needed water. The train gave a smooth, silent ride and did not shake at all.

One night, everyone went to bed as usual, and the next morning, when they woke up, they were already in a foreign country.

Matt had just finished washing and dressing when the envoy of the foreign king appeared to pay his respects. The envoy had boarded the train during the night, but he had not wanted to disturb King Matt. The envoy just kept an eye on things, since, once they crossed the border, Matt was under his protection.

'When will I be in your king's capital?'

'In two hours.'

Matt thought it was very nice that the royal envoy spoke to him in Matt's own language, for, although Matt could now speak and understand a couple of foreign languages, it was always nicer to speak his own.

Words cannot describe the welcome Matt was given. He entered that foreign capital not as a conqueror of cities, fortresses, and walls but as a conqueror of people's hearts. The old gray-haired king of that kingdom was waiting for Matt at the station with his grownup children and his grandchildren. The station had been decorated with so many leaves, branches, and flowers that it looked more like a beautiful garden than a train station. The branches and flowers had been woven into a sign: A WARM WELCOME TO OUR YOUNG FRIEND. There were four welcoming speeches in which Matt was called a good, kind, and valiant king. They predicted that he would rule longer than any king before him. He was offered bread and salt on a silver tray. Their highest medal, the Order of the Lion, containing an enormous diamond, was pinned to Matt's chest. The old king kissed him so tenderly that it made Matt think of his dead parents and tears filled his eyes. There was a band and banners and an arch of triumph, and flags hanging from every balcony.

Matt was carried on people's shoulders to a waiting car. There were so many people on the street that it seemed as if the whole world had come to see him. The children had all been excused from school for three days, and so they were out thronging the streets.

His own capital had never yet shown Matt a welcome like this one.

After they drove up to the palace, a huge mob gathered in the square and wouldn't disperse until Matt came out on the balcony.

'Say something to us,' they cried.

It was almost evening time when Matt finally appeared on the royal balcony.

'I am your friend!' cried Matt.

The cannons roared out a salute, followed by fireworks. Red, blue, and green stars showered down from the sky-rockets. It was exquisite.

Then it all started—the balls, evenings at the theater, trips outside the city where there were tall, beautiful mountains and castles set in old forests. Then came the hunt, the inspection of the troops, another gala dinner, and then back to the theater.

The old king's grandsons and granddaughters wanted to give Matt all their toys. His presents included two handsome horses, a little cannon made of real silver, and a new magic lantern with the most beautiful pictures.

Then came the best thing of all: the entire court went by car to the ocean, where a mock sea battle was staged for them. Matt had his first ride on the sea, in a flagship which had been named after him.

And so Matt was entertained for ten whole days. He would gladly have stayed longer, but he had to go see the second king.

This was the king whom Matt had set free. This king was poorer than the first, and so he welcomed Matt more modestly but even more warmly. This king had many friends among the kings of countries that were still wild, and he had invited them, too. There were very interesting balls for Matt, attended by Africans, Chinese, and Australians. Some were yellow and wore pigtails, some were black and wore decorations made of shells and ivory in their noses and ears. Matt became friends with these kings; one of them gave him four beautiful talking parrots, another one gave him a crocodile and a boa constrictor in a huge glass cage, and another one gave him two trained monkeys who knew such funny tricks that Matt laughed every time he looked at them.

It was in this kingdom that Matt saw the greatest zoo in the world, which had penguins that looked like people, polar bears, bisons, big Indian elephants, lions, tigers, wolves, foxes—everything, right down to the smallest creatures of land and sea. And fish and birds of every kind and color.

'These are all presents from my African friends,' said the king.

Matt decided to invite the Africans to his capital so he, too, could have a zoo like that. If he liked these animals so much, all the other children would, too.

'Oh, well, I have to leave. Too bad. I wonder what the third king will show me. The huge building Felek told me about is in his capital.'

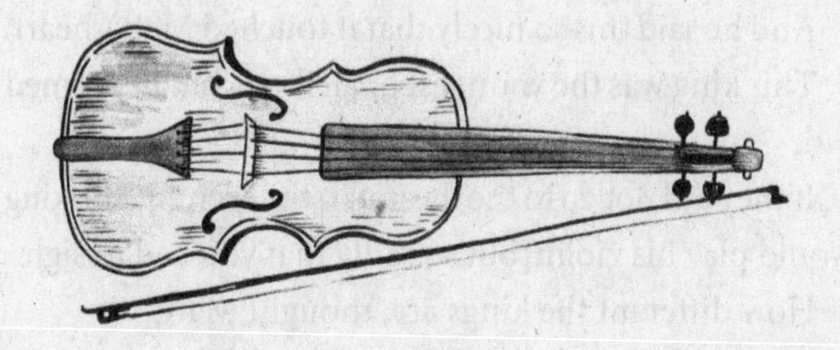

THE third king's reception was very modest but just as friendly. But the modesty of the reception surprised Matt a little, and he even thought it a bit unpleasant.

Is he stingy or what? thought Matt. Even his palace doesn't look like a castle, it's not all that much better than a nice house.

One footman even had slightly soiled gloves, and there was a small hole in the tablecloth which had been neatly sewn up with silk thread.

And so Matt was all the more surprised when the king took him to his treasure room. There was so much gold, silver, and precious stones that it made Matt blink his eyes.

'Your Royal Majesty is awfully rich.'

'Oh, no,' said the king. 'If I gave all this wealth away to the citizens of my country, they'd each only get a few copper coins.'

And he said this so nicely that it touched Matt's heart.

This king was the youngest of all three, but he seemed sad.

If they did not go to the theater in the evening, the king would play his violin, but so sadly that you had to sigh.

How different the kings are, thought Matt.

Matt said: 'I heard that Your Majesty had an enormous building in your country. This one is big, very big, but it's not enormous.'

'Oh, that's right. I didn't show Your Royal Majesty the parliament building. You don't have democracy in your country, and so I didn't think it would interest you.'

'But I would very much like to see that … that … parliament.'

Matt hadn't understood what the king had said, and again he thought: That's strange; they teach me so much about what kings did a hundred, two hundred, even a thousand years ago, but they don't teach me what kings are doing now and what they are like now. If I'd known them before, we might not have had a war at all.

The king began playing his violin again, while Matt, Helenka, and Stash listened.

'Why does Your Royal Majesty play such sad music?'

'Because life is no fun, my friend. And a king's life is probably the saddest of all.'

'But,' said Matt in surprise, 'the other kings are so jolly.'

'They're sad, too, dear Matt, they only pretend to be happy for their guests, that's the custom, that's what etiquette demands. How could they be jolly when they just lost the war?'

'Oh, so that's why Your Royal Majesty is worried.'

'I'm the least worried of the three kings. I am even pleased.'

'Pleased?' Matt was even more amazed.

'Yes, because I didn't want that war.'

'So why did you go to war, then?'

'I had to. There was nothing else I could do.'

What a strange king, thought Matt. He doesn't want to go to war but he does, and then he's happy when he loses. A perfectly strange king.

'It's very dangerous to win a war,' said the king, as if talking to himself. 'That can make you forget what a king is for.'

'And what is a king for?' asked Matt naïvely.

'Not just to wear a crown—but to bring happiness to the people of his country. But how can you bring them happiness? What I did was to make various reforms.'

Oho, that's interesting, thought Matt.

'But reforms are the hardest thing of all, yes, the hardest.'

And then the king began playing his violin so sadly that it seemed to be weeping.

Matt stayed up late into the night, thinking and thinking. He tossed and turned, the sad violin music still in his ears.

I'll ask him for advice. He must be a good person. I am the Reformer King and I don't know what reforms are. But he says they are very hard.

Then Matt thought some more: But maybe he's lying. Maybe the three kings have a plan, and the third one will try to give me some document to sign.

Matt had been surprised that none of the kings discussed the loan or anything else with him. After all, kings get together to talk about politics and other important things. But not them. He thought they didn't want to talk to him because he was little. Then why was the third king treating him like a grownup?

Matt liked the sad king, but he didn't trust him. Because kings soon learn not to trust.

Matt wanted to fall asleep quickly and began to hum a sad song to himself, when suddenly he heard footsteps in the next room.

Maybe they're going to kill me, flashed through Matt's mind. He had heard about kings lured into ambush and murdered treacherously. All his thoughts and the sad king's mournful song had made Matt edgy.

Matt quickly pressed the button on the electric lamp. Then he slid his hand under his pillow, where he kept his revolver.

'Not sleeping, Matt?'

It was the king.

'I can't fall asleep.'

'So dark thoughts are even driving sleep from the eyes of little kings?' said the king with a smile, sitting down by the bed.

He said no more but only looked at Matt. Matt remembered that his own father had often looked at him like that and that he hadn't liked it when his father looked at him like that. But now it felt nice.

'Yes, yes, Matt, you were very surprised when I told you that I didn't want a war with you but that I went to war anyway. Because you still think kings can do what they want to.'

'That's not so. I know we have to follow etiquette and obey many laws.'

'Oh, so you do know. Yes, we make bad laws ourselves, and then we have to obey them.'

'But can't we make good laws?'

'We can, and we have to. You are young, Matt. You must study and learn to make good, wise laws.'

The king took Matt's hand and placed it on his as if comparing his own large hand to Matt's little one; then he stroked it very tenderly, bent forward, and kissed it.

Matt felt terribly embarrassed, but the king began to speak quickly and softly: 'Listen, Matt. My grandfather gave his people freedom, but it didn't turn out well. He was assassinated. And people ended up even more unhappy than before. My father built a great monument to freedom. You'll see it tomorrow. It's beautiful, but what does that matter when there are still wars, still poor people, still unhappy people? I ordered that great parliament building built. And nothing changed. Everything's still the same.'

The king seemed suddenly to remember something. 'You know, Matt, we always did the wrong thing by making reforms for adults. Try doing it with the children, maybe you'll succeed ... Sleep now, dear child. You came to enjoy yourself, and I've been keeping you up late. Good night.'

The next day Matt tried to continue this conversation, but the king was no longer in the mood. However, he did give Matt a very clear explanation of what parliament was. Parliament was a huge and beautiful building whose interior looked a bit like a theater and a bit like a church. The members of parliament sat on a sort of stage at a table, just as they did in Matt's palace during conferences. Except that here there were an awful lot of chairs with all sorts of people sitting in them. Speakers would get up, go to a sort of pulpit, and speak as if they were delivering a sermon. There was a special section where the ministers sat. To one side, at a large table, sat the people who wrote for the newspapers. The public was up above.

When Matt and the king entered, someone was addressing the ministers very angrily. 'We won't allow it,' he shouted, brandishing his fists. 'If you don't do what we want, you won't be our ministers any more. We need intelligent ministers.'

Another man said that the ministers were very intelligent and they didn't need any others.

Then they started quarreling and everyone began to shout. Someone shouted: 'Down with the government.' Someone else shouted: 'Shame on you.' And while Matt was leaving the chambers, someone yelled: 'Down with the king.'

'Why are they quarreling like that?'

'Things are going badly for them.'

'But what will happen if they really kick the ministers out?'

'They'll elect new ones.'

'What about the one who shouted "Down with the king"?'

'He always shouts that.'

'Is he crazy?'

'No. He just doesn't want a king.'

'But can they kick the king out?'

'Of course they can.'

'What would happen then?'

'They'd elect someone else and call him something else.'

It was almost as interesting as the two monkeys he'd been given by the African chief, Vey-Bin.

MEANWHILE, in Matt's capital, the newspapers were constantly writing about the welcome the foreign kings had given Matt, how much they liked and respected him, and what lovely presents he was receiving. Hoping to put these new friendships to good use, the ministers wanted to borrow a great deal of money, and to do so quickly. They were worried that Matt would return to the capital and spoil everything at the last moment. It was a good thing that the foreign kings had not been offended by Matt's postscript to the document, though never before in all the world had any king, even the greatest Reformer King, ever written on an official document: 'Don't be piggy.'

So the ministers had arranged for Matt to spend an extra month abroad, saying that he was tired and needed a rest.

Matt was very happy and asked if they could go to the seashore. And so Matt, the captain, Stash, Helenka, and the doctor traveled to the seashore together. This time Matt wore civilian clothes and stayed in an ordinary hotel, not a palace. And now he was called prince, not king. All this was done so that Matt could stay by the sea—incognito. Because there is a rule that kings can go abroad only when they are invited, and if they want to be by themselves, they must pretend not to be kings.

Matt didn't care, he even liked it, because he could play with all the children and be like everyone else.

It was wonderful. They went swimming in the sea, collected seashells, built castles, ramparts, and fortresses out of sand. They went boating, horseback riding; they went berry picking in a nearby forest, and found mushrooms, too.

The time went even faster because Matt had started his lessons again, and as I've already said many times, he was glad to study and loved his teacher and so three hours of classes did not spoil his fun in the least.

Matt was very fond of Stash and Helenka. They were very well brought-up children and never quarreled with him, or only very rarely, and then just for a very short while.

Once Matt quarreled with Helenka about a mushroom, an enormous mushroom. Matt said that he had seen it first, and Helenka said that she had. Matt would have given in to her, because one mushroom didn't mean very much, especially to a king. But why was she bragging and lying?

'As soon as I saw the mushroom, I shouted, "Oooo, look," and pointed my finger at it,' said Matt. 'And all you did was run over to it.'

'I picked it.'

'Because you were closer, but I saw it first.'

Helenka grew angry, threw down the mushroom, and stomped on it with her foot. 'I don't need that old mushroom.'

But she immediately saw that she had been bad. She felt very ashamed of herself and burst into tears.

Girls are strange, thought Matt. She stomped on it herself, and now she's the one crying about it.

Another time, Stash had built a very fine fortress with a tall tower. It's hard to make a tall tower from sand because you need very damp sand for that and have to dig deep. Stash was tired from digging. He put a stick in the middle of the tower to give it support and was waiting to see what the waves would do to his fortress. Then Matt suddenly got an idea and shouted: 'I'm going to conquer your fort.'

He jumped on the tower at a run and knocked it over. Stash was angry, but he had to admit that it was hard for a king to restrain himself when he saw a fortress, and so he only pouted a little. Then they made up.

Sometimes the captain told them stories about the times when he had fought against savage tribes in the African deserts. And sometimes the doctor would tell them how a disease is like an enemy who attacks a person, that there are little red and white specks like soldiers in the blood which attack the infection and they either win and the person is healthy again or they lose and he dies. There are glands in a person very much like forts. Inside those glands are many corridors, trenches, and places to wait in ambush, and when the infection is drawn into the gland, it gets lost, and then those little soldiers in the blood attack and kill the infection.

They made friends with fishermen who taught them how to tell from the sky if a storm was coming, and whether it would be a big storm or not.

It was interesting to listen to people and nice to play, but sometimes Matt ran off deep in the forest or broke away from the group as if he were going to look for seashells; then he would sit down and think for a long time about what he should do when he returned home.

Maybe things should be as they were in the country of the sad king who played the violin. Maybe it's even better when all the people rule, and not just the king and the ministers. Why not? A king might be too young and his ministers might not be too wise, or even just plain dishonest. But what could you do then? He had put all his ministers in jail, but then he'd been all alone and not known what to do. But this way he could go to parliament and say: 'Choose new, better ministers.'

Matt devoted a lot of time to thinking, but he wanted to get advice from someone. So one day he went out alone with the doctor and asked him: 'Are all children healthy like me?'

'No, Matt.' (The doctor didn't call him king because Matt was at the seashore incognito.) 'No, Matt, there are very many children who are weak and sick. Many children live in unhealthy, damp, dark houses, they don't go out to the country, they don't eat enough and often go hungry, and so they become ill.'

Matt had already seen some dark, airless houses, and he had also known hunger. Matt remembered how he had often preferred to sleep outside on the cold ground rather than in a poor peasant's hut. Matt remembered the pale children with crooked legs who would come to their camp and ask the soldiers for a little soup, and he remembered how greedily they had eaten. He thought it was only like that during a war, but now he learned that children often suffered from cold and hunger even when there was no war.

'But can't something be done,' asked Matt, 'so everyone could have nice little houses with gardens and nourishing food?'

'That's very difficult. People have been thinking about that a long time, but so far nobody has come up with a good idea.'

'Do you think I could?'

'You could, of course you could. A king can do a lot. For example, the king who plays the violin built many, many hospitals and homes for children, and in his kingdom most children go to the country in the summertime. He made it a law that every city has to build camps in the country where children in poor health can spend the whole summer.'

'Do we have any summer camps like that?'

'No, we don't, because we haven't made a law like that yet.'

'Well, then, I'll make one,' said Matt, stamping his foot. 'Doctor, I need your help, because naturally the ministers will say it's too difficult again, that they don't have this and that, and I don't know if they're telling the truth or just giving me a song and dance.'

'No, Matt, they're right. It isn't easy.'

'All right, I know. I wanted chocolate given out in one day and they promised to do it in three weeks. And then it took them two months. But they did do it.'

'Sure, but it's easy to give away chocolate.'

'But if it was easy for the king with the violin to make that law, why should it be hard for me?'

'It was hard for him, too.'

'All right. Hard or not, I'll do it anyway.'

Just then, the sun, huge, red, and beautiful, began to set behind the sea. Matt was thinking how to make it possible for all the children in his country to see the sun and the sea, go boating and swimming, and pick mushrooms.

'All right,' said Matt on the way back from their walk, 'but if that king is so good, why did somebody yell "Down with the king"?'

'Some people are never satisfied. There is no king or minister in the world who could win everyone's praise.'

Matt remembered how the soldiers at the front had made fun of kings and said all kinds of things about them. If Matt had not been to war, he would have thought that everyone really loved him so much they just had to throw their hats up in the air for joy every time they saw him.

After that conversation, Matt studied even harder, and began to ask when they'd be going home.

I have to begin my reforms, he thought. I am the king and I must do just as good a job as the other kings who send all their children out to the country for the summer.

MATT returned to the capital just when all the arrangements had been made to borrow the money from the foreign kings. Matt only needed to sign the papers and say when and how he would repay the loan.

As soon as King Matt signed the papers, the Chancellor of the Exchequer left with sacks and boxes to contain all the foreign silver and gold.

Matt waited impatiently for the money, because he wished to introduce three reforms:

1. To build camps in all the forests, in the mountains, and at the seashore so that poor children could spend the entire summer in nature.
2. To supply all schools with seesaws and merry-go-rounds of the type that play music.

3. To construct a zoo in the capital, with cages for wild animals—lions, bears, elephants, monkeys, snakes, and birds.

But Matt was soon to meet with disappointment. When the money arrived, it turned out that the ministers couldn't spare any for Matt's reforms, because they had only calculated how much was required for their own needs.

A certain amount had to go for new bridges, a certain amount for the railways, a certain amount to build new schools, and a certain amount to pay war debts.

'Had Your Royal Highness told us earlier, we would have borrowed more,' said the ministers, while thinking to themselves: It's a good thing Matt wasn't at the meetings. The foreign kings wouldn't have wanted to lend us money for Matt's reforms.

'Well, all right. You've tricked me, but I know what to do now.' He wrote a letter to the king who played the violin: 'I want to introduce the same reforms in my country that Your Royal Highness did in yours. I need a lot of money. My ministers borrowed for themselves, and now I want to borrow for myself.'

Matt waited a long time and had begun to think he would never receive an answer, but then one day during a lesson he was informed that a royal envoy had arrived for an audience. Matt knew what this meant and went to the throne room at once.

The envoy requested that everyone leave, because his business was secret and could only be communicated to the king. When everyone had left, the envoy told Matt that they could lend him money, but only if he created a constitution that would allow the country to be ruled by the people.

'Because if we lend money to Matt, we could lose it, but if we lend it to the people, that's a completely different story. The only problem is,' said the envoy, 'the ministers will never agree.'

'They have to agree,' said Matt. 'What else can they do? They agreed to my becoming a reformer king, and so that's that.'

But the ministers agreed with unexpected ease. They were terribly afraid that Matt would put them in jail again.

Now, when something has to be done, thought the ministers, we'll say that this is what the whole nation wants and there's nothing we can do about it. We have to do what the people tell us to. And Matt can't put the whole country in jail.

Meetings began. The wisest people came to the capital from all the cities and all the villages. And they discussed everything for days and nights on end. It was very difficult to make sure that the whole nation had said what it wanted.

The newspapers wrote so much about the parliament that they didn't even have any room for pictures. But Matt was a good reader now and didn't need pictures any more.

Separate meetings were held by the bankers to calculate how much money would be needed to build the camps for the children in the country, the merry-go-rounds, and the seesaws.

Traders came from every corner of the world to find out which animals, birds, and snakes would be needed for the zoo. Their meetings were the most interesting, and Matt always attended them.

'I can sell you four beautiful lions,' said one trader.

'I have the wildest tigers,' said a second.

'I have pretty parrots,' said a third.

'Snakes are the most interesting,' said a fourth. 'I have the most dangerous snakes and crocodiles. My crocodiles are big and live a long time.'

'I have a trained elephant. He used to perform in a circus when he was young. He rode a bicycle, danced, and walked a tightrope. Now he's a little old, so I can sell him cheaply. He'll be great fun for the children, because he can take them for rides. Children love elephant rides.'

'Don't forget about bears,' said the man who sold bears. 'I can sell you four regular bears and two polar bears.'

All the men who sold wild animals were brave hunters; one of them was a real Indian, and two of them were black. The children came from every part of the capital to gaze at the traders and were happy that their king was buying so many interesting animals for them.

One day another black man came to the meeting. He looked less civilized than the other two. They wore regular clothes and spoke European languages; they lived some of the time in Africa and some of the time in Europe. But this black man did not say a single word you could understand; he wore practically no clothes, had on a necklace made of shells, and had so many decorations made of bone in his hair that it was hard to believe anyone's neck could support that much weight.

In Matt's country there was one very old professor who knew fifty different languages, and Matt sent for him to translate what the man was saying. Because the other black men could not understand him, or maybe they didn't want to translate for him, so as not to hurt their own business.

The black prince—yes, he was a African prince—said: 'Oh, King Matt, you are great as the baobab tree, mighty as the sea, swift as lightning, and bright as the sun.

I bring you the friendship of my sovereign, may he live seven thousand years and have one hundred thousand great-great-grandsons. In his forests my sovereign has more wild animals than there are stars in the sky or ants in an anthill. Our lions eat more people in one day than the royal court does in a month. And the royal court is made up of the king, his hundred wives, and his thousand children, may they all live five thousand years. Magnificent King Matt, don't trust these tricksters who have toothless lions, tigers without claws, old elephants, and painted birds. My monkeys are smarter than theirs, and my king's love for you, Matt, is even greater than their stupidity. They want money from you, but my king needs no gold because his mountains are full of gold. All he wants is for you to let him come here and be your guest for two weeks, because he is very curious to visit your land. The kings of Europe will not invite him because they say that he is a savage and it does not behoove them to be friends with him. If you went to visit him, King Matt, you'd see for yourself that everything I say is the pure truth.'

The wild-animal traders saw that things had taken a bad turn, and so they said: 'Does Your Royal Highness know that this man is an envoy from the land of the cannibals? We advise Your Royal Highness not to go visit them or let them come here.'

Matt told the professor to ask the envoy if his king was really a cannibal.

'Oh, King Matt, bright as the sun, I said that the lions in our forests eat more people in one day than the whole royal court in a month. I will tell you only one thing, oh King Matt, white as the sand, my king will not eat you or any of your subjects. My king is hospitable and would rather eat all his hundred wives and his thousand children, may they all live five thousand years, than gnaw off even one finger of your hand.'

'All right,' said Matt, 'I'll go.'

The wild-animal traders left immediately, angry that their deals had fallen through.

THE Prime Minister returned home in such a bad mood that his wife was even afraid to ask him what happened. The Prime Minister ate his dinner without saying a word. His children were very quiet, so they wouldn't be spanked. The Prime Minister usually drank a glass of vodka before dinner but only drank wine with his meal. That day, he pushed the wine aside and drank five glasses of vodka.

'My dear husband,' his wife began timidly, so as not to make him even angrier. 'I can see that there's been more trouble at the palace. All this is ruining your health.'

'It's unheard of!' the Prime Minister finally burst out. 'Do you know what Matt is doing now?'

His wife sighed deeply.

'Do you know what Matt is doing now? He's going to visit the king of the cannibals! Can you believe it?

Cannibals! No European king has ever been there. Can you believe it? They'll eat Matt, no question of that. I'm at my wit's end.'

'Isn't there any way of talking him out of it?'

'Try if you want to, but I have no intention of going to jail again. Matt is a stubborn, foolish boy.'

'All right, but what would happen if, God forbid, the cannibals did eat Matt?'

'Use your head, woman. Our country is going to be a democracy soon. The king has to sign a paper called a manifesto, and then the parliament will be opened with great ceremony. Who will sign the manifesto, who will open the parliament, if Matt is inside some savage's belly? They can eat him a year from now, but Matt must remain here until everything is finished.'

The ministers had another problem: it was not fitting to let Matt make such a dangerous journey alone, but no one wanted to go with him.

Meanwhile, Matt was making serious preparations for his journey.

The news spread throughout the city that the king was going to travel to the land of the cannibals. The grownups shook their heads, but the children were very envious of Matt.

'Your Highness,' said the doctor. 'To be eaten by cannibals is bad for your health. They'll probably want to roast Your Royal Highness on a spit and cut off the white meat right away, so Your Royal Highness—'

'My dear doctor,' said Matt. 'I have already come close to being beaten, shot, and hanged, but I got out of it one way or the other. Maybe the cannibal prince is telling the truth, maybe they are hospitable people and won't cook me. I've already made up my mind and given my promise, and kings must keep their word.'

The captain also tried to persuade Matt not to go through with it. 'It's hot there, you'll have to travel two weeks on camelback. There are all kinds of diseases in those countries that you could die from. Besides, you can't trust cannibals, they're treacherous. I know, I fought against them.'

Matt agreed that his journey would be dangerous but continued with his preparations.

Matt had to have a zoo in his capital city. He had to bring back lots of lions, tigers, elephants, and monkeys of every sort. A king had to do his duty.

The African prince requested that Matt hurry, because he could not live without human flesh for more than a week. He had secretly brought a barrel of salted flesh with him and had been taking nibbles from it every so often. Now his supply was starting to run out, and so he wanted to get going.

It was decided that the old professor who knew fifty languages and the captain would travel with Matt. Stash and Helenka couldn't go, because their mother was too afraid for them. But then, at the last moment, Felek and the doctor joined the group.

The doctor did not know about African diseases and so he brought along a thick book on those diseases in his suitcase, which was full of all the medicines they might need. Just as they were leaving, an English sailor and a French traveler came to ask Matt if they could accompany him.

None of them took much baggage, because they wouldn't need warm clothing, and besides, camels can't carry lots of suitcases.

They boarded the train, and off they went. They rode and rode and rode, until they reached the sea. There they embarked on a ship and sailed away. A big storm overtook them at sea, and everyone got seasick. This was the first time the doctor used his medicines.

The doctor was very angry about the trip. 'What good is it being the royal doctor?' he complained to the ship's captain. 'If I were a regular doctor, I could sit in a comfortable office and walk to the hospital. But this way I have to wander all over the world. And besides, to be eaten at my age would be very unpleasant.'

On the other hand, the captain grew more cheerful every day. The trip made him remember running away from home, joining the Foreign Legion, and fighting African tribes. He had been young and very jolly then.

Felek was the happiest of them all. 'When you went to see the European kings, you only took the captain's fancy children, not me. But when you go to see the cannibals, Felek is the only one by your side.'

'My dear Felek,' said Matt, feeling embarrassed, 'you were not invited by the foreign kings. It would have been against etiquette to bring you. Stash and Helenka wanted to come with me this time, but their mother wouldn't let them.'

'I'm not mad,' said Felek.

When their ship arrived in port, they boarded another train and traveled for two more days. Then palm trees, date and fig trees, and beautiful banana trees came into view. Matt kept squealing with glee. But the black prince only smiled, flashing his white teeth, which was somehow frightening.

'This is not the African forest. Later on, you'll see what a real forest is.'

But it wasn't a forest they came to. It was a desert.

Nothing but sand and more sand. An ocean of sand.

In the last village before the desert, there was a detachment of white soldiers and a couple of stores belonging to white people. Matt told them that they were travelers going to the land of the cannibals.

'Go if you want to. Many people have gone there, but we don't remember anyone coming back.'

'But maybe we'll succeed,' said Matt.

'Well, don't say we didn't warn you. Those are very savage people you're going to visit.'

The black prince bought three camels and rode on ahead to get everything ready, telling them to wait until he returned.

'Listen,' said the officer of the little garrison. 'You can't fool me. I know what's what. You're not ordinary travelers. You've got two little boys and an old man traveling with you. And that savage who came with you must be some sort of very important person. Only members of the royal family can wear shells like the one he had in his nose.'

They saw no reason to hide the truth and told the officer everything. The officer had already heard of Matt from the mail and newspapers they received every couple of months.

'Well, that's another story, then. Maybe you will succeed. I do have to admit they are very hospitable. And I'll tell you one thing—either you'll never come back or you'll be given an awful lot of presents, because they have so much gold and diamonds that they don't know what to do with it all. They'll give you a couple of handfuls of gold for any silly old thing—a little gunpowder, a mirror, a pipe.'

The travelers' mood improved. The old professor spent all day out in the sun lying on the sand because the doctor had told him that this was very good for the legs and the professor's legs had been bothering him. In the evening, he would go to the black people's huts, talk with them, and write down their language, which had never been recorded before.

Felek ate so much fruit that the doctor had to give him a spoonful of castor oil from his first-aid kit. Sometimes the Englishman and the Frenchman would take Matt out hunting. Matt also learned how to ride a camel. They all had a very nice time.

THEN, one night, a black servant came rushing, terrified, into their tent, shouting that they had been betrayed and were about to be attacked.

'I should never have gone to work for white people. My own people won't forgive me for that, they'll kill me. Oh, poor me, what will I do now?' said the servant.

They all leaped from their cots, grabbed whatever weapons they had, and looked outside.

The night was dark. Nothing could be seen. Far away on the desert, a huge mass of people was approaching, making a great hubbub. Oddly enough, none of the soldiers had started shooting. The garrison seemed peaceful and quiet.

The garrison commander knew the customs of the savage tribes well and had realized at once that it was not an attack. But because he did not know what was going on, he sent a messenger to find out.

It was a caravan coming for King Matt.

The caravan was led by an enormous royal camel with a beautiful little booth on its back. It was followed by a hundred more, beautifully decorated camels. And there were many men on foot, cannibal soldiers guarding the caravan. What would have happened if the officer of the garrison had not been so experienced? He might have started shooting, and that would have made for a massacre. Matt thanked him warmly for being so wise, awarded him a medal, and the first thing next day they set out on their way.

The terrible heat made it a very hard journey. The natives were used to the scorching heat, but the white people could barely breathe.

Matt rode in the little booth. Two cannibals fanned him with large fans made of ostrich feathers. The caravan moved slowly, and the leader kept looking around anxiously to see if any whirlwinds were coming, those awful winds that fling hot sand on travelers. There had been cases of entire caravans being covered in sand, with everyone dying.

No one said a word all day, and the white people only started feeling a little better in the cool of the evening. The doctor gave Matt some cooling powders, but they didn't help very much. Matt had been tempered by the war and been through many a rough spot, but that journey was the hardest thing he had ever done in his life. His head ached, his lips were swollen, his tongue felt like wood. His skin became dark and dry; the white sand irritated his eyes, and there were red, itchy sores all over his body. Matt slept badly; he kept having terrible nightmares that the cannibals were eating him or burning him at the stake. Oh, water was much better than sand, it was so much nicer to travel by ship. But what could he do, he couldn't go back, people would laugh at him.

Twice they stopped at oases. What a pleasure it was to see green trees again and drink cool water, not that nasty, warm, smelly water they'd been drinking from animal-skin pouches.

They stopped for two days at the first oasis, and they had to spend five whole days at the second, because even the camels were so tired they couldn't go a step farther.

'Only four more sunrises and sunsets in the desert and we'll be there,' said the cannibal prince happily.

They got a good rest in those five days. Before they left, the cannibals felt so happy that they built a fire and danced a terribly wild war dance.

The last four days of the journey were not as hard, because the desert was coming to an end. The sand wasn't as hot, and now there were even a few bushes. One time they spotted some people.

Matt wanted to make their acquaintance but was told not to, because they were desert robbers. The robbers didn't attack the caravan because it was so large, but they would have gladly if there had been fewer travelers.

At last!

Now a forest could be seen in the distance, and they could feel a damp forest coolness in the air. Their journey was over, but no one knew what awaited them now. They had avoided death on the burning sands but still might perish at the hands of savages.

Things got off to a wonderful start. The king of the cannibals and his entire court came riding out to meet them. Musicians walked out ahead, but they made a terrible, ear-splitting racket. Their trumpets were animal horns, their flutes were made of bone, and they used kettles for drums. A terrible racket. And they were also screaming and yelling, which, after the silence of the desert, was enough to drive a person out of his mind.

The welcoming ceremony began with a religious service. They set up a huge wooden statue with frightening animal faces carved on it. The witch doctor was wearing a frightening mask, too. They all started shouting again, and the translator said that the king of the cannibals was putting Matt under the protection of his gods.

When Matt got down from his camel, after the service, the king and all his sons began doing somersaults in the air and jumping up and down. That went on for half an hour, and then the king made a speech to Matt.

'Oh, my white friend who is brighter than the sun, I thank you for coming. To see you makes me the happiest person in the world. Please, I beg you, make one little signal with your hand and I will bury this great sword in my heart and then I will have the highest honor of all—to be eaten by my own guest.'

Through his translator, Matt said that he did not want that in the least, that he wanted to make friends with the king, to talk with him and enjoy his company, not eat him.

Then the king, his hundred wives, and all his children began to weep loudly and crawl around on all fours and make sad little back somersaults. This meant that their white friend looked down on them and didn't love them because he didn't want to eat them and might even think they weren't tasty and not worth eating. Matt had no desire to laugh at these strange customs. He pretended to be serious and did not say a word.

There's no reason to describe everything Matt saw and did at the court of the cannibal king, because the learned professor who was Matt's translator has recorded it all in a fat book entitled *Forty-nine Days at the Court of King Bum Drum in the Savage Land of the Cannibals.*

Poor King Bum Drum did everything he could to make Matt's stay at court full, varied, and amusing, but the cannibals' games were so wild that Matt could only look on them with curiosity, and sometimes even with displeasure.

Matt did not want any part of many of their games.

For example, Bum Drum had an old rifle which was carried out from the treasury with great pomp and circumstance, and Matt was supposed to shoot it, using Bum Drum's eldest daughter for a target. Matt didn't want to, and that hurt Bum Drum's feelings. Again they started making sad somersaults. And, worst of all, Matt had offended the witch doctor.

'He pretends to be our friend, but he doesn't act like one,' said the witch doctor. 'Now I know what to do.'

That evening, the witch doctor slipped some poison into the shell Matt used as a wineglass.

This poison made everything turn red, then blue, then green, and then black. Then you died.

In the finest royal tent, on a chair of gold at a golden table, Matt was saying: 'Why is everything turning red? The cannibals are red. Everything's red.'

As soon as Matt's doctor heard that, he jumped up and began to wave his arms in despair, because he had read about this poison. The book said there was a cure for every African malady except the one this poison caused—and the doctor didn't have the antidote in his first-aid kit.

But Matt had no idea what was happening. He was very merry and said: 'Oh, now everything's turned blue. Everything looks so pretty.'

'Professor,' cried the doctor. 'Tell those savages that Matt has been poisoned.'

The professor translated quickly. The king of the cannibals clutched his head, did a sad somersault, and ran off like an arrow.

'Here, drink this, my white friend,' he cried, handing Matt some terribly bitter, sour liquid in an ivory bowl.

'Phooey, I don't want any,' cried Matt. 'Oh, now everything's green. The gold chair is green, and the doctor's green, too.'

Bum Drum grabbed Matt by the waist, put him on the table, propped his mouth open with an ivory arrow, and forced the bitter drink down Matt's throat.

Matt struggled and spat, but he swallowed the drink, and his life was saved.

In fact, black circles had already started spinning around in front of Matt's eyes. But there were only six of them, and all the rest were still green. Matt didn't die, but he slept for three days.

THE witch doctor was very ashamed that he had tried to poison Matt. But Matt forgave him. To make up for what he had done, the witch doctor promised to show Matt his greatest magic tricks, which he had been allowed to perform only three times in his entire life.

Everyone sat in front of a tent on tiger skins. Matt couldn't understand all of the witch doctor's tricks. A few were explained to him.

For example, the witch doctor took a little animal out of a box and held it in one hand. The animal, a sort of little snake, wound itself around the witch doctor's finger, stuck out its thin little tongue, made a strange hiss, and then, taking hold of the finger in its mouth, stood with its tail straight up in the air. The witch doctor pulled off the snakelike creature and showed everyone the drop of blood on his finger. Matt could see that the savages thought this was the best trick of all, though some of the others really were better. But then Matt was told that the snakelike creature was worse than a leopard or a hyena because its bite caused instant death.

The witch doctor walked through fire, flames burst out through his mouth and nose, but he never even said 'Ouch.'

Then the witch doctor made forty-nine enormous snakes dance to the tune of his flute. Then he blew on an enormous palm tree, which was about a hundred years old; the palm tree began slowly bending, until it finally broke. Then he stretched a rope between two trees and walked through the air on it as easily as if he were on a plank. Then he threw an ivory ball in the air. As it fell, he tilted back his head—the ball struck his head and disappeared without a trace. Then he whirled around for a very long time, and when he stopped, everyone saw that he now had two heads and two faces, one of which was laughing and the other crying. Then he took a little boy, cut off his head with a sword, and put it in a box. The witch doctor danced wildly around that box, and when he kicked the box, someone inside began playing the flute. The box was opened and there was the little boy, fine as could be. The boy stepped out and began doing gymnastics. The witch doctor repeated the trick with a bird: he let the bird go, it flew high in the air, and then he shot it with an arrow. The bird fell, pierced by the arrow. Then the bird pulled out the arrow with its beak, fluttered its wings, and flew over to the witch doctor to return the arrow.

Matt thought it was worth it to be poisoned a little to see so many tricks.

Matt toured his friend's country, traveling mostly by camel and elephant. He saw many villages in the enormous and beautiful forests. The huts where people and animals lived together were very dirty inside. Many of the people were sick, but it was easy to cure them. The doctor gave them medicine, and they were very grateful to him. In the forests, they often came across the bodies of people who had been torn apart by wild animals or bitten by poisonous snakes.

Matt felt very sorry for these poor people who had been so good to him.

Why didn't they build railroads for themselves, put in electric lights, why didn't they have movie theaters, why didn't they build themselves comfortable houses, why didn't they buy rifles to defend themselves against those terrible animals? After all, they had so much gold and so many diamonds that the children used them for toys.

These poor people suffered so much because their white brothers did not want to help them and were afraid of them. Then Matt got an idea—when he returned home, he would write at once to the newspapers that anyone who couldn't find work should go help Bum Drum's people by building stone houses and railroads for them.

Matt was thinking how to help the cannibals, but he was also wondering where he would find the money he needed to make reforms in his own country.

One day, they visited a large gold mine, and Matt asked King Bum Drum to lend him a little gold. Bum Drum started laughing wildly; he said that he had no use for gold and would give Matt as much as his camels could carry.

'Me, make loans to a friend? No, my friend can have anything he wants. Bum Drum loves his friend and wants to serve him all his life.'

When Matt was getting ready for his journey back, the king of the cannibals arranged a great celebration in honor of their friendship. This is what it was like.

Once a year, all the tribesmen gathered in the capital and selected those who would be eaten by the royal court during the upcoming year. The people who were chosen were terribly happy, and those whom the king did not choose were very upset. The people who would be eaten danced a wild dance of joy, and those who had not been chosen crawled around on their hands and knees in a sort of mourning dance. They sang, too, but a sad song which made it sound as if they were crying.

The king scratched his finger with a sharp shell, and then Matt scratched his own. The king of the cannibals licked a drop of blood from Matt's ring finger, and Matt had to do the same. Matt found this ceremony unpleasant, but the sad experience of almost being poisoned had taught him not to refuse anything and to do everything required of him. There was one more ceremony after the licking of the blood; Matt was thrown into a pond full of snakes and crocodiles, then King Bum Drum jumped into the pond and pulled Matt out. Then Matt was greased up with some sort of oil and he had to jump into a roaring fire. But Bum Drum jumped in right behind him and pulled Matt out of the fire so swiftly that only a few of Matt's hairs were a little singed. Then Matt had to jump to the ground from a very tall palm tree, but Bum Drum caught him so deftly that Matt was not hurt in the least.

The professor explained to Matt what all this was about: licking blood meant that if Matt was in the desert without water, his friend would give him his own blood to drink so Matt wouldn't die of thirst; the other ceremony meant that if Matt was ever threatened by danger—by fire, or in the air, or surrounded by enormous crocodiles in the water—his brother Bum Drum would risk his own life to rush to Matt's rescue.

'We Europeans,' said the professor, 'write everything down on paper, but they don't know how to write and so this is how they make their contracts.'

Matt was sorry to leave. Now he very much wanted to convince the foreign kings that even though the cannibals were wild they were still good people, and all the kings should become friends with them and help them. But, first, one reform would have to be made—they would have to stop being cannibals.

'Bum Drum, my friend,' said Matt when they were talking on their last evening together, 'I urge you to stop being a cannibal.'

Matt spent a long time explaining that it was wrong to eat people, that the foreign kings would never forgive that, and that Bum Drum had to introduce a reform against eating people; if he did, lots of Europeans would come and help them make progress, so that all the people in their beautiful country would have a good life.

Bum Drum listened to Matt sadly and then said that, once before, a king had tried to do just that, but he had been poisoned. It was a very hard reform to make, but he would give it some more thought.

Matt walked a little way into the forest after their conversation. The moon was shining beautifully. The world was lovely and still. But then Matt heard a rustling sound. What could that be? A snake or tiger coming at him?

He walked a little farther. There was another rustling sound. Someone was behind him. Matt pulled out his revolver and waited.

But it was just a little girl, jolly Klu Klu, the cannibal king's daughter. Matt saw her clearly in the bright moonlight. He wondered what she wanted.

'What do you want, Klu Klu?' asked Matt, using the cannibal language, which he could now speak a little.

'Klu Klu kiki rets—Klu Klu kin brum.'

She said a lot more, but Matt could understand only a few words of it. He saw that Klu Klu was very sad and had tears in her eyes. Matt felt sorry for little Klu Klu. And so he gave her his watch, a mirror, and a pretty little bottle. But Klu Klu didn't stop crying.

What could the matter be?

They went back, and Matt asked the professor to interpret. The professor told Matt that Klu Klu was saying that she loved Matt very much and wanted to go with him back to his kingdom.

Matt asked the professor to tell Klu Klu that she could not come to his kingdom alone, but her father, Bum Drum, would soon be invited to Europe, and then, of course, she could come with her father.

And that was the last Matt thought of little Klu Klu, especially since there was so much work to do before they left.

Fifty camels were loaded with boxes of gold and precious stones, delicious fruits of every kind, drinks, African delicacies, and also wine and cigars as gifts for the ministers. Matt said that in three months he would send cages to transport the wild animals for his zoo; he also warned Bum Drum that he might send some things by airplane and not to be frightened if a white man came flying in on a great iron bird.

The next morning, they climbed up on their camels and started on their way. The journey was hard, but they were all seasoned travelers now and so the desert did not exhaust them as much as before.

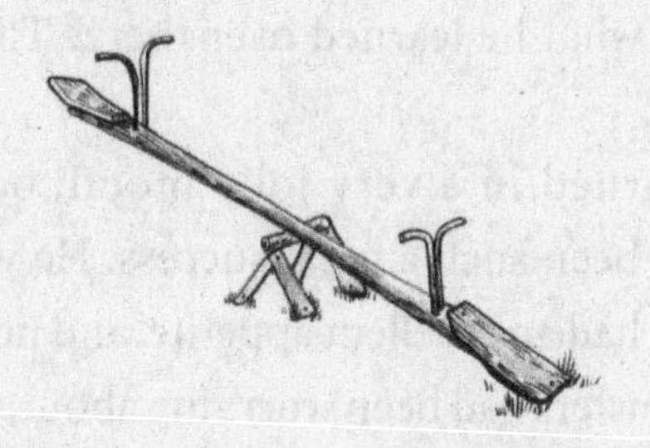

MEANWHILE, Matt's ministers had written the entire constitution and now were just waiting for him to return.

They waited and waited, but there was no sign of Matt. No one had any idea where Matt was. They knew that Matt had gone by ship to Africa and then taken a train to the garrison at the beginning of the desert; that Matt's group had lived in tents and the garrison officer had spoken with Matt. Then camels sent by the cannibal king had arrived, and that was the last anyone had heard of Matt.

Then one day a telegram arrived, saying that King Matt was alive and well and that he had set sail for home.

'He never fails, that Matt,' said the foreign kings enviously.

'That lucky Matt,' said the ministers, sighing. If it was hard to deal with Matt when he came back from war, what would it be like when he returned from the land of the cannibals?

'When he came back from the war, he put us in jail. Who knows what he learned over there? This time he might eat us.'

Matt returned in a very jolly mood, because his journey had been such a great success. He was tanned and taller, he had an excellent appetite, and not knowing what the ministers had been worrying about, he decided to joke around a little.

When they had all assembled for the royal conference, King Matt asked: 'Have the railroads been repaired?'

'They have,' said the minister.

'That's good, because otherwise I would have ordered you cooked in crocodile sauce. And have new factories been built?'

'Many,' said the Minister of Industry.

'That's good, because otherwise I'd have you stuffed with bananas and roasted.'

The ministers looked so frightened that Matt burst out laughing.

'Gentlemen,' said Matt, 'there's no reason to be afraid of me. I didn't become a cannibal, and I even hope I may have convinced my friend Bum Drum to quit his savage habit of eating people.'

The ministers would never have believed Matt's tales of adventure if he hadn't arrived with an entire train full of gold, silver, and gems. The ministers finally cheered up when Matt handed out the presents King Bum Drum had sent them—excellent cigars and delicious African wines.

Matt's proclamation of democracy was soon made public. It said that the newspapers would print a list of what the ministers and the king wanted to do and then everyone could voice his opinion, either by writing to the paper or by speaking out in parliament. At last the whole country could express its approval or disapproval of the ministers.

'All right, then,' said Matt. 'Now please write down what I want to do for the children. Now I have money of my own and can take care of them. And so every child is to be given two balls to play with in the summer and skis for the winter. Every day after school, all children are to be given a piece of candy and a nice piece of cake. Each year, the girls will be given dolls, and the boys will get jackknives. Every school should have a seesaw and a merry-go-round. Also, pretty color pictures are to be added to all school-books. That is only the beginning, because I am thinking of introducing many other reforms. So please figure out how much it will cost and how much time will be needed to get everything done. I would like your answer in a week.'

You can imagine how happy the children were when they found out about all this. Matt had already given them a lot, but the newspapers said it was only the beginning and there would be much more to come.

Any child who knew how to write wrote to King Matt requesting this, that, or the other. Sacks of letters from children began arriving at the royal chancellery. The secretary would open the letters, read them, then throw them away. That's how things were always done at royal chancelleries. Matt didn't know that. One day he saw a servant carrying a basket of papers to the royal rubbish heap.

Maybe he's got some rare stamps in there, thought Matt, who collected stamps and had a whole album of them. 'What are those papers and envelopes?' he asked.

'How should I know?' said the servant.

Matt looked and saw that they were all letters to him. He immediately ordered those letters brought to his room, and then he summoned his secretary.

'What sort of papers are these, Mr Secretary?' Matt asked.

'Those are unimportant letters to Your Royal Majesty.'

'And you ordered them thrown out?'

'That's how it has always been done.'

'Then it was badly done,' cried Matt impulsively. 'If a letter is written to me, then I am the only one who can know if it's important or not. Don't read my letters, send them to me. I'll know what's to be done with them.'

'Your Royal Majesty, a great many letters of all sorts are sent to kings. And if people found out that the kings actually read them, there'd be such mountains of letters that there'd be no dealing with them. As it is, there are five officials whose only job is to read those letters and choose which ones are important.'

'And which letters are important?' asked Matt.

'The letters from foreign kings, various manufacturers, and various great writers.'

'And which ones are unimportant?'

'It's mostly children who write to Your Royal Highness. Any time they get an idea, they sit down and write a letter. And some of them scribble so badly, you can barely read what they write.'

'All right, then. If it's too hard for you to read letters from kids, I'll read them. And you can give those officials other jobs. I'm a kid, too, for your information, but I've won a war against three grownup kings and I've made a journey that no one else dared to.'

The royal secretary made no answer but only bowed and left. Matt began reading the letters.

Matt was the sort of boy who did everything with enthusiasm. Hour after hour passed, but Matt kept on reading and reading.

Several times, the master of ceremonies peeped through the keyhole of the royal study to see what Matt was doing and to find out why he wasn't coming to dinner. But he saw the king bent over his papers, and so he was afraid to go in.

Matt soon saw for himself that it was too big a job for him. Some letters were very hard to read, and Matt began throwing them away. But some were very nicely written and very interesting. One boy wrote Matt a letter telling him how to make ice skates. Another boy told Matt his dreams. And there was a boy who wrote about his beautiful doves and rabbits and said that he wished to give King Matt two doves and one rabbit as a present but didn't know how to go about it. One girl wrote a little poem about King Matt and sent it to him with a pretty drawing. Another girl told about her doll, who was very happy because soon she would have a little sister. Many of the letters came with drawings. One boy sent Matt a present of a book of drawings entitled *King Matt in the Land of the Cannibals.* They were not very accurate, but they were pretty and gave Matt pleasure.

But most of the letters were requests. The children usually asked for ponies, bicycles, or cameras. One boy asked if he could be given a real soccer ball instead of just a plain old ball. One girl wrote that her mother was sick and they were poor and couldn't buy medicine. There was a student who had no boots and couldn't go to school; he even sent his school report, which said that he was a good student but had no boots.

Maybe it would be better to give the children boots instead of dolls and balls, thought Matt, who had learned to respect boots during the war.

Matt kept reading, but now he had started to feel awfully hungry. So he rang his bell and ordered his dinner brought to his study because he had urgent work and had to stay at his desk.

Matt sat up late into the night with those letters. The master of ceremonies peeped through the keyhole again to see why the king wasn't going to bed. All the servants wanted to go to bed, but they couldn't before the king did.

Matt put the letters with requests in a special pile. After all, that girl's mother had to be given medicine. And that good student really needed a pair of boots.

By then, Matt's eyes hurt from reading. He threw away all letters that were too hard to read, though that really didn't seem fair. Not long ago, Matt's handwriting hadn't been very good, even though he did sign important papers. A child might have something important to tell

Matt and would write as best he could—it wasn't his fault that his writing wasn't nice and clear yet.

Clerks could copy out all the poorly written letters for me, thought Matt.

But when a couple of more hours passed and there were still about two hundred letters on his desk, Matt realized that he had done all he could.

I'll finish them tomorrow, thought Matt. Feeling very sad, he went off to the royal bedroom.

Matt could see that it wasn't a very good situation. If he had to read that many letters every day, he wouldn't have time for anything else. But it seemed pretty rotten just to throw those letters out with the trash. Those were important letters, interesting letters. There were just so many of them!

THE next day Matt got up very early, drank only a glass of milk for breakfast, then went right to his study. He had no lessons and he read letters right up until lunchtime. It made him as tired as a long march or a trip through the desert. Just as Matt had started to think about lunch, the royal secretary came into his study, followed by four people.

'Today's mail for Your Royal Highness,' said the secretary.

Matt thought the secretary was smiling. That made him so angry that he stamped his foot and shouted: 'A hundred cannibals and crocodiles! What's going on here? Do you want me to go blind? No king could read through a stack of letters like this. How dare you joke with the king? I'll put you in jail.'

The more Matt shouted, the more he realized he was wrong, but it was too hard to admit it.

'All these freeloading officials who don't do a thing! All they know how to do is throw letters in the trash or give them to me to read.'

Fortunately, just then the Prime Minister came in.

He ordered that the sack of letters be taken away and told the secretary to wait in the next room while he discussed the royal correspondence with the king in private.

Matt felt much calmer when he saw the four servants carrying the sacks of letters out, but he pretended he still was angry.

'Mr Prime Minister, I cannot allow letters to me to be thrown out in the trash without being read. Why shouldn't I know what the children of my country need? Why should a boy stay out of school just because he has no boots? That isn't fair, and I'm very surprised that the Minister of Justice allows such things to happen. My friend King Bum Drum doesn't wear shoes, but he lives in a hot climate.'

The meeting between King Matt and the Prime Minister lasted a long time. They called in the secretary, who had spent more than twenty years reading the letters sent to Matt's father the king, and even to his grandfather the king, and so had a lot of experience in these matters.

'Your Royal Highness, when your grandfather was king, we used to receive a hundred letters a day. Those were good times. In the entire country, only a hundred thousand people knew how to write. Then King Stephen the Wise built schools and two million citizens learned to write. We started receiving six hundred to a thousand letters a day. I could no longer manage them all myself, and so I took on five officials to help. After our gracious King Matt gave the fire captain's daughter a doll, the children started writing letters. Between five and ten thousand letters arrive every day. Most of the letters come on Monday, because the children don't go to school on Sunday and have time to write letters. They love their king, and that's why they write to him. I was just about to ask for five more clerks, because it's too much for the ones I have, but—'

'I know, I know,' said Matt. 'But what's the good of reading the letters if they're thrown out with the trash?'

'The letters must be read, because there is a book where every letter is given a number and we record who wrote it and what it was about.'

To be sure the secretary was telling the truth, Matt asked: 'And was there a request for boots in one of those letters the servants were about to throw out yesterday?'

'I don't remember, but we can check.'

Two clerks carried in an enormous book and there, indeed, next to number 47,000,000,000, was the boy's name and address, and in the column headed 'Contents of Letter' it said: 'A request for boots to wear to school.'

'I have been an official for twenty years, and my chancellery has always been in order.'

Matt was fair. He shook the secretary's hand and said: 'My warmest thanks.'

They thought up a solution.

The letters would be read, as they had been, by the clerks. The most interesting letters would be selected for Matt but would be limited to no more than one hundred. Two special clerks would check up on the letters containing requests to make sure they were telling the truth.

A boy could write that he needed boots. But maybe he was lying. If the king sent him boots, he might sell them and buy himself all sorts of stupid things.

Matt had to admit that was a good point. He remembered that during the war there was one soldier in their division who sold his boots to buy vodka and then asked for a new pair.

'It's a terrible shame that you can't trust people.'

'There's another way of doing it. The clerks can check to see if they're telling the truth. Then the royal chancellery can send for the children to come for an audience where Your Royal Highness can grant their requests in person.'

Yes, that's a good idea, thought Matt. I want to have audiences with children, not just foreign envoys and ministers.

Things had turned out well. Now Matt knew how he should act as the king of the children. He would have lessons until twelve o'clock. The royal snack would be served at noon. Then an hour's audience for envoys and ministers; then he would read letters until lunchtime. After lunch, he would hold the audience for the children, then meet with his ministers until suppertime. Then to bed.

But his schedule made Matt sad. There wasn't even an hour left to play. That was too bad, but he was the king. Even a little king can't worry about himself. A king has to care for his subjects all the time.

Maybe later on, when he'd given everyone what they needed, Matt would have an hour a day for himself.

Well, thought Matt, I did do some traveling. I saw many wonderful things, I was by the sea for a month, I was in the land of the cannibals, but now I can't play any more. Now I must do my duty as king.

That was that.

Matt studied in the morning, and then the letters were read to him. The clerks read very quickly, but it was hard for Matt to sit still for such a long time, and so he listened while pacing the room with his hands clasped behind his back.

The doctor said that since the weather was so beautiful and warm, the reading of the letters could take place in the royal gardens. And it really was much nicer there.

There were a great many audiences. The foreign envoys came to ask when Matt would open the parliament, because they wanted to come and see his democracy at work. The ministers came with the manufacturers who were building the seesaws and merry-go-rounds to ask the king how he wished them to be made. And savages came from the whole world over to tell Matt that their kings wanted to live in friendship with him.

They thought that if King Matt was now friends with Bum Drum, the king of the cannibals, then he wouldn't look down his nose at them, because even though they were savages, they had already stopped eating people.

'We haven't eaten any people for thirty years now,' said one.

'The last person we ate was forty years ago. And even that was an unusual case. That person was a good-for-nothing lazybones. And he was fat, too. When he was brought to trial for the fifth time for refusing to work, everyone voted that he should be eaten.'

King Matt was more careful now. He made no promises, he ordered that everything be written down and told everyone to come for an answer in a week because he had to confer with his Minister of Foreign Affairs, and as a rule, such questions could only be discussed at a meeting of the ministers.

Matt enjoyed the audiences with the children very much. The boys and girls were allowed into the throne room, where Matt granted the requests they had made in their letters. Every child was given a number, which was also on the package he was to be given. No one was admitted to an audience until the official had checked that the child really needed what he was asking for, and until it had been bought in a store on Matt's command. Everything was orderly and all the children were happy.

One child would be given a warm coat, another the books he needed but couldn't afford to buy. The girls usually asked for combs and toothbrushes. Children with artistic talent were given paints. One boy very much wanted a violin, because he had been playing the accordion for a long time and was bored with it. He even played Matt a tune on his accordion and was very happy when he received a new violin in a handsome case.

Matt would become very angry if anyone changed their request during an audience. Matt had given one girl a new dress to wear to her aunt's wedding and then she asked for a doll that reached up to the sky.

'You're a dope,' said Matt, 'and because you asked for too much, I won't even give you the dress.'

Matt was a pretty experienced king now and harder to fool.

ONE day, during the afternoon audience, Matt heard an unusual hullabaloo in the waiting room. At first he was not very surprised, because now the children were used to coming to the palace and did not sit still while waiting for their audience. But this was a different sort of hullabaloo, more like an argument. Matt sent a footman to find out what was going on. The footman returned to say that some stubborn grownup was insisting on seeing the king. Matt was curious and ordered that the man be admitted.

A long-haired young man with a briefcase under his arm came in and, without even bowing, began to speak loudly.

'Your Royal Highness, I am a journalist. That means I write for the newspapers. I have been trying to get an audience for a month now, but they wouldn't let me in. They kept saying 'Tomorrow, tomorrow.' But then they'd say the king was tired and to come back the next day. And so finally today I pretended to be the father of one of the children, thinking I might get in quicker. I have several very important matters to discuss, and I'm sure Your Royal Highness will want to hear what I have to say.'

'All right,' said Matt. 'But wait until I'm done with the children, because this is their time. And then I will talk to you.'

'Would Your Royal Highness permit me to stay in the throne room? I won't make any noise, and I won't interfere. And tomorrow I will write about the audience in the newspaper. That will be very interesting for our readers.'

Matt ordered that the journalist be given a chair. The journalist kept jotting things down in his notebook throughout the remainder of the audience.

'Well, let's hear,' said Matt, when the last child had left the throne room.

'My king,' the journalist began. 'I won't take much of your time. I'll be brief.'

In spite of his promise, the journalist spoke for a long time, but what he said was interesting. Matt listened closely, then finally interrupted him. 'I can see that this really is an important matter. And so won't you please have dinner with me now? Then we'll go to my study and you can finish.'

The journalist talked until eleven o'clock that night. Matt paced back and forth in his study, his hands clasped behind his back, listening carefully. This was the first person Matt had met who wrote for a newspaper. Matt had to admit that the journalist was an intelligent person, and even though he was a grownup, he did not act like Matt's ministers.

'Do you draw, too?'

'No, every newspaper has some people to do the writing and others to do the drawings. We would be most pleased if Your Royal Highness visited our newspaper.'

Matt hadn't been away from the palace for quite some time, and so he was very glad to accept the invitation.

He was driven to the newspaper offices first thing the next morning.

The large building had been decked with flags and flowers for Matt's arrival. On the ground floor were the enormous machines that printed the newspaper. The office where the papers were mailed out and distributed was upstairs. There was a separate little office where people brought advertisements and payments. Even higher up was the editorial office, where people sat at desks writing the stories that would immediately be printed down below. Telegrams came in from all over the world, the telephones were ringing constantly, grimy boys ran around carrying the copy to the typesetters, people were drawing pictures, machines were clattering. It reminded Matt of war.

Matt was given a silver platter with a fresh copy of the newspaper, which contained a photograph of Matt and a story about the children's audience. They had printed everything—what the children had said to Matt, and what Matt had said in reply.

Matt spent two whole hours in the newspaper building and very much liked how swiftly everything moved there. Now he was no longer surprised that the newspapers could carry stories about everything, no matter where it happened — fires, robberies, traffic accidents, or what the kings and ministers were doing throughout the world.

The journalist was right—the newspapers knew everything. The newspapers had been quick to write about what Matt did when he was the guest of the foreign kings, they reported everything about the war and even had seemed to know before anyone else when Matt was on his way back from the land of the cannibals.

'But how come you didn't know that I ran away to the front and there was only a porcelain doll here?'

'Oh, we knew all that perfectly well, it's just that we don't write about everything. We only write what needs to be written in the papers. The whole country doesn't have to know everything. And there are many things that shouldn't be known abroad.'

That evening, Matt had another long conversation with the journalist, who now said that Matt was not making real reforms. Matt was not a real reformer yet, but he could become one. Matt wanted all the people to govern, but children were part of the people, too. And so he should create two parliaments, one for the grownups and one for the children. The children could elect their own members of parliament and tell them what they wanted the most— chocolate, dolls, jackknives, whatever. Maybe they'd rather have candy, maybe boots, or maybe they'd rather get money and everyone could buy what he wanted. The children should have a newspaper like the grownups did, one that came out every day. And they could use the newspaper to inform the king of what they wanted; otherwise, the king would do whatever came into his head. After all, a king can't know everything, but a newspaper could. For example, not all children had received their chocolate that first time, because some officials just ate the chocolate themselves. And the children didn't even know that they had chocolate coming to them, because they had no newspaper of their own.

All this seemed so obvious to Matt now that he even thought it was his own idea. After four evenings talking with the journalist, it all came together in his mind, and at the next meeting of the ministers he brought up the subject.

'Gentlemen,' began Matt, and then took a drink of water, because he intended to speak for a long time. 'We have decided on a democratic form of government. But, gentlemen, you forgot that our country has children as well as grownups. We have several million children, and they should help govern the country, too. Let there be two parliaments—one for the grownups with grownup senators and grownup ministers. And the other one will be the children's parliament, and there children will be the delegates and the ministers. I am the king of the grownups and the children, but if the grownups consider me too little for them, let them elect themselves a grownup king and I will be the king of the children.'

Matt spoke so long that he had to stop for water four times. The ministers realized that this was no joke, this wasn't chocolate, skates, or seesaws, this was a very serious reform.

'I know this is difficult,' concluded Matt. 'All reforms are difficult. But we have to begin somewhere. If I don't succeed in everything, then my son, or my grandson, will finish these reforms of mine.'

The ministers bowed their heads. Never before had Matt spoken at such length and so wisely. And what he said was true—children were part of the nation, and they had the right to govern, too. But could it be done? Could they succeed, or were they too foolish?

The ministers couldn't say that children were foolish, because Matt was a child. There were no two ways about it —they'd have to give it a try.

Setting up a newspaper for children was no problem. Matt had brought back a lot of gold, and so there was money to pay for it. But who would write for the children's newspaper?

'I know a good journalist,' said Matt.

'And who'll be the Prime Minister?'

'Felek will be the Prime Minister.'

Matt was very anxious to convince Felek that he was still his friend. Felek teased Matt often, saying: 'Your good graces aren't too reliable. Felek is fine when it comes to bullets and war. But Stash and Helenka are better for going to balls and theaters and collecting shells at the seashore. But Felek went to the land of the cannibals because that was dangerous and Stash and Helenka's mother didn't let them go. Oh well, my father's just a platoon leader, not a captain. But the next time there's trouble, you'll turn to Felek for help.'

It is very unpleasant to be accused of being haughty or, even worse, of being ungrateful.

But now there was a way to show Felek that he was wrong and that Matt did not think of him only when he was in trouble. Felek would be just right for the job—he was always running around town and would be certain to know what the children needed.

POOR Matt. He wanted to be a real king, to rule the country, to understand everything. And now his wish had come true. But Matt had never imagined how much work, trouble, and worry would come down on his head.

Everything was going well throughout the land. Construction of the children's camps was under way, and so the architects, bricklayers, carpenters, tilesetters, plumbers, locksmiths, and glaziers were satisfied because they were earning a lot of money. The brickyards, the sawmills, and the glass factories had orders to fill; a special ice-skate factory was being built, and four large candy and chocolate factories were under construction. Special railroad cars were being manufactured to cage and transport the wild animals; the cars for the elephants and camels were difficult and very expensive to produce, and a special car had to be designed for the giraffes because of their long necks. The zoo was nearing completion, not to mention the two large buildings where delegates from the entire country would gather to deliberate, govern, and make laws.

One of the parliament buildings was for the grownups, and one for the children. The children's parliament was just like the grownups', except that the door handles were lower, so that even the littlest delegates could open the doors themselves; the chairs were low, so their legs wouldn't dangle in the air, and the windows were lower, too, so the children could look outside if a meeting wasn't too interesting.

The craftsmen and workers were happy to have work, the manufacturers were happy to be making profits, and the children were happy that their king cared about them. The children liked having their own newspaper in which anybody could say what he wanted to. Now the children who didn't know how to read and write were in a rush to learn, because they wanted to know what was going on and to write to their newspaper about what they thought should be done.

Parents and teachers were happy that the children were studying so hard. And now there were fewer fights in school, because everyone wanted to be liked and be elected a delegate.

Now practically everyone loved Matt, not just the soldiers. People marveled that so young a king had learned so quickly and ruled so well.

But people didn't know what troubles Matt had. And the worst thing of all was that the foreign kings were growing more and more envious of Matt.

'What's Matt up to?' they asked. 'We've already been ruling for a long time. Does he want to surpass us all in a day? It's no big deal to do good deeds with somebody else's money. Bum Drum gave him gold, and now Matt orders people around. And is it proper for a civilized king to make friends with cannibals?'

Matt had learned of all this from his spies. The Minister of Foreign Affairs warned him that there might be another war.

Matt did not want another war. He did not want to tear himself away from his work. War would mean that the construction crews would have to go back to the trenches and the children's camps would be left unfinished. Matt wanted the children to spend the next summer in the country, and he also wanted both parliaments, the one for the grownups and the one for the children, to open in the fall.

'What can be done to avoid another war?' asked Matt, pacing his office, taking long strides, his hands clasped behind his back.

'If the foreign kings quarreled, and the stronger ones became friends with you, war could be avoided,' said the Minister of Foreign Affairs.

'Oh, that would be perfect. I think the sad king who plays the violin might become friends with us. He told me that he had no desire to go to war with me the last time, and he suffered the least because his army was kept in reserve. And it was he who advised me to carry out reforms for the children.'

'What Your Royal Highness is telling me is very important,' said the Minister of Foreign Affairs. 'Yes, he might make friends with us. But the other two will always remain our enemies.'

'Why?' asked Matt.

'One of them is angry now because the people will govern here.'

'What does he care?'

'He cares a lot, because if his people find out, then they'll want to govern, too, they won't want him giving them any more orders. And there'll be a revolution there.'

'And the other king?'

'The other one? Hm, you might be able to come to an understanding with him. He's mostly angry because now the Oriental and African kings love us more than they love him. They used to send him presents, but now they send them to us. We could make an agreement with him—he can be friends with the Oriental kings and we'll be friends with the African kings.'

'All right, then, we have to try, because I don't want another war,' said Matt firmly.

That same evening, King Matt sat down to write a letter to the sad king who played the violin.

> My spies have informed me that the foreign kings are envious because Bum Drum gave me gold, and are going to attack me. So I am requesting that Your Royal Highness remain my friend and be on my side this time.

Matt wrote a great deal about his reforms and asked for advice about what to do next. He had so much work, it was so hard to be a king. He told the sad king not to worry if somebody shouted 'Down with the king' in parliament—you couldn't make all of the people happy all of the time.

It was late at night when Matt put down his pen. He went out onto the royal balcony and looked at his capital. The streetlights were on, but the windows in the houses were dark, because by now everyone was asleep.

Matt thought: All the children are sleeping peacefully. I am the only one still up. I have to write letters at night so there won't be a war, so that the camps can be finished in peace and the children can spend this summer there. Children only think about schoolwork and games, but I don't even have time to study or play, because I have to think about all the children in my country.

Matt went to his room and looked at his toys, which were all dusty, because he had not played with them for a long time.

'My little puppet,' said Matt to his puppet, 'you must be angry at me for not playing with you for so long. But what can I do? You're a wooden puppet, and as long as you're not broken, you don't need anything. But I have to think about real people who need lots of things.'

Matt lay down, turned off the light, and was just about asleep, when he remembered that he still hadn't written a letter to the second king to say that Matt would be friends with the Africans and the second king could keep on receiving presents from the Oriental kings.

What to do now? Both letters had to be sent at the same time. It couldn't wait—otherwise, war might be declared before the letters arrived.

So Matt got up, even though his head ached from weariness, and he wrote a long letter to the second foreign king, which took until dawn.

And then, after a night without any sleep, he did a whole day's work again. That was a very hard day for Matt, because a telegram arrived from the seaport. It said that King Bum Drum had sent him a whole boatful of wild animals and gold, but one of the foreign kings would not allow it to be transported across his country.

The foreign kings' ambassadors arrived and said that they didn't want presents from cannibals to be transported across their countries and that just because they allowed it once didn't mean that they had to do whatever Matt wanted. Matt was taking too many liberties. Matt had defeated them once, but that didn't mean anything, because they had bought new cannons and weren't in the least afraid of Matt.

All in all, they spoke as if they wanted to start an argument. One of them even stamped his foot. The master of ceremonies remarked that etiquette did not permit people to stamp their feet when talking with a king.

At first, Matt flushed red with anger, because the blood of Henryk the Hasty flowed in his veins, and when they said they weren't afraid of Matt, he almost shouted: And I'm not afraid of you, either! We can have another go at it, and then we'll see what's what.

But a moment later Matt had regained his composure and began to speak as if he had no idea what they were up to.

'My dear ambassadors, there's no reason for your kings to be afraid of me. Just last night, I wrote them letters saying that I want to be friends with them. Please hand me those letters. There are only two letters, but I'll write to the third king right away. I'll be glad to pay if you don't want Bum Drum's presents shipped across your countries for nothing. I didn't know it was causing your kings any unhappiness.'

The ambassadors didn't know what Matt had written to their kings, because the envelopes were closed and sealed with the royal seal, and so they said no more. They only muttered under their breath and went away.

Matt had a meeting with the journalist, another with Felek, and then one with the ministers. And then an audience, followed by the signing of papers. Then he inspected the troops, because it was the anniversary of the battle won by the royal army during the time of Witold the Conqueror.

In the evening, Matt was so tired and pale that the doctor was very worried.

'You have to respect your health,' said the doctor. 'Your Royal Highness is working a lot, and eating and sleeping very little. Your Royal Highness is still growing and could fall ill with tuberculosis and start spitting blood.'

'I was spitting blood yesterday,' said Matt.

The doctor became even more frightened. He examined Matt, but it turned out not to be tuberculosis; Matt had just lost a tooth, and that was why he had been spitting blood.

'Where is the tooth?' asked the master of ceremonies.

'I threw it in the wastepaper basket.'

The master of ceremonies didn't say anything, but thought to himself: Fine times these are, when a king's teeth are thrown out with the trash.

Court etiquette required that when a royal tooth fell out it was to be set in gold and placed in a diamond-studded box that was kept in the treasury.

A MEETING of the kings had become an absolute must. First, Matt had been their guest, and so now he should invite them to visit his country. Second, the parliaments should be opened with great ceremony and with all the kings attending. Furthermore, they had to be shown the new zoo. And, most important, they had to discuss whether they wanted to live in friendship or not.

Letter after letter, telegram after telegram was sent, the ministers were always on the move. It was an important issue: either there would be friendship, peace, and prosperity—or another war.

There were meetings day and night, both at Matt's palace and at those of the foreign kings.

One ambassador came and said: 'My king wants to live in friendship with Matt.'

'But why is your king recruiting troops and building new fortresses? You don't build new fortresses unless you're thinking about war.'

'My king,' said the ambassador, 'lost the last war, and so now he must be on his guard, but that doesn't mean that he intends to attack Matt.'

But Matt's spies had reported that the first king posed the greatest threat.

Actually, the king did not want a war, because he was old and tired. But his eldest son, the heir to the throne, wanted war with Matt.

Matt's spies had even overheard a conversation between the old king and his son.

'Father, you're old and weak now,' said the son. 'It would be best for you to hand the throne over to me so I can deal with Matt.'

'What harm did Matt do to you? He's very nice, and I like him very much.'

'You like him, but so what? He wrote a letter to the sad king telling him to leave us and be friends with him. He wants to give the second king all the Oriental kings and keep Bum Drum and the African kings for himself. And who will be with us then, who will send us gold and presents? Then we'll be all alone and they'll be friends with Matt and so all three of them will attack us. We must build two new fortresses and draft more soldiers.'

The old king's son knew everything, because he had his own spies who reported to him.

The old king had to agree to draft more men and to build one more fortress, for he was afraid that if there was a war and they lost again, his son would say: 'Didn't I tell you, Father, it would turn out like this? You should have given me the throne and the crown so this wouldn't have happened.'

And it went on like that all through the fall and winter, no one knowing who would be friends with whom.

It was only when Matt sent out the letters inviting them all to be his guests that they were forced to show their true colors—would they come to see him or not?

Matt received one reply to the invitation, which said: 'Of course, we will be glad to come, but on the condition that Matt does not invite Bum Drum. We are civilized kings and we do not wish to sit at the same table with cannibals. Our fine breeding and our royal honor does not permit us to socialize with savages.'

That answer hurt poor Matt's feelings, because it seemed to say that he was not well-bred and had no royal honor. The Minister of Foreign Affairs advised him to pretend that he had not noticed the insult, but Matt would not agree.

'I don't want to pretend that I didn't notice it. And I won't. Not only have they offended me, they have insulted my friend who has sworn to be true to me in danger, who is ready to go through fire for me, and who wanted to be eaten by me as proof of his great love. It's too bad that he's so uncivilized, but he wants to change his ways. He is my true friend, he trusts me, and we do not have spies in each other's countries. But those civilized kings are false and treacherous. And I am going to write them all this.'

The Minister of Foreign Affairs was very frightened. 'Your Royal Highness does not want war, but a reply like that means war. You can write them, but not like that.'

Again, Matt did not sleep the whole night. He composed his reply with the aid of his ministers. It read: 'King Matt made friends with Bum Drum precisely so that Bum Drum would stop being a cannibal. Bum Drum promised Matt that he would not eat people any more. If Bum Drum has not kept his word, that is only because he is afraid that the witch doctors would poison him because they do not want their people to stop being cannibals. Besides, Matt is prepared to check whether Bum Drum has stopped being a cannibal or not and to let you know.'

At the end of the letter, Matt wrote: 'And I assure Your Royal Highnesses that both my honor and that of my African friend are dear to me and I am prepared to defend that honor at the cost of my own life and blood.'

That meant that the foreign kings should beware, for Matt would not allow himself to be offended, and though he did not want war, he wasn't afraid of one, either.

The foreign kings wrote back: 'All right, if Bum Drum has ceased being a cannibal, he can come to see Matt along with us.'

The foreign kings, actually only the first one, wanted to delay things because his new fortress was not ready yet. This is what they thought: If Matt writes us that Bum Drum is no longer a cannibal, we'll reply that African kings break their word and can't be trusted. And for that reason we don't accept his invitation.

What they didn't expect was that Matt would outfox them again.

As soon as he received their answer, Matt declared: 'I will go by airplane to see King Bum Drum to make certain that he is no longer eating human flesh.'

The ministers advised Matt against such a dangerous journey, but to no avail. The wind could make the plane crash, the pilot could get lost, they could run out of fuel, something could go wrong with the motor.

Even the manufacturer who was to build the airplane, and would of course earn a lot of money from it, advised Matt against it. 'I can't guarantee that the airplane won't have any problem during five days in the air. Airplanes usually fly in the cooler countries, and we still don't know whether heat can cause anything to go wrong. A part might break, and there aren't any mechanics in the desert.'

Besides, the airplane could carry only the pilot and Matt. And how would Matt communicate with Bum Drum without the professor who knew fifty languages?

Matt nodded his head that yes, he understood that it was a very difficult and dangerous journey, that he really might die in the desert sands, that it would be very difficult to communicate with Bum Drum without the professor, but in spite of everything, he had made up his mind to go and go he would.

He urged the manufacturer to spare no expense, to hire only master craftsmen, to use the best equipment and materials, and to make the best airplane possible as fast as he could.

The manufacturer set all other work aside; the best mechanics worked three shifts, day and night. The chief engineer at the factory did so many calculations that he went out of his mind and had to spend two months in the hospital. Matt would go to the factory every day in the royal car and spend a few hours there, carefully examining every hose and every screw.

It's not difficult to imagine the impression this made both at home and abroad. The newspapers wrote about practically nothing but the king's journey. Matt was called 'King of the Air,' 'King of the Desert,' 'Matt the Great,' and 'Mad Matt.'

'It's curtains for him this time,' said some spiteful people. 'Matt pulled off two good ones, but he won't succeed this time.'

Matt spent a long time searching for a pilot. Two people applied for the job. One was an older man who had no legs and only one eye. Felek was the other applicant.

The legless pilot was actually the senior mechanic who had assembled the plane. He had been flying since the early days of aviation, when airplanes were rickety and crashed often. He had crashed seven times, been seriously hurt four times, but had lived through it all. Once he lost an eye, once his legs were mashed, and once he broke two ribs and his brain was so badly shaken that he was in the hospital for a year, unable to speak. He still did not speak very clearly. His last accident had made him reluctant to fly, but he loved airplanes so much that he took a job at the factory so he could work on them and be around them, even though he could no longer fly them.

But he would go with King Matt. He had powerful hands, and one good eye was enough.

Felek understood that he couldn't be compared with such an experienced pilot, and at heart he was glad not to be going. He thought the same thing as everyone else—you could go on a journey like that, but coming back was another story.

And so Mad Matt and the legless, one-eyed pilot set out on their journey to the land of King Bum Drum.

THE officer in charge of the garrison was sitting with the telegraph operator, smoking his pipe and chatting on about one thing and another.

'It's a lousy life, I tell you. Stuck in this godforsaken African village at the edge of the desert. Since King Matt left, King Bum Drum's been shipping wild animals in cages and sacks of gold through here every day. Those animals will get to live in Matt's capital, a beautiful, civilized city—and me, a human being, will have to stay in the desert until the day I die. Before, the natives revolted once in a while and you could have a fight. But since they made friends with King Matt, they've been peaceful and haven't attacked us once. What the hell are we doing here? Another year or two like this and we'll forget how to shoot a gun.'

The telegraph operator was about to say something, when suddenly the telegraph began tapping.

'Oho, it's a telegram.'

Letters began to appear on the white strip of paper.

'Ohoho, interesting news.'

'What is it?'

'I don't know yet. One second. "King Matt will arrive by train tomorrow at sixteen hundred hours to fly by plane across the desert to King Bum Drum. While unloading his plane, break some part that will ground it. This is a secret." '

'I see,' said the captain. 'Our kings don't want Matt friendly with Bum Drum. I don't like this order. They don't want to make friends with the cannibals, but still they're standing in Matt's way. That's really rotten. But what can I do? I'm an officer, I have to obey orders.'

The officer immediately summoned a soldier he trusted and ordered him to disguise himself as a porter.

'All the railroad porters are black. When Matt sees a white porter who speaks their language, I'm sure he'll hire you to keep an eye on them. Then you can unfasten a bolt to keep the plane from flying.'

'Yes, sir,' said the soldier. Then he disguised himself as a porter and set off for the station.

Matt was surrounded by natives as soon as he arrived. Matt told them in sign language to unload the plane carefully, but he was afraid that they hadn't understood. Then suddenly a white porter appeared. Matt was relieved.

'I'll pay you well,' said Matt. 'Just explain everything to them and keep an eye on things.'

The captain came running up as if he had just learned of Matt's arrival.

'What? By airplane. Ho-ho, that's a fine trip. When, tomorrow? The king should spend a couple of days with us and rest up. Anyway, come have breakfast with us, gentlemen.'

Matt was quick to agree, but the pilot absolutely refused to go.

'I'd rather keep the one eye I have on what's happening here, to make sure nobody pulls any fast ones on us.'

'I'll keep watch,' said the soldier disguised as a porter.

But the legless pilot was a stubborn man. No, no. He wasn't budging an inch until the airplane was unloaded from the train and fully assembled.

Well, how can you beat someone that stubborn? First the black porters unloaded the wings, then the case with the motor, then the propeller. Directed by the pilot, they began assembling the plane. The disguised soldier kept trying to get rid of the pilot, but he couldn't find a way. So he treated him to a cigar doused with knockout drops. The pilot fell asleep after a couple of puffs.

'Let the man sleep, he's very tired from his trip. And you're tired from working, too,' said the soldier to the black porters. 'Here's some money, go buy yourselves a drink.'

Now the black porters were gone and the pilot was out cold. The soldier unscrewed the most important bolt on the motor, then buried it deep in the sand by a palm tree.

The pilot woke up an hour later, a little ashamed of having fallen asleep on the job. He put the finishing touches on the plane, which the porters had rolled to the edge of Matt's camp.

'And so?' the officer asked the soldier in a soft voice.

'Everything's under control,' answered the soldier. 'I buried the part by a palm tree. Or should I have brought it to you?'

'No, no need to. It can stay where it is.'

Matt was up before dawn, preparing to leave. He had a four-day supply of water, a little food, and two revolvers. They filled up with gas and took along some spare oil for the motor. That was all; the airplane had to be kept light.

'All right, we can leave.'

Now what's wrong? The motor won't start. What's the problem? After all, the pilot had packed the plane himself and then assembled it himself.

'The main bolt is missing!' shouted the pilot suddenly. 'Who could have taken it?'

'What bolt?' asked the officer.

'Right here, there was a bolt here. We can't fly without it.'

'And didn't you bring a spare bolt?'

'Do you think I'm crazy? I brought parts that could break or get damaged on the way, but bolts don't break or go bad.'

'Maybe they forgot to pack it?'

'Not a chance! I packed it myself at the factory. And I saw it yesterday when the motor was out of its crate. Somebody took it on purpose.'

'If it was a shiny bolt,' said the officer, 'the natives might have taken it, they're crazy about shiny things.'

Standing by the plane, furious at his bad luck, Matt suddenly noticed something shiny in the sand. 'What's that over there? Go take a look, gentlemen.'

Everyone was astonished—it was the missing bolt.

'What a devilish country this is,' cried the pilot. 'The strangest things happen here. I swear I've never fallen asleep on the job in my entire life, but yesterday I did. I've had all sorts of problems with airplanes, but that bolt is always on the tightest, and I've never seen one come loose. And how did it end up here?'

'Let's hurry,' said Matt. 'We've already lost an hour.'

The officer was very surprised by what had happened, and the soldier who had stolen the bolt was the most surprised of all. Those black devils have played some sort of trick, he thought. And he was right.

When the natives went to the tavern, they began talking about the strange machine they had unloaded from the train.

'It's like a bird. The white king will fly in the bird to see Bum Drum the cannibal.'

'What won't those people think of next.' They nodded their heads in amazement.

'But for me,' said one old native, 'that white porter is even stranger than the bird. I've been working with white people for thirty years, and I don't ever remember a white man feeling sorry because a black worker was tired, and giving him money before the work was done.'

'And where did he come from? Did he come with them?'

'I tell you he's one of the white men from around here disguised as a porter. He speaks our language too well for a white man.'

'And didn't you notice the man with no legs fell asleep when the white porter gave him a cigar? It must have had knockout drops in it.'

'There's something going on here.' They all agreed to that.

The white porter had left when the job was done, and then the natives sat down not far from the palm tree where he had buried the bolt. Suddenly one young native cried: 'This sand's been freshly dug. Something's been buried here. I remember that the sand by this palm tree was smooth when we started working.'

They began to dig, found the bolt, and figured out the rest.

What to do? The white people wanted to play a dirty trick on Matt, but the blacks loved Matt. After all, weren't they earning plenty of money unloading the cages, boxes, and sacks from Bum Drum's camels and loading them onto that fire-breathing dragon which the white people called a train?

But what should they do? If they went to Matt and gave him back the bolt, the officer from the garrison would punish them severely. After talking it over, they decided to slip into the camp that night and dig away some sand so the bolt could be spotted.

And so it was that, with the help of some honest natives, Matt was again on his way, in spite of a three-hour delay.

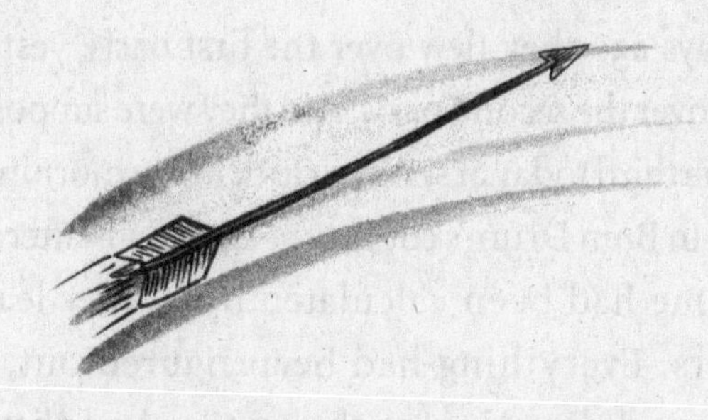

THEY were lost!

If you've never been lost, you can't know what it's like. At least, if you're lost in a forest, there are trees around you and you might come upon a forester's cottage. There are berries and streams in the forest; you can drink some water and fall asleep under a tree. If your ship goes off course, the other people on board can cheer you up and make you feel better. There's always food on a ship, and sooner or later you'll catch sight of an island. But to lose your way in the air above a desert is probably the most terrible thing that can happen to anyone. There's no one to ask directions from, no landmarks, and you can't even take a nap when you're tired.

You just sit there in that god-awful bird, which is flying like an arrow, though you have no idea where. All you know is that it will fly as long as it has fuel and oil, and then it will drop like a stone. When the bird dies, your hopes die with it, and that means certain death on the hot desert sand.

Two days ago they flew over the first oasis, yesterday they flew over the second oasis, and they were supposed to fly over the third today at seven o'clock in the morning and then land in Bum Drum's country at four in the afternoon.

The time had been calculated by twenty learned professors. Everything had been figured out, even the force and direction of the winds. And they had been flying straight all the time because there were no obstacles to be avoided in the air.

So what had gone wrong?

They were supposed to fly over the third oasis at seven o'clock in the morning, and here it was seven-forty and all they could see was sand and more sand.

'How long can we stay up in the air?'

'Nine hours at most. There might be enough fuel for more, but the beast drinks too much oil. What can you do? It's hot here, the beast wants to drink, nothing surprising about that.'

That made sense to them, because their own water supply was running low.

'Your Royal Highness should drink some water,' said the pilot. 'I need less than you, because I left my legs back home.'

He was trying to joke, but Matt saw that the brave pilot had tears in his eyes.

Seven forty-five.

Seven-fifty.

Eight o'clock.

No oasis in sight.

'I wouldn't mind dying in a storm or something. But everything had been going so well. We passed the first oasis ten seconds ahead of schedule, and the second oasis four seconds behind. We've been flying at the same speed, so we might have been five minutes late. But not a whole hour.'

And they were so close to their destination! And this journey was so important! Now what?

'Maybe we should change direction,' advised Matt.

'It's easy to change direction. My airplane only needs one little turn of the wheel. It flies so beautifully! It's not to blame for what happened. So don't you worry, my little bird. Change direction, but why? And where to? I think we should keep flying. Maybe it's another devilish trick, like what happened to the bolt. How did it get lost, then turn up again right away? The motor wants another drink of oil. Here's another glassful, you silly plane, but don't get drunk, that's asking for disaster.'

'An oasis!' cried Matt, who had kept his eyes glued to the binoculars.

'All right,' said the pilot, who was just as calm now when he was happy as he had been a moment before, when he was worried.

'Any oasis is good. We're an hour and five minutes late. But that's not so terrible. We have enough gas for an extra three hours, because we're not heading into the wind. And so let's have a drink.'

The pilot poured a cup of water for himself and tapped it against the oil tank, saying: 'To you, buddy.'

After he gave the plane a good squirt of oil, he drank the whole cup of water.

'Would Your Royal Highness allow me to have the binoculars for one moment, so I can see this miracle with my one good eye?

'Ah, what beautiful trees Bum Drum has. Is Your Royal Highness certain that Bum Drum has quit being a cannibal? Being eaten is not so bad if you know that you'll taste good. But I'm tough and stringy, of course, and without legs there's not much meat on me. And a soup made from my carcass wouldn't be very nourishing.'

Matt could not help wondering why this quiet man who had said practically nothing the whole trip had now suddenly become talkative and cheerful.

'Is Your Royal Highness certain that this is the right oasis? Should we keep flying over these cursed sands, or should we land here?'

Matt couldn't tell from the air, but landing was out of the question—they'd end up surrounded by desert bandits or wild animals.

'Maybe we should descend and have a closer look.'

'All right,' said Matt.

They had been flying very high to keep the plane cool and conserve their oil. But now they had no need to be afraid, because there were only a few hours between them and their destination.

'What was that?' asked Matt in surprise. Then he suddenly cried: 'Up, up, as fast as you can!'

There were a dozen arrows stuck in the plane's wings.

'Are you hurt?' Matt asked the pilot, worried.

'Not at all. That was a nice reception those devils gave us,' he added.

A few more arrows whizzed past the airplane as they rose to a higher altitude to escape them.

'Now I'm certain that was the right oasis. The desert robbers always stay near the oasis. There's more chance of robbing people there. They wait near the oasis closest to Bum Drum's forest.'

'Is Your Royal Highness certain that we'll be returning by camel?'

'Of course. Bum Drum will send us back the same way he did the first time. You might be able to find oil in Bum Drum's country, but there won't be any fuel, of course.'

'In that case,' said the pilot, 'we can risk it. When a good railroad engineer is running late, he speeds up to arrive on time. That's what I'll do. I'll go full speed so we can land on schedule. This may be the last flight of my life, I might as well enjoy myself.'

He pulled the throttle, and a minute later they had left the oasis and the robbers far behind.

'Won't the arrows be a problem?' asked Matt.

'Not at all. Let them just dangle there.'

They flew and they flew and they flew. The well-oiled motor worked perfectly. Finally, a few bushes and low trees began to appear again.

'Ho-ho, my little horse can smell the stable already,' joked the pilot.

They drank all their water and ate the rest of their food, because they had no idea how long the welcoming ceremonies would last before they were fed. Besides, it wouldn't be polite for them to arrive ravenously hungry.

They began to descend carefully, reducing their speed. Matt had already spotted the gray strip of Bum Drum's forests in the distance.

'All right, then,' said the pilot. 'Is there a clearing in the forest? We can't land on top of the trees, after all. I did land in a forest once, though it was the airplane that did most of the landing. That's when I lost my eye. I was still a young man then, and the planes were young, too, and didn't always obey.'

There was a large glade in front of Bum Drum's palace. And now, swinging low over the forest, the plane began heading for that glade.

'A little to the right,' cried Matt, looking through his binoculars. 'Too far, go back.'

The plane circled back, tried again, and missed again.

'To the left, less of a turn, good.'

'Oh, I see it, I see it, that's the clearing, but what's that?'

'Go back up!' shouted Matt with fear in his voice.

The plane roared up and away from what sounded like a screaming forest.

The entire field in front of the royal tent was full of people standing shoulder to shoulder.

Something must have happened. Either Bum Drum had died or it was some sort of holiday.

'All right, then, but we can't land on their heads, you know.'

'Well, we'll just have to keep going up and down until they understand that if they don't get out of our way we'll come crashing down on them.'

Seven times they rose in the air and came back down before the tribesmen realized that the great bird wanted to land in the clearing. Finally, they moved away into the forest, which wasn't easy because there were so many of them, and Matt's airplane landed without any more problems.

Matt's feet had barely touched the ground when a curly-haired little creature came running up to him and squeezed him with all its might.

A moment later, no longer dizzy, Matt saw that it was a black child. And when the child raised its head and looked him in the eye, Matt knew at once who it was—nice little Klu Klu, King Bum Drum's daughter.

MATT had no idea what was going on. Everything happened so fast that Matt thought he was dreaming or seeing things.

The first thing he saw was Bum Drum tied up with ropes and lying on a pyre surrounded by witch doctors. All the witch doctors were fearsome-looking, but one was more fearsome-looking than the rest—he had two wings, two heads, four arms, and two legs. That was his costume. In one hand the witch doctor held a board on which something had been drawn or written in human blood, and in the other a flaming torch. Matt realized they were going to burn Bum Drum. Off to one side were Bum Drum's hundred wives— they, too, were bound with ropes, and each one held a poison arrow to her heart. Bum Drum's children were crying something terrible and crawled around on all fours or did sad little somersaults. Little Klu Klu pulled Matt by the hand toward her father and said something, but Matt didn't understand. Just to be on the safe side, he pulled out his revolver and fired twice in the air.

Right then, Matt heard a cry from behind him. It was the pilot shouting and flapping his arms; his legless torso flew up in the air, he turned blue, and fell dead to the ground.

All the tribesmen began to scream so loud Matt thought they had gone mad. But then the witch doctor with the two heads untied the ropes on Bum Drum and began dancing the wildest of dances; he climbed up onto the pyre where Bum Drum had been lying a moment before and touched the lighted torch to the wood. The wood must have been doused with some highly flammable liquid, for it immediately burst into flames so huge that Matt and Klu Klu barely managed to leap aside in time.

The airplane was not far from the pyre. One wing caught on fire, and the fuel in the motor exploded with a roar. Bum Drum's wives grabbed hold of Matt and seated him on a golden throne. Then Bum Drum and all the lesser kings and princes placed their heads at the foot of the throne and hit themselves in the neck three times with Matt's right foot while uttering words that made no sense to Matt.

The pilot's body was wrapped in a shroud that had been drenched with so much perfume that Matt felt his head spin when he knelt beside the pilot to say a prayer for him.

What's all this supposed to mean? Matt asked himself.

Something extraordinary had happened, that was clear, but what? It looked as if Matt had saved Bum Drum and all his hundred wives from death. If that was true, Matt was not in any danger. But could you be certain of anything in this savage land?

Where had that fearsome mob of tribesmen come from? What would they do next? In the meantime, they had lit a few thousand fires in the forest and were dancing, playing music, and singing. Each tribe had its own kind of music and its own different songs.

Matt could tell by their costumes that they weren't all Bum Drum's subjects. Some must have been from the forests because they were dressed in leaves and feathers, some had huge sea-turtle shells on their backs, some wore monkey skins, and some were naked except for the decorations on their noses and ears.

Matt was not afraid, because he had already looked death bravely in the eye more than once. But still, to be all alone, far from home, surrounded by thousands of savages, just little him ... No, that was too much even for Matt's valiant heart. And when he thought of his good companion who had perished so mysteriously, such sorrow overcame him that he burst into tears, weeping loudly.

Matt was now alone in a tent made of lion and tiger skins, and so he thought he could cry freely, without being heard. But he was mistaken. Little Klu Klu was keeping watch over him, little Klu Klu had never left Matt for a single second. And now he could see her again in the light that came from an enormous diamond. Klu Klu was crying, too; she placed her little hand on his forehead while sad tears streamed from her eyes.

Oh, how Matt regretted not knowing the cannibals' language. Klu Klu would have told him everything. She was saying something, speaking very slowly and repeating the same words again and again, hoping Matt might understand. Then she showed him something in sign language. But there were only two things that Matt understood: Klu Klu was his most faithful friend in the world, and he was in no danger now, nor would he be in the future.

Weary as he was, Matt did not sleep a wink that night.

It was only toward morning, when the tribesmen quieted down a bit, that Matt caught a little sleep. But they woke him up and seated him on the throne again. A group from each tribe brought Matt presents. Matt smiled and thanked them, but he realized that there weren't enough camels in all the world to carry everything back across the desert. And besides, before Matt's departure, the foreign kings had announced that they would allow cages of wild animals to pass through their countries and nothing else, no matter how much Matt paid them.

Oh, what a shame that my country doesn't have its own seaport and its own ships, thought Matt.

But, to tell the truth, Matt also thought that if a new war broke out and he won that one, too, he would make one of the foreign kings give him a seaport, so he would not have to depend on their good graces ever again.

Matt would have been glad to stay a week to rest up, but he could not: what would happen if war broke out, and besides, how would he ever catch up on all his mail? After all, he had to read one hundred letters a day and at every audience give one hundred children whatever they needed most.

'I have to go back,' said Matt to Bum Drum, pointing at a camel and waving his hand toward the north.

Bum Drum understood.

When the perfumed rags on the dead pilot were unwound, Matt saw that he was now all white and hard like marble. The pilot was placed in an ebony box, and using sign language, Matt indicated that he should be loaded for the return trip.

What was left of the burnt airplane was packed into another box. Matt made a gesture that meant he would not be taking that box. He was very surprised how happy that made Bum Drum, as if a burnt airplane were something special and important.

But Matt still didn't know the most important thing—had Bum Drum stopped being a cannibal or not? He had to take Bum Drum back with him, there was no other choice.

And so Matt took Bum Drum with him. And the royal caravan set off through the desert on a route that was familiar by now.

And it was only back in his study, in his own capital, that Matt understood all the strange goings-on he had witnessed in the land of the cannibals. The professor who knew fifty languages explained everything to Matt.

'One of Bum Drum's ancestors was poisoned when he decided to stop being a cannibal. And it was then that the head witch doctor had told of an old legend. He said: "A time will come when the cannibals will change their ways. This is what will happen. One day, toward sundown, an enormous bird will appear in the sky. It will have an iron heart and a dozen poison arrows hanging from its right wing. The bird will circle the royal glade seven times and then swoop to the ground. The bird will have enormous wings, four arms, two heads, three eyes, and two legs. One of the bird's heads and two of its arms will be poisoned by one of the dozen arrows and die. Two thunderbolts will strike. Then the head witch doctor will be burned and the great bird's iron heart will break. And all that will remain of the bird are a piece of marble, a handful of ashes, and a white man who will become the king of all the cannibals. Then the cannibals will stop eating people and begin learning the arts and sciences. But nothing can be changed until that bird appears. Any king who wishes to change things before the bird comes has to die, by fire or by poison."

'Bum Drum had chosen fire. And just when the ceremonial burning of Bum Drum and the poisoning of his hundred wives was about to take place, the plane with the two travelers had appeared. Two thunderbolts had flashed from Matt's pistol, and the pilot—who was two of the bird's arms and one of its eyes—had been killed when he accidentally touched one of the dozen arrows shot by the desert robbers. The head witch doctor had gone onto the fire of his own free will, the plane was burned, and Matt became not only king of all the cannibals but the leader of all the black kings as well. Now the cannibals would stop eating people and start learning how to read and write; they would no longer put shells and bones in their noses but would dress like everybody else.'

'That's wonderful,' cried Matt. 'Let Bum Drum send a hundred of his tribesmen here. Our tailors will teach them how to make clothes, our shoemakers will teach them how to make shoes, and our masons will teach them how to build houses. We'll send them record players, so they can hear beautiful music. Then we'll send them horns, drums, and flutes, and violins and pianos a little later. We'll teach them our dances and send them toothbrushes and soap.'

'Good idea.'

'I know what to do,' cried Matt suddenly. 'I'll install a wireless telegraph in Bum Drum's capital. Then it will be easy for us to communicate. I can't keep making these long trips every time I need to talk with him.'

Matt called in the royal tradesmen and ordered them to make twenty suits for Bum Drum, twenty coats, twenty pairs of boots, and twenty hats. The barber cut Bum Drum's hair. Bum Drum agreed to everything. And the only thing he didn't like was the taste of the shoe polish and a piece of sweet-smelling soap he ate without knowing it wasn't food. From that time on, four footmen kept watch on Bum Drum so he wouldn't make any more silly mistakes.

ON THE day after Matt's return, the Prime Minister called a meeting, but Matt requested that it be postponed. Beautiful wet, white snow was falling, and about twenty boys, including Felek and Stash, were playing in the royal gardens. It would be sheer torture to have to miss all that fun.

'Mr. Prime Minister,' said Matt, 'only yesterday I returned from a hard and dangerous journey. And it was a total success. Can't a king have even one day off? I'm still a boy, you know, and I love to go out and play. If there's nothing that can't wait a day, I'd prefer to have the meeting tomorrow. Today I want to play with the other boys. The snow's beautiful, and it's probably the last of the year.'

The Prime Minister felt sorry for Matt, because even though he was the king, he still asked for permission to go out and play.

'Oh, it can wait a day,' said the Prime Minister.

Matt was thrilled. He put on a jacket so he could run freely, and one minute later he was with the other boys, throwing snowballs. At first, they didn't throw any snowballs at Matt, because they weren't sure if they were allowed to or not. But then Matt noticed this and shouted: 'What fun is it if nobody throws any snowballs at me? Don't worry, I can take care of myself. Snowballs aren't poison arrows, you know.'

Now everything was fine. They divided up into two sides. One side attacked the snow fort, and the other one defended it. There was so much noise that the footmen came running out. Then they saw the king, and though they were surprised, they said nothing and went back into the palace.

Nobody could have recognized the king now without looking very closely. Matt was covered with snow—he had fallen twice and had been hit by snowballs in the back, the head, and the ear. But he was defending himself furiously.

'Listen,' he shouted suddenly, 'let's make it a rule that anyone who gets hit by a snowball is dead and out of the game. That way, we'll know who won.'

That wasn't a good idea, because everyone was dead after a couple of minutes. So then they decided that three hits meant you were dead. But some of the boys cheated and didn't stop, even after they'd been hit three times. But it was still a better way to play. They talked less, made better snowballs, and took closer aim. Then they changed the rules so the dead ones could rejoin the game.

It was great fun.

Then they made an enormous snowman who had coal eyes, a carrot nose, and held a broom in one snow hand. Matt kept running back and forth to the royal kitchen.

'Cook, two pieces of coal, please.'

'Cook, please give me a carrot for our snowman's nose.'

The cook was angry because all the other boys came running in after Matt; the kitchen was so hot that the snow on them melted and made a mess of the floor.

'I've been the royal cook for twenty-eight years, but I don't remember my kitchen ever being turned into such a pigsty,' grumbled the cook. Then he barked at the kitchen boys and ordered them to mop the floor.

Too bad there's no snow in Bum Drum's country, thought Matt. I could teach the children how to make snowmen.

When the snowman was all done, Felek suggested they go for a sleigh ride. There were four sleighs and four ponies in the royal stables. The grooms hitched the ponies up to the sleighs.

‘We’ll drive them ourselves,’ said Matt to the grooms. ‘We’ll race around the gardens. The first one to go around five times wins. All right?’

‘All right!’ agreed the other boys.

Matt had just climbed onto his sleigh when he caught sight of the Prime Minister walking quickly toward them.

It must be for me, thought Matt with a sigh.

He was right.

‘A thousand pardons, Your Royal Highness, that I must interrupt Your Royal Highness’s play.’

‘That’s my tough luck. Play without me,’ said Matt to the boys. ‘So what’s happened now?’

‘Our most important spy has just returned to the country,’ whispered the Prime Minister. ‘He has brought news that he could not put in writing for fear the letter would fall into the wrong hands. We must have a meeting immediately, because the spy has to leave the country again in three hours.’

A sleigh had just tipped over, because the pony had not been in harness for a long time and was so angry that he jumped to the side instead of going forward. Matt watched sadly as the boys got up laughing from the snow and began to turn the sleigh back over. But there was no sense in thinking about it, his fun was over for the day.

Matt was curious to see a real spy. He'd heard about them but had never laid eyes on one.

Matt thought they would bring in some barefoot boy or an old beggar with a sack on his back, but the spy was elegantly dressed. For a moment, Matt even mistook him for the Minister of Agriculture, who worked out in the countryside and only rarely came to meetings.

'I am your number-one spy in the old king's country,' said the elegant gentleman. 'I have come to warn Your Royal Highness that the king's son finished building his fortress yesterday. But that's not the worst of it. A year ago he built a top-secret munitions factory in the forest and is now completely ready for war. He has six times more gunpowder than we do.'

'That rat!' exclaimed Matt. 'I've been building summer camps for children while he's been making shells and cannons to attack my country and destroy what we've built here.'

'There's more to it even than that,' the spy said in his soft, pleasant drawl. 'He has something even viler in mind. Knowing that Your Royal Highness will send the foreign kings invitations to the ceremonies for the opening of parliament, he bribed your Secretary of State to send out forged declarations of war instead of invitations.'

'That sneak! I could tell he couldn't stand me when I visited his country.'

'I still haven't finished yet, Your Majesty. The old king's son is very tricky. If the Secretary of State fails to switch the letters here, the same papers have been prepared with your forged signature at the court of the sad king and at the court of the friend of the Oriental kings. And now if Your Royal Highness will permit me to say a word in defense of the old king's son.'

'But how can you defend such a treacherous bandit?'

'It's not easy, but he's really just looking out for his country, as we look out for ours. We want to be top dog, and so do they. There's no need to get angry, we just need to be vigilant and make the right moves in time.'

'So what should I do?'

'Your Royal Highness can sign the invitations to the three kings right now, and I will take them with me and deliver them in secret. At tomorrow's meeting, discuss the invitations as if the letters had not been sent yet. Let the Secretary of State switch the letters, then open the envelopes at the last moment and arrest him.'

'Fine, but what about the fortress and the munitions factory?'

'Simple as pie,' said the spy, with a smile. 'The fortress and the factory can be blown up. And that is precisely why I am here—to request Your Royal Highness's permission.'

Matt turned pale. 'But how can we? This isn't war, after all. Blowing up your enemy's ammunition in wartime is one thing. But inviting someone for a visit while playing a dirty trick on him is another.'

'I understand,' said the spy. 'Your Royal Highness thinks such actions are ignoble and ugly. I will do nothing without Your Royal Highness's permission. But don't forget—he has six times more gunpowder than we do.'

Now Matt was very upset and began pacing back and forth. 'But how would you do it?' he asked.

'We have bribed the assistant to the factory's chief engineer. He knows the factory like the back of his hand. There's a small building near the factory. It's full of wood shavings—the shavings will be set on fire and a fire will break out.'

'And so they'll put it out.'

'No, they won't,' said the spy, with a smile and a wink. 'For some strange reason, the main water pipe will have burst and there won't be a drop of water in the entire factory. Your Royal Highness can rely on it.'

'But will any workers die?' Matt asked.

'The fire will break out at night, and not many workers will die. Nowhere near as many as will die if there's a war.'

'I know, I know,' said Matt.

'Your Royal Highness, we must do it,' the Prime Minister interjected timidly.

'I know we must,' said Matt in anger, 'and so why are you asking for my permission?'

'We don't have the right to act on our own.'

'All right, all right, burn down the factory, but don't touch the fortress for now.'

Matt quickly signed the letters inviting the three foreign kings to the opening of parliament, and went off to his room.

Matt sat by the window watching Stash, Felek, and all the other boys laughing as they raced around in their sleighs. He rested his heavy head on his hands and thought: Now I understand why the sad king plays such sad music on his violin. And now I understand why he went to war with me even though he didn't want to.

IT WAS time for the meeting at which the signed invitations would be placed in their envelopes and sealed with the royal seal. Matt couldn't wait to see how the Secretary of State would put the forged declarations of war into the envelopes instead of the invitations to attend the opening of parliament. He was very surprised when the Secretary of State did not come to the meeting but sent his assistant instead.

'And so will both houses of parliament be ready?' asked Matt.

'They most certainly will.'

'Excellent.'

This was the schedule. The festivities would last a week. First day: a religious service, a review of the troops, a gala dinner, and a grand presentation at the theater.

Second day: opening of the grownups' parliament. Third day: opening of the children's parliament. Fourth day: opening of the zoo. Fifth day: a parade of the children who were going off to the country to spend a whole summer in the camps Matt had built for them.

Sixth day: a grand farewell ball for the foreign kings. Seventh day: departure of all guests.

Matt decided that the fourth day should also include the unveiling of a monument to the valiant pilot who had lost his life, and some special entertainment for the African kings.

Delegates from both parliaments would be present at all the festivities. Prime Minister Felek would sit at Matt's left, and the other Prime Minister at his right. This would show that the grownups' and the children's ministers were entirely equal in the king's sight. Felek, too, would be called Mr. Prime Minister.

When everything was agreed upon, Matt signed the invitations to all the foreign kings—to the European kings on white paper, to the Oriental kings on yellow paper, and to the African kings on black paper. The invitations on white paper were written in black ink, those on yellow paper in red ink, and those on black paper in gold ink. Bum Drum was to pass on the invitations to the other African kings, while the invitations to the

Oriental kings were to be sent on through the European king who was their friend. But he was going to keep the invitations and not send them on—then the Oriental kings would feel insulted and stay friends with him.

The master of ceremonies carried in the box which contained the royal seal. One after the other, the invitations were inserted into their envelopes and the Secretary of State's assistant sealed them with red or green wax.

Matt watched carefully. He had always thought the ceremony of sealing foolish and unnecessary, and was annoyed by how long it took. Only now did he understand its true importance.

All the letters were sealed except the final three.

Bored by the ceremony, the ministers lit cigars and started chatting, even though the regulations prohibited talking while the royal seal was being affixed to letters. They had no idea what was going to happen. Matt, the Prime Minister, and the Minister of Justice were the only ones in on it. Later on, the Minister of Foreign Affairs would feel very insulted that he had not been informed.

The Secretary of State's assistant was a bit pale, but his hands were not trembling in the least. He suddenly began coughing just as he was about to insert the last three invitations into their envelopes. He began to search through his pockets, pretending that he couldn't find his handkerchief. And then he pulled the forged letters from his pocket, along with his handkerchief, so skillfully that only those in the know could have spotted this.

'Excuse me, Your Royal Highness,' he said humbly. 'There's a broken window in my office and I've caught a cold.'

'No need to apologize,' said Matt. 'Actually, it's my fault, because I broke that window during our snowball fight.'

The assistant was very happy because he thought he had brought it off. Then, suddenly, the Minister of Justice said: 'Gentlemen, your attention, please. If the ministers would set their cigars aside ...'

They knew immediately that something had happened. The Minister of Justice put his spectacles on his nose and turned to the Secretary of State's assistant. 'I arrest you in the name of the law as a spy and a traitor. In accordance with paragraph 174, you will be hanged.'

The assistant's eyes bulged as he started wiping the sweat from his forehead, but still he pretended to be calm. 'Mr. Minister, I don't know anything, nothing. I'm sick, I have a cough. They broke the window in my office. I have to go home and go to bed.'

'No, my friend, you're not going anywhere. They'll cure your cold in prison.'

In came five guards and chained the assistant hand and foot.

'What's going on?' asked the ministers in astonishment.

'You'll see in a moment, gentlemen. Would Your Royal Highness please break the seal on these letters.'

Matt opened the envelopes and showed them the forged letters.

The letters said: 'Now that all the savage kings are my friends, I couldn't care less about you. I beat you once, I'll beat you again. And then you'll do whatever I say. I hereby declare war on you.'

One of the guards pulled the invitations to the European kings out of the assistant's pocket. The invitations were balled up in his handkerchief.

Bound in chains, the assistant was ordered to sign an official statement admitting everything. The Secretary of State was summoned by telephone and arrived at once, trembling in fear.

'Oh, that no-good bum!' he cried. 'I was going to come here myself, but he begged me to let him come instead. He bought me a ticket to the circus and told me the show was great. And, like a fool, I believed the whole thing!'

Five generals were summoned to hold the trial.

'If the defendant tells the truth, it may help him. But if he tries to wriggle out of it, it's all over.'

'I'll tell the truth.'

'How long have you been a spy?'

'Three months.'

'Why did you become a spy?'

'Because I lost a lot of money at cards and couldn't pay. And gambling debts have to be paid within twenty-four hours. And so I borrowed some government money.'

'You mean you stole it.'

'I thought I'd be able to just put it back.'

'And what happened?'

'I played cards again to win back my money, and I lost even more.'

'When was that?'

'About six months ago.'

'What happened next?'

'I was afraid there would be an audit and I'd be sent to prison. So I became a spy for one of the foreign kings.'

'How much did he pay you?'

'Different amounts. For important information I got a lot, less if it wasn't so important. I was supposed to receive a great deal of money for this job.'

'Generals, judges, gentlemen,' said the Minister of Justice. 'This man is guilty of three crimes. The first is stealing government money. The second is spying. And the third is trying to start a war that would have cost the lives of many innocent people. In accordance with paragraph 174, I demand the death penalty for him. The accused is not in the military, so there is no need for a firing squad. An ordinary hanging will do. As for the Secretary of State, he is responsible for his assistant's actions. I have nothing against going to the circus, but he should have come to such an important meeting himself and not sent his assistant, who turned out to be a spy. That is very great negligence, and he deserves six months in prison for it.'

The generals retired to deliberate. Matt walked up to the Prime Minister and whispered: 'Why did our spy tell us that the Secretary of State was going to switch the papers, not his assistant?'

'Oh, a spy's information can't be one hundred percent accurate. A spy can't ask too many questions, that would attract too much attention. Spies have to be very careful.'

'Still, it was very intelligent advice not to hurry with the arrest but to wait for the meeting,' marveled Matt. 'I was itching to arrest him the whole time.'

'Oh, no, that would have been wrong. Best to pretend that you know nothing and catch them red-handed. Then they can't wriggle out of it.'

The master of ceremonies struck the table three times with his silver gavel as the generals filed back in.

'Here is our verdict: The Secretary of State is sentenced to one month in prison, his assistant is to be hanged.'

The condemned man began to plead for mercy and to weep so loudly that Matt felt sorry for him.

Matt also remembered that he, too, had once been before a military court and had survived only because the judges had quarreled about whether to shoot him or hang him.

'Your Royal Highness has the right to commute the sentence from death to life in prison.'

Matt wrote on the verdict: 'I commute the sentence to life in prison.'

And can you guess what time Matt went to bed?

At three o'clock in the morning.

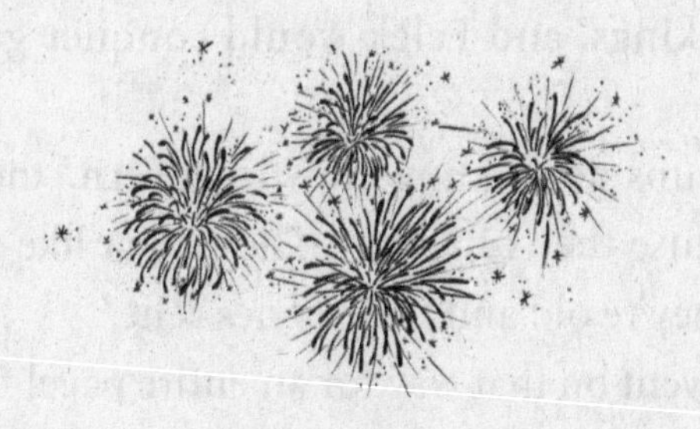

MATT was still eating his breakfast when the journalist walked in.

'I wanted to be the first to bring Your Royal Highness today's paper. I think Your Royal Highness will be pleased.'

'What's the news?'

'If you would be so good as to see for yourself.'

On the front page was a drawing of Matt on his throne, with thousands of children, holding bouquets, kneeling in front of him. Beneath the drawing was a poem that praised Matt, calling him the greatest king in the history of the world, the greatest reformer, child of the sun and brother of the gods.

Matt did not like either the drawing or the poem, but he didn't say so because he did not want to hurt the journalist's feelings.

On page 2 there was a photograph of Felek and an article: *First Child Prime Minister in the World*. Felek was praised for being wise and brave; Matt had conquered grownup kings, and Felek would conquer grownup ministers.

'Grownups don't know how to govern,' the article said, 'because they can't run. They don't like running because they're old and their bones ache.'

And it went on that way for an entire page!

Matt didn't like it at all. What good was all this praise when the future was still cloudy? And it wasn't nice to attack old people, either. Since Matt had really taken charge of the government, he had lived in harmony with his ministers, was glad to listen to their advice, and had learned a great deal from them.

But the most interesting news was buried in the back of the paper: *A Fire in the Royal Forests*.

'The foreign king's largest forest has burned,' said the journalist.

Matt nodded his head to indicate that he had seen the article, which he then read very carefully.

The article said that one of the men cutting timber had been careless with a cigarette and caused a terrible fire.

'Still, it's strange,' said the journalist. 'I can understand a forest catching on fire in the summer when it's dry, but there was snow on the ground not long ago. And apparently there was a huge, great explosion. Forests don't explode.'

Matt finished his breakfast without saying a word.

'What does Your Royal Highness think about it?' asked the journalist. 'There's something suspicious about that fire.'

The journalist said this in a soft and very pleasant tone of voice. And without quite knowing why, Matt thought: I have to be careful with this one.

The journalist lit a cigarette and changed the subject. 'I've heard that the Secretary of State was sentenced to a month in prison yesterday. I did not inform our paper about this because the children aren't very interested in what the grownups are doing. But it would be another story if there were problems with their own ministers. Your Royal Highness made an excellent choice in appointing Felek Prime Minister. The soldiers are thrilled that a platoon leader's son has become a minister. The newspaper boys know Felek because he used to sell newspapers before the war. All the other children are happy about it, too. But why did the poor Secretary get tossed in jail?'

'There were irregularities in his ministry,' answered Matt evasively. For some strange reason, he suddenly thought that the journalist might be a spy.

Matt thought about the journalist for a long time after he left. I'm imagining things. I'm not getting enough sleep. I've heard so much about spies the last couple of days that now I'm suspicious of everyone.

But Matt soon forgot all about it, because he had so much work to do before the kings arrived.

There were endless meetings with the master of ceremonies. The summer palace in the gardens was renovated in great haste for the African kings. A small, separate palace was built in case any of the Oriental kings did arrive. The European kings would stay in Matt's palace.

Cages of wild animals kept arriving. They had to hurry to finish the zoo in time.

They were building summer camps for the children and two huge parliament buildings all at the same time.

Elections for delegates to parliament were held throughout the land. It was decided that the delegates to the small, or children's, parliament should not be younger than ten or older than fifteen. Two delegates were elected from each school, one from the upper grades and one from the lower. This caused a lot of confusion, because it turned out that there were so many schools that all the delegates could not be accommodated in one hall. So many letters kept arriving that Matt had to spend long hours in his study. The letters were important and contained all sorts of questions.

Can girls be elected delegates?

Of course they can.

Can children who still don't know how to write very well be elected delegates?

Where will the delegates who come from the towns and the country live?

Would there be a school for the delegates so they would not lose a year while they were in the capital for sessions of parliament?

The Secretary of State's sentence was changed to house arrest, which meant that he had to stay in his house for a month and could not even go out for a walk. But he was brought to the palace each day by car, because Matt could not manage without him.

The master of ceremonies set up the schedule for the festivities. There were many questions: What sorts of triumphal arches should there be for the foreign kings, and where should they be situated? On which streets were the bands to play? What sorts of flowers were to be imported? Plates, knives, and forks had to be bought. More automobiles were needed. And what seats should the kings be given in the theater, and what places at the dinner table? The important kings had to be given the best places, and kings who didn't like each other should not be seated side by side. Wines, fruits, and flowers were being imported from the warm countries. Run-down houses were being repainted and streets repaired. Matt wasn't sleeping or eating, all he did was work, work, work.

'The architects are here to see Your Royal Highness.'

'The gardener wishes to speak with Your Royal Highness.'

'The Minister of Foreign Affairs is waiting to see you.'

'The ambassador of an Oriental king wishes to see you.'

'Two gentlemen to see Your Royal Highness.'

'What do they want?' asked Matt impatiently, called away from lunch for the third time.

'They want to talk with you about the fireworks.'

Angry and hungry, Matt went back to his study. He rarely received people in the throne room now. There just wasn't any time for ceremony.

'What do you gentlemen want? Please be brief, I'm short of time.'

'We heard that some savage kings are coming here. They should be shown something that will amaze them. The zoo won't interest them, because they've seen plenty of wild animals at home. And the theater won't mean much to them, either.'

'All right, all right,' said Matt. 'And so you want to put on a fireworks display?'

'That's right.'

Rockets would be placed on all government buildings. A tall tower, a windmill, and a 'waterfall' would be built in the royal gardens. All the fireworks would be set off at night. Rockets with red tails would shoot into the air from the top of the tower and send down showers of green and blue as they fell. The arms of the windmill would spin circles of green and red. Fiery flowers would blossom in the sky. And then, last but not least, the flaming waterfall.

'Here are the sketches. Perhaps Your Royal Highness would care to have a look at them.'

The pyrotechnicians had brought one hundred and twenty sketches of what the fireworks would look like. Matt looked them over, but meanwhile his lunch was getting cold.

'And how much will it cost?' asked Matt cautiously.

At the last meeting, the Minister of Finance had spoken of the need for new loans.

'How can that be, with all the gold we had?' Matt had said in surprise.

'That's true, but Your Royal Highness's reforms are awfully expensive.'

Then they began calculating how much the summer camps, the two huge parliament buildings, the monthly chocolate, the dolls, and the skates would cost altogether.

'We'll be lucky to have enough money to pay for all the festivities for our guests from abroad.'

'You mean we might run short?' asked Matt, truly frightened.

'It's not really a problem, because we can always levy new taxes. Now everyone is earning good money; they can chip in.'

'Oh,' sighed Matt, 'if only we had our own seaport and our own ships, Bum Drum could send us as much gold as we wanted.'

'That can be fixed,' said the Minister of War. 'But you can't stint on cannons, rifles, and forts if you want a seaport. Yes, cannons are more important than chocolate and skates.'

Matt turned red. Yes, it was true, a couple of new fortresses would come in very handy right now. At their meetings, the Minister of War was always saying that some of the gold from Bum Drum should be allocated for the army. But Matt was so busy that he kept telling the minister to wait a while.

Matt agreed to the fireworks display, but with a heavy heart.

'There's no way out of it. We'll economize later. But we have to do something for the African kings, too.'

Matt went to bed late that night and thought: Maybe I was wrong not to order the spy to blow up the fortress, too. Then the old king's son would have always been one fortress short. If he wants war, let there be war.

But Matt wouldn't be stupid next time around. He'd say: I beat you, so give me one seaport and ten ships.

MATT had already visited the foreign kings, and so he knew how guests should be treated. They had done things very beautifully. But no one had ever seen anything like the reception Matt prepared for his friends the kings, and they were the first to admit it. Nearly everything had been arranged well in advance, but Matt thought up several surprises only after the kings had arrived. It was something new each day—hunts, outings, circus shows with trained animals, wrestling matches.

The African kings were the first to arrive. But, good heavens, were there problems with them! Bum Drum had taken on the responsibility of maintaining order in the summer palace, but some of the kings could not be controlled.

The worst thing was that they had started fighting among themselves, and those were terribly savage fights.

They scratched and bit each other, and it was impossible to tear them apart. First they would stuff themselves with the delicacies prepared by the royal cook, then they would cry because their stomachs hurt, but when the doctor told them not to eat for a day, they'd start yelling and breaking chairs and windows. And they were afraid of all sorts of things, too. King Lum-Bo was so terrified when he saw himself in the mirror that he had to take medicine to stop from shaking. Instead of walking down the stairs, King Du-Nko slid down the banister, fell, and broke his leg. In a fit of anger, King Mup bit off a servant's finger. And there was no counting the bumps and bruises. King Pu-Bu-Ro brought along twenty wives who had received no invitations whatsoever. King Dul-Ko-Tsin had smuggled in a sausage made from the flesh of four different men. There was a tremendous uproar when the sausage was taken away from him. King Braput climbed up a tree, sat there for five hours, and spat, kicked, and bit whenever people tried to get him down. The firemen were called in. They knocked him out of the tree with a powerful stream of water and he fell into their outstretched net.

Bum Drum was very ashamed of the kings who ran wild and was afraid they would ruin the whole celebration. It was bad enough that they fought in the little palace where they were staying, but what if they took it into their heads to start brawling at the theater or during a gala dinner?

'We have to punish them—either whip them or put them in jail,' said Bum Drum.

Matt refused for a long time, but then he saw that Bum Drum could not keep them under control without punishments.

One room in the royal palace had been made into a museum. It contained various instruments which Henryk the Hasty had used to punish his subjects. There were jabbers for poking out eyes, pliers for pulling out fingernails, thumbscrews, terrible saws for cutting off arms and legs, and iron scourges, straps, sticks, and clubs of every type. It made your hair stand on end just to look at them. Matt did not like that museum. Henryk the Hasty had also had a deep well dug in the gardens, but there was no water in it. People condemned to starve to death used to be thrown down that well.

Bum Drum decided to put all these things to good use. On the day before the European kings were to arrive, he brought the wild kings to the well and then to the torture museum and gave them a long talking-to.

Matt didn't know what Bum Drum said, but he must have threatened them fiercely, because they started behaving properly as could be everywhere they went.

Bum Drum punished only two of the wild kings. One received ten lashes for biting off the servant's finger, and another had to spend an entire day in an iron cage for what he had done one night.

This is what happened: That night, he had felt like playing the flute. He was told that the other kings were tired and wanted to sleep, but he didn't care. When the palace servants tried to take away his flute by force, he hopped up on a bureau and started hurling vases and figurines at their heads. And worse, he jumped out the window into the gardens and made such a hullabaloo on the terrace of the winter palace that he woke up all the European kings. They were angry because they had not been able to sleep, and complained to Matt the next day.

'It's bad enough that we have to sit at the same table with them and watch them eat with their fingers. Now we can't sleep at night!'

Matt had to do a lot of talking. He explained that the wild kings would change their ways, that Bum Drum had once been wild, too, but in two months he had learned to wash with scented soap and even how to use a toothpick.

The European kings threatened to leave. It wasn't easy for Matt to convince them to eat apart if they preferred. And only the best-behaved African kings would sit with them. Three of them were completely respectable and educated; they even wore jackets and trousers and knew how to use a record player.

The European kings would not have given in so easily, but some of them were waiting for the hunt, others for the wrestling matches, and all of them—African, Oriental, and European—were waiting for the fireworks.

Only two Oriental kings had come. King Kito-Sivo wore glasses and spoke just like a European. But Tsin-Dan, though he wasn't very European, was not uncivilized either, because he knew etiquette.

Tsin-Dan caused other problems. He wanted to say hello and goodbye to everyone. You might not think that was so bad unless you knew how he did it. First he would make fourteen preliminary bows to each king, then twelve ordinary bows, then ten bows of etiquette, eight ceremonial bows, then six solemn bows, four additional, and finally two concluding bows. So, all together, that was fourteen plus twelve plus ten plus eight plus six plus four plus two bows, which took forty-nine minutes; the preliminary bows took a half minute each, and the others a minute.

'My ancestors have been doing this for five thousand years, and so I will do it as well.'

'All right, then, you can greet one or two kings like that, but that's all.'

It's a strange world, thought Matt. Some people aren't polite enough, and others are too polite.

King Tsin-Dan had come with two scholars who convinced him that he needn't exchange greetings with the African kings, who were the most numerous. And he did not have to bow to the European kings in person; their pictures would do. All the European kings had been photographed, and so every day, morning and evening, Tsin-Dan performed his bows to photographs of them in his own room. When he was finished with one king, his servants would set up the photograph of another. Tsin-Dan never made it to breakfast, although he rose two hours earlier and went to sleep two hours later than the other kings.

At least the African kings weren't causing any more trouble. Some of them stuck out their tongues twice when greeting each other, while others stuck their tongues out four times; some put the ring finger of their right hand into their left nostril, others pounded each other's back with their fists, jumping up three times, though some others jumped six times.

Matt was very surprised when Bum Drum told him that in the last century there had been a terrible war between two kings that had lasted fifteen years and it had all started because one king greeted the other by putting his right index finger into his left nostril and the other had done the exact opposite. Both nations were furious. The witch doctors and other kings joined the quarrel. Everybody had a different opinion and they began to fight over who was right. They burned down huts and entire villages; they killed women and children, took prisoners and threw them to the lions. Then a plague broke out and there was such a famine that they couldn't fight any more. But neither king had ever apologized and so now they would exchange no greetings whatsoever and sat far away from each other at the table.

And just getting them to sit at the table was a tricky business. King Bum Drum wore himself out before they understood that chairs were for sitting on and not for whacking people's heads with.

But it was the children of the capital city who had the most fun. The schools had been closed, because no one was going anyway.

The savage kings still didn't like automobiles and went about the city on foot, with a mob of boys behind each of them. The police, too, had their hands full. When the festivities were over, the prefect of police complained that he had lost more than fifteen pounds.

'Just think about it. Those wild men were all over town, and you had to keep an eye on them so some rascal wouldn't throw a stone at them, and so they wouldn't get themselves run over or eat anybody. That's all we would have needed.'

Matt had to give him a medal. Matt distributed all sorts of medals during the festivities: the African kings hung their medals from their noses, and the European kings wore theirs on their chests. Everyone was happy.

Matt had yet another disagreeable experience, because the African kings did not like the hunt. There was nothing so surprising about that—hunting rabbits and deer couldn't seem much fun to people who were used to killing elephants, tigers, and crocodiles. Some of the European kings may not have liked the hunt very much either, but they were well brought up and pretended to like everything, for they knew that Matt was trying hard. But the wild kings were not well brought up and may even have thought that Matt was making fun of them. They raised an infernal uproar and began to brandish their bows and spears menacingly. The European kings got into their automobiles and were about to drive away, but Bum Drum came running up like a madman and began waving his arms to calm the excited savages. Finally, he succeeded.

There was no further trouble during the hunt. The European kings even shot two boars and one bear and hoped that now the African kings would understand that there were wild animals in Europe, too. The king who had killed the bear became friendly with the Africans at the end of the hunt and bragged in sign language that he knew how to shoot and was a very great hunter. He examined their bows and arrows and even asked if he could spend the night with them in the summer palace. And the next day at breakfast he said that Africans were very nice, a lot could be learned from them, and, who knows, food just might taste better if you ate it with your fingers rather than with sharp, cold forks.

NO ONE could have foreseen the next development. Bum Drum's daughter, brave little Klu Klu, arrived at Matt's palace in a crate full of monkeys.

This is what happened: The zoo had been completely finished. All the animals were in their cages. The opening ceremonies were to take place on Wednesday, and on Thursday the zoo would be given over to the children to enjoy. But they were still waiting for one crate to arrive, which contained three monkeys so rare that none of the other European kings had any.

The crate was to be opened during the ceremonies in such a way that the monkeys would jump right into their cage. Everyone stood and watched. A board was pried from the crate, and a monkey jumped into the cage, followed by a second. The third one wouldn't come out. As soon as the crate was pulled away from the entrance to the cage, little Klu Klu jumped out and threw herself at Bum Drum's feet, saying something to him in their language.

Bum Drum was terribly angry, and though he was no longer as wild as he'd once been, he was about to kick his disobedient daughter when Matt came to her defense.

'Klu Klu was bad to run away from home. Klu Klu was wrong to break open the box in the night, let one monkey go, and then take its place. But Klu Klu has already been punished. Because it's no fun to spend six weeks in a box with two monkeys. And, after all, Klu Klu is not an ordinary child, but one who's used to all the comforts of a king's daughter. And things were even tougher for her than for the monkeys—Klu Klu could not go to the little window in the box where the monkeys were handed in their food, because she was afraid someone might spot her and send her back home.

'King Bum Drum, Bum Drum my friend,' said Matt, very moved, 'you can be proud of your daughter. No European girl could have done what she did. And no European boy either.'

'I'll give you this brat as a present,' said Bum Drum, still furious.

'Fine,' agreed Matt. 'Let her stay in my palace and learn things. When Klu Klu becomes the queen, she'll make reforms for her people just the way I do for mine.'

Strange as it may seem, just one hour after the fuss at the zoo, Klu Klu was acting as if she felt right at home in Matt's country.

The old professor who knew fifty languages spoke to her in her own language. He explained Matt's plans for her, and she replied at once: 'That's a great idea. Please, Professor, you're strong as a lion and wise as a crocodile. Please start teaching me your language right away so I can say what I'm thinking. I have very important plans, and I hate waiting around.'

It turned out that Klu Klu had already learned one hundred and twelve expressions during Matt's stay in Africa.

'It's remarkable how talented that little wild girl is,' marveled the professor. 'She has an extraordinary memory.'

Klu Klu not only remembered all one hundred and twelve expressions, but who she heard use them, and where. And she had also picked up some new expressions from the sailors while she was in the crate on the boat.

'Klu Klu,' said the professor, 'where did you learn those nasty expressions? You probably don't know what they mean.'

But Klu Klu answered: 'Three of those expressions were used by the porter when he put the monkey crate on his back. He said four more when he tripped and almost fell. I heard some from the boatman when he gave us our food and from the sailors when they were drunk.'

'Klu Klu, it's too bad that these are the first expressions you learned from our people,' said the professor. 'You must forget them right away. I'll be very glad to teach you our language, poor dear brave Klu Klu.'

Klu Klu was out in front during all the festivities. She turned up in more photographs than anyone else. The boys never shouted 'Hurrah!' louder or tossed their caps higher than when Klu Klu went by in a car. At the opening of the children's parliament, Klu Klu made a little speech in the language of Matt's country: 'In the name of my fellow Africans and all the children of Africa, I salute this, the first children's parliament in the world.' Her words were followed by such a storm of applause and such howls of delight that Felek, who always kept cool, lost his temper and shouted to the delegate who was howling the loudest: 'Shut up, or I'll punch you in the mouth.'

Felek's choice of words made a bad impression on the European kings, even though they did not let it show.

I would be glad to describe all the games and feasts in detail, but then I wouldn't have enough space for more important things. And this, after all, is a book about a reformer. Besides, Matt had important political reasons for inviting all those people.

Among the guests were the old king and his son, Matt's sworn enemy. The king who was the friend of the Oriental kings had also come. And so had the sad king. Matt had already had a couple of long talks with him.

'My dear Matt,' said the sad king, 'I have to say that your reforms are very interesting and important. You've made a brave beginning. Things have been going well for you; everything's wonderful so far. But remember: reforms are paid for with hard work, tears, and blood. Don't fool yourself into thinking that everything will always be the way it is right now. Don't think you can make everything just the way you want it.'

'Oh, I know how hard it is,' answered Matt. He told the sad king how much he had been working, how many sleepless nights and cold dinners there had been.

'The worst thing is that I don't have a seaport of my own,' complained Matt. 'And there are problems getting my gold shipments.'

The sad king thought for a moment, then said: 'You know, Matt, I think the old king would give you one of his ports.'

'Oh, come on. His son would never allow him to.'

'I think he would.'

'But he hates me. He's envious of me. He's suspicious of me, and he feels insulted by me.'

'Yes, that's true, that's all true. But he'll agree all the same.'

'Why?' said Matt, astonished.

'Because he's afraid of you. He can't count on my friendship,' said the sad king, with a smile. 'And the other king is happy because you've left all the Oriental kings to him.'

'Well, I can't take everything for myself,' grumbled Matt.

'Of course, it isn't intelligent to want to rule the whole world. But there are always people who try. Maybe you'll try, too, Matt.'

'Never!'

'Oho, people change. Success spoils people.'

'But not me.'

Just then, in walked the old king and his son. 'And what are Your Royal Highnesses discussing?'

'Matt was just complaining that he doesn't have a seaport. Matt has mountains, forests, cities, fields, but he doesn't have a seaport or ships. And now that he's friends with the African kings, he absolutely needs a port.'

'I think so, too,' said the old king. 'But a solution can be found. Matt defeated us in the last war, but he ceased hostilities and demanded no reparations from us. That was very noble on his part. Now it is our turn to show that we can be grateful. My son, we can yield Matt a stretch of our seacoast and one port without any harm to ourselves.'

'But Matt has to pay us for the ships,' the son was quick to add. 'He has lots of rich friends now.'

'I'd be more than glad to,' Matt said happily.

The Minister of Foreign Affairs and the Secretary of State were summoned immediately, and the proper papers were drawn up and signed by all the kings. The master of ceremonies brought in the box containing the royal seal. Then, his hand trembling, Matt applied his seal.

It was high time to finish, for the fireworks had just started.

It was really something to see. The whole city had poured into the streets. The gardens were full of delegates, soldiers, and officials. There was a separate section for the journalists who had come from all over the world. The kings gathered on the balconies, at the windows, and on the palace terrace. Some of the savage kings climbed up onto the roof to have a better view.

A tower of fireworks went off. Bengal fire, rockets, and red and green comets went streaking up into the sky. Then came serpents of fire and windmills, one color after another. And a gasp of admiration came from every single throat when the waterfall of fire was set off.

'More, more!' cried the African kings, amazed and delighted. They began calling Matt the King of the Hundred-Colored Sky and the Conqueror of Fire.

But they all had to go to bed early because everyone was scheduled to depart the next morning.

A hundred bands played in the streets as the royal automobiles brought Matt's guests to the station. Then all the kings—European, African, and Oriental—left Matt's hospitable capital on ten royal trains.

'We have achieved a great diplomatic success,' said the Prime Minister, rubbing his hands on the way back from the station.

'What does that mean?' asked Matt.

'It means you're a genius,' said the Prime Minister. 'Your Royal Highness has done a great thing without even intending to. Not all conquering is done by going to war. In war, you fight and win and take what you want. But this is a diplomatic victory, which means getting what you need by bargaining, not war. Now we have a seaport, and that's the important thing.'

NOW Matt had to get out of bed at six o'clock in the morning. Otherwise, he wouldn't have time for everything. He changed his schedule so that now he studied two hours a day. He had parliamentary sessions to attend, and besides all the letters, he had to read two newspapers, the one for the grownups and the one for the children, to know what was going on in the country.

And so one day, when the royal bedchamber was still quiet at eight o'clock, worry spread through the palace.

'Matt must be sick.'

'We should have seen it coming.'

'No grownup king works as much as Matt.'

'He's been looking pale and thin lately.'

'And he's hardly been eating at all.'

'But you can't say a word to him about it because he gets so angry.'

'Yes, he's been very impatient lately.'

'We'd better send for the doctor.'

Very worried, the doctor drove to the palace, and without any formalities, without even knocking or taking off his coat, he ran right into the royal bedchamber.

Matt woke up, rubbed his eyes, and asked anxiously: 'What happened? What time is it?'

The doctor came right to the point, speaking rapidly because he was afraid Matt would interrupt him.

'Matt, my dear child, I have known you since you were in the cradle. I'm an old man. My own life doesn't matter to me. You can order me hanged, shot, thrown in prison, I don't care. When he lay dying, your father entrusted you to my care. I will not allow you out of bed, and that's that. If anyone tries to bother you, I'll have him thrown down the stairs. Matt, you're trying to do in one year what takes other kings twenty. It can't be done. You should see what you look like. Not like a king, but like the lowliest beggar's child. It would be good if the prefect of police lost some weight. He's too fat. But you shouldn't be losing weight while you're still growing, Matt. You take care of all the children. Twenty thousand children will go off to camp tomorrow. Why should you be wasting away? It makes an old man like me ashamed, so ashamed.'

The doctor handed Matt a mirror. 'Just look, Matt, look.'

And the old doctor burst into tears.

Matt took the mirror. It was true! He was white as a sheet of paper, his lips were pale, his eyes looked tired and sad, his neck was long and thin.

'You'll get sick and die,' said the doctor, weeping. 'And you won't finish your work. You're already sick.'

Matt laid the mirror aside and blinked his eyes. For some reason, he was glad that the doctor had not once called him king, would not allow him out of bed, and would have anyone who wanted to see Matt on business thrown down the stairs.

How nice to be sick, thought Matt, stretching out comfortably in his bed.

Matt had been thinking he was just very tired. Too tired to eat even when he was hungry, too tired to fall asleep at night or to sleep without having bad dreams. Sometimes he dreamed that cannibals were attacking the children and eating them. Or that a fiery rain was scorching him. Or that both his legs had been cut off and one eye gouged out. Or that he was down in the well, sentenced to death by starvation. He had frequent headaches and couldn't follow the teacher in class. He felt ashamed to be seen like that by Stash, Helenka, and especially Klu Klu, who, after three weeks of school, could read the newspaper herself, made no spelling mistakes, and could show on a map the route from Matt's capital to her father's country.

'But what will happen? Who'll rule the country if the king is sick?' Matt asked in a quiet voice.

'Both parliaments are in recess for the summer. The country has enough money. All we have to do is bring in the gold. And now we have a seaport and ships. The camps have been built. The officials and ministers can take care of everything. What you need is to go away for two months and rest.'

'But I'm supposed to go to the port and inspect the ships.'

'I won't allow it. The Minister of Commerce and the Prime Minister can stand in for you perfectly well.'

'I'm supposed to attend the military maneuvers.'

'The Minister of War will attend.'

'And the children's letters?'

'Felek will read them.'

Matt sighed. It's not easy to let other people replace you when you're used to taking care of everything yourself, but Matt really had no strength left.

Matt ate breakfast in bed while Klu Klu told him some lovely African folk tales. Then he played with his favorite puppet and looked at picture books. Then he was brought a three-egg omelet, a glass of hot milk, and a roll with fresh butter. And only after he had eaten everything did the doctor allow him to dress and sit on the balcony in a comfortable armchair.

Matt sat in his chair without thinking about anything. He had no worries, no fears. No one was coming to see him on business; no minister, no master of ceremonies, no journalist, nobody, nobody at all. Matt sat listening to the beautiful songs of the birds out in the gardens. He listened and listened until he finally dozed off, and he slept until lunch-time.

'And now we'll have some lunch,' said the doctor, with a smile. 'After lunch, we'll take a ride around the gardens in a carriage. Then another nap. Then a bath, and back to bed for another nap. And then supper and a good night's sleep.'

Matt slept and slept; he couldn't have been more willing to sleep. Now there were fewer bad dreams. He was eating more and gained more than three pounds in three days.

'If things continue like this,' said the doctor happily, 'in a week I'll be able to call you Your Royal Highness again. But I still don't see a king. I still see a skinny, worn-out little orphan who tried to take care of the whole world but had no one to take care of him—no father, no mother.'

A week later, the doctor handed him the mirror again. 'Almost a king again, right?'

'Not yet,' answered Matt, who for some strange reason liked the doctor's tender tone of voice, liked being treated like a child and not being called Your Royal Highness.

Matt was becoming lively and cheerful again, and the doctor had trouble making him go back to bed after meals.

'What do the papers have to say?'

'The papers say that King Matt is sick and that he's leaving for vacation tomorrow like all the rest of the children in the country.'

'Tomorrow?' asked Matt happily.

'Yes, at noon sharp.'

'Who's going?'

'Well, me, the captain and his children, and probably Klu Klu, too, because who'd she stay with here?'

'Of course, Klu Klu's coming with us.'

Matt signed only two documents before leaving. One said that the Prime Minister would be in charge of all grownup affairs, and the other, that Felek would see to all matters concerning the children.

For two weeks, Matt did nothing but play. Klu Klu thought up all sorts of hunting and war games. She built beautiful huts from tree branches and then taught the other children how. Sometimes they played up in the trees and sometimes on the ground.

At first, Klu Klu couldn't walk with shoes. 'What a barbaric custom,' she complained. 'Wearing clothes on your feet.'

And dresses made her furious.

'How come boys and girls wear different kinds of clothes here? That's barbaric. No wonder the girls here are so awkward. You can't climb a tree or hop a fence in a dress. The stupid dress always gets caught on something.'

'But, Klu Klu, you can climb trees even better than the village boys, not to mention Matt and Stash.'

'Those are trees?' laughed Klu Klu. 'Those little sticks are for two-year-olds, not big girls like me.'

One day, the children were admiring a squirrel jumping nimbly from tree to tree.

'I can do that, too,' cried Klu Klu quickly. And before Matt, Stash, or Helenka realized what Klu Klu was about to do, she tossed off her dress and sandals and went bounding after the squirrel. The race was on. The squirrel jumped from one branch to another, but Klu Klu was always right behind it. Then the squirrel jumped from one tree to another, but Klu Klu was still right behind it. The race went on for about five minutes, until the tired squirrel began scampering down to the ground, with Klu Klu right behind it. The children thought now Klu Klu would be killed, but she knew how to get down from a tree in a hurry, clinging to some branches and pushing others away. She even managed to grab the squirrel by the nape of the neck so it couldn't bite her.

'Is this little northern monkey of yours poisonous?'

'Not at all. Only snakes are poisonous here.'

Klu Klu asked detailed questions about the snakes, studied their pictures, and then one day she disappeared into the forest. They searched for her all day long, but Klu Klu was nowhere to be found. It was dark when she returned, covered with scratches, her hair a mess, and hungry as can be. She was carrying three live snakes in a glass jar.

'How did you catch them?' asked Matt in astonishment.

'The same way you catch all poisonous snakes,' she answered simply.

At first, the village children were afraid of Klu Klu, but later they came to respect and love her very much.

'She may be a girl, but she outdoes all the boys. Good God, can you imagine what African boys are like?'

'Just the same as the girls, not the least bit better,' said Klu Klu. 'It's only European girls who have long hair and wear long dresses, and that's the reason they can't do things.'

KLU Klu was best not only at throwing stones and shooting bows and arrows but also at collecting mushrooms and nuts. Not to mention botany, zoology, geography, and physics. All she needed was one look at a picture of a plant or an insect to be able to recognize it in a meadow or a forest. When she found out that a certain plant grew in swamps, she ran right to the village boys to ask them where the swamps were.

'They're pretty far away, about two miles.'

That might be far for some people, but not for Klu Klu. She broke into the storeroom, grabbed a hunk of bread and cheese, and off she went.

They didn't even try to find her.

'Aha, Klu Klu's been at the storeroom again. That means she's out after something.'

Evening, night, no Klu Klu.

She spent the night in the forest and returned the next morning, triumphantly carrying a bouquet of marsh flowers, as well as some frogs, newts, lizards, and leeches.

Her herbarium was the most complete, her collection of insects, butterflies, and rocks was the largest. The most snails were born in her aquarium, which also had the most little fish swimming around in it.

Klu Klu was always cheerful, her sharp white teeth flashing when she smiled.

But Klu Klu knew how to be serious, too. 'Oh, Matt, when I was watching those beautiful fireworks and that waterfall of fire, I kept thinking how wonderful it would be for African children to see all these miracles of yours. I have a big, big favor to ask of you, Matt.'

'What is it?' asked Matt.

'That you bring fifty African children to your capital so they can study like me. Then they could go back to Africa and teach all the children everything.'

Matt did not answer, because he had decided to give Klu Klu a surprise. That evening he wrote a letter to the capital:

Dear Felek, When I left, a wireless telegraph was being installed on the roof. Work on it was to be completed by the first of August. We need that telegraph to be able to communicate with Bum Drum. Please send the first telegram to Bum Drum. Tell him to send me one hundred of his tribe's children. I am opening a school for them in my capital. Please don't forget.

MATT

Matt had licked the envelope and was just about to seal it, when the door opened.

'Felek! Good to see you! I was just about to send you a letter.'

'I have come on an important official mission,' said Felek in a serious voice.

Felek pulled out a gold cigar case and offered Matt a cigar. 'Your Royal Highness should try one—first-class, extra-special, an aroma worthy of the royal nose.'

'I don't smoke,' said Matt.

'That's just it,' said Felek, 'that's not right. A king should have the best of everything. Anyway, I'm here on official business—to see about the ratification of my counterproposal. Here's my ultimatum: First, my name won't be Felek any more, but Baron Felix von Rauch. My parliament is not to be called the children's parliament any more, but the Progress Parliament—Proparl, for short. Further, you should stop calling yourself Matt.

Your Royal Highness is twelve years old now. You should be formally crowned and be called Emperor Matthew the First. Otherwise, all our reforms will go down the drain.'

'I have a different plan,' said Matt. 'I want the grownups to choose themselves a king, and I'll stay Matt, the king of the children.'

'Your Royal Highness's concept could be codified even in its current rough form,' said Felek. 'I do not dare impose my moratorium on the person of the king. However, as far as my own official person is concerned, I wish to be Baron von Rauch, Minister of the Proparl.'

Matt agreed.

Felek also demanded his own office, two automobiles, and a salary twice as large as the Prime Minister's.

Matt agreed.

Felek also demanded the title of count for the journalist from *Progzette*, which was short for *Progress Gazette*, the name of the newspaper for the children.

Matt agreed.

Felek had brought all the documents, ready for signature, and Matt signed them.

The whole conversation made Matt terribly sad. He would have agreed to anything to get it over and done with. Matt had been feeling so fine that he had forgotten about meetings and sessions. He had no desire to remember all the hard work he had already done or to think about what awaited him when his vacation was over. And that was why he wanted Felek to leave as quickly as possible.

When the doctor learned of Felek's arrival, he came running angrily into Matt's room. 'My dear Felek, please don't bother the king.'

'My dear doctor, please don't raise your voice to me, and please call me by my *real* name.'

'And what is your real name?' asked the doctor in surprise.

'I am Baron von Rauch.'

'Since when?'

'Since the moment His Royal Highness graciously conferred that title on me with this official document.'

Felek pointed at the paper, freshly signed, the ink still wet.

Years of service at court had taught the doctor self-control. So he changed his tone at once and said, calmly but firmly: 'Baron von Rauch, His Royal Highness is on vacation for reasons of health, and I am responsible for his progress. And, in view of that responsibility, I demand that Baron von Rauch beat it at once.'

'You'll pay for that,' said Felek, who stuffed the papers in his portfolio and then left the room.

Matt was especially grateful to the doctor, since Klu Klu had just invented a new game—lassoing horses.

The children would each attach a lead ball to one end of a long, strong rope and then hide behind trees like hunters. The stable boy would let ten ponies out of the royal stable. The children would lasso the ponies, jump up on them, then gallop away bareback.

Klu Klu did not know how to ride a horse, because in her country people rode camels and elephants. But she learned quickly. Except she didn't like riding with a saddle—she couldn't stand any kind of saddle.

'Saddles are for old ladies who like to be comfortable. But when I ride a horse, I want to sit on the horse, and not on some pillow. Pillows are good at night in bed, not when you're playing.'

It was a delightful summer for the village children, because they were included in practically all the games. Klu Klu taught them not only new games but new fairy tales and songs, how to make bows and huts, how to weave baskets and hats, and new ways of finding and drying mushrooms. And Klu Klu, who couldn't speak their language two months before, was now teaching the shepherds how to read.

Klu Klu compared every letter of the alphabet to an insect or bug.

'What's the problem? You know hundreds of different flies, bugs, insects, and herbs, and you can't memorize twenty-six silly little letters? You can do it, you just think there's something hard about it. It's the same as the first time you tried to swim, or ride a horse, or go ice skating. Just tell yourself it's easy and it'll be easy.'

And so the shepherds started saying: 'Reading's easy!' And before they knew it, they could read. Their mothers were astonished.

'That black girl is really something! The teacher hollered at them for a whole year, beat them with a ruler, pulled them by the ears and hair, but those dummies didn't learn a thing. But she just tells them that the letters look like insects and they learn in a minute.'

'And you should see her milk a cow!'

'My calf got sick. Klu Klu's just a child, but she takes one look and says: "Your calf'll die in three days." She didn't have to tell me, I've had calves die on me before. Then she says: "I can save the calf with a certain herb, if it grows around here." I went with her, I was curious. She looks and looks, she sniffs and she bites. "The right one's not here," she says, "but we'll have to try this one, it has the same bitter taste." She gathers a bunch of them, adds a little hot ash, and mixes it all together like a real pharmacist, then she pours it in some milk and gives it to the calf. And the calf drinks it, like it understood, even though the milk is bitter and doesn't taste good. The calf bleats, but it drinks and licks its chops. And what do you think? The calf's all better. Now isn't that something?'

When the summer was over, all the men, women, and children in the village were sorry to see Matt go because he was the king, and the captain and his wife because they were polite, and the doctor because he helped quite a few people, but most of all they were sorry to see Klu Klu go.

MATT returned to the capital with a heavy heart. He was welcomed at the station, but Matt noticed that something was wrong. The train station was surrounded by soldiers. There were fewer flags and flowers than usual. The Prime Minister looked troubled. The prefect of police was there, too, and he hardly ever came to welcome Matt home.

Their cars did not take the usual route.

'Why aren't we going through the center of town?'

'Because the workers are having a parade.'

'The workers?' said Matt in surprise, remembering the jolly processions of children leaving for summer camp. 'And are they going away, too?'

'On the contrary, they just returned a little while ago. They're the ones who built the summer camps for the children. They're all done with that job, and now they're out of work. And so they're kicking up a fuss.'

Suddenly, Matt caught sight of the march. The workers were carrying red flags and singing.

'Why do they have red flags? Our flag's not red.'

'The workers in all countries carry the same red flag. They say that the red flag is for all the workers in the whole world.'

That gave Matt an idea. Why couldn't all the children in the world have their own flag, too? But what color should it be?

Just then, Matt's car was passing down a sad, gray, narrow street. Matt remembered the green forest and the green meadows he had seen in the country and said out loud: 'Would it be possible for all the children in the world to have their own green flag?'

'It would,' said the Prime Minister with a grimace.

Feeling sad, Matt walked around his palace, along with Klu Klu, who was feeling sad, too.

'I've got to get to work. I've got to get to work,' Matt kept saying, even though he didn't feel like working at all.

'Baron von Rauch,' announced the footman.

In came Felek.

'Tomorrow will be the first session of the Droparl after vacation,' said Felek. 'No doubt, Your Royal Highness will wish to make a little speech to parliament.'

'And say what?'

'Kings usually say they are happy that the people are making their voices heard, and they wish them success.'

'All right, I'll go,' agreed Matt.

But he didn't want to go, because it would be noisy with so many children there, and they'd all be staring at him.

But when Matt saw that children had come to parliament from all over his land to discuss how to govern the country, when he saw how happy they were, and when he spotted his village playmates from that summer in the crowd, he came to life and made a very fine speech.

'You are the delegates,' he said. 'Until now, I was all alone. I wanted to make life good for everyone. But it's very hard for one person to know what everybody needs. It'll be easier for you. Some of you know what the cities need, and some of you know what the countryside needs. The little children know what little children need, and the big children know what big children need. I hope that someday children from all over the world will meet together, the way the kings did recently, and all the children will present their own special needs. For instance, African children don't need skates, because they don't have skating rinks. The workers have their own special flag. A red one. The children should have a flag of their own, too. Maybe they'll choose green, because children love the forest, and the forest is green ...'

Matt spoke for a very long time, but the delegates paid close attention, and that made Matt happy.

Then the journalist stood up and said that the newspaper for children was coming out every day, so they could read the latest news, and they could write articles for it themselves if they wanted. Then he asked if they'd had a good time at camp.

The children responded with a terrific uproar. Felek called in the police and things quieted down.

Felek said that anyone who shouted would be thrown out the door and that they should take turns talking.

The first to speak was a barefoot boy wearing a tattered jacket.

'I'm a delegate and I want to say that we didn't have a good time at all. There were no games to play, the food was bad, and when it rained, water dripped on your head because there were holes in the roof.'

'And they didn't change the sheets,' someone shouted.

'And they gave us slop for lunch.'

'Like we were pigs.'

'Things were a mess.'

'And they beat us.'

'And locked us in our cabins for any little thing.'

Again, such an uproar arose that a ten-minute recess was needed.

The four delegates who were making the most noise were thrown out. Then the journalist made a brief speech saying that nothing was perfect in the beginning and that next year would be better. He called on the delegates to state their requests.

There was another uproar.

'I want to keep pigeons,' one shouted.

'I want a dog.'

'Every child should have a watch.'

'Children should be allowed to use the telephone.'

'We don't want people kissing us.'

'Let them tell us fairy tales.'

'We want kielbasa.'

'And headcheese.'

'We want to go to bed late.'

'Every child should have a bicycle.'

'And his own bookcase.'

'And more pockets. My father has thirteen pockets and I only have two. I can't fit everything in them, and I get yelled at if I lose my handkerchief.'

'Every child should have a trumpet.'

'And a revolver.'

'And drive a car to school.'

'Abolish girls and little children!'

'I want to be a magician.'

'Every child should have his own boat.'

'And go to the circus every day.'

'Every day should be Halloween.'

'And April Fool's Day. And Mardi Gras.'

'Every child should have his own room.'

'And scented soap.'

'And perfume.'

'Every child should be allowed to break a window once a month.'

'And smoke cigarettes.'

'And there shouldn't be any blank maps with countries to fill in.'

'Or spelling tests.'

'We want a special day when the grownups have to stay home and the children can go wherever they want.'

'All kings should be children.'

'Grownups should go to school.'

'We want oranges instead of chocolate all the time.'

'We want boots.'

'We want people to be like angels.'

'Every child should have his own car.'

'And his own ship.'

'And a house.'

'And a railroad.'

'Children should have money and be able to buy things.'

'There should be a cow for every little child.'

'And a horse.'

'Every child should have ten acres of land.'

It went on like that for an hour. The journalist kept smiling and taking notes on everything. At first, the village children felt shy, but then they started talking, too.

Matt was very tired.

'All right, you've written everything down, but what next?'

'They need to learn some manners,' said the journalist to Matt. 'Tomorrow I'll write a story for the paper telling them how to behave.'

Later on, one of the boys who wanted to abolish girls walked by in the corridor.

'Mr. Delegate,' asked the journalist, 'what have girls done to you?'

'There's one horrible girl in our courtyard. All she does is pick fights, and when you do something back, she starts hollering, then runs off to tattle. And she's like that with everyone. So we've decided to fix her good.'

The journalist stopped another delegate. 'Mr. Delegate, why don't you want to be kissed?'

'If you had as many aunts as I do, you wouldn't ask. Yesterday was my birthday, and they slobbered over me so much that I threw up my whole dessert. If grownups are so crazy about that mushy stuff, let them kiss each other and leave us alone, because we hate it.'

The journalist wrote that down, too.

'And you, Mr. Delegate, does your father really have so many pockets?'

'Count for yourself. He has two side pockets in his pants and one in the rear. He has four little pockets in his vest and one in the lining. His jacket has two in the lining, two on the sides, and one on top. He has a separate pocket for his toothpick, and I don't have a pocket for my yo-yo. And they also have drawers, desks, bookcases, and shelves. Then they brag that they never lose anything and put everything back where it belongs.'

The journalist made a note of this as well.

Then came two delegates who disliked little children. But why?

'And who has to babysit them and rock their cradles?'

'And big people tell us to give in to them because they're little.'

'And they tell us to set a good example. But when one of the kids does something bad, they don't yell at him, they yell at me: "He learned it from you." But who told him to act like me?'

And the journalist wrote that down, too.

THE journalist wrote an article that said no parliament in the world could make people angels or magicians; every day can't be Halloween, and children can't go to the circus all the time. And girls and little children could not be abolished.

The article had been written carefully, so as not to offend the delegates. And so there were no expressions like 'silly talk,' 'nonsense,' or 'they need a good whack.' The newspaper only listed the various proposals.

More pockets? No problem. The tailors could be ordered to make a couple of extra pockets on all children's pants.

And so on and so forth.

Klu Klu was upset after reading the newspaper. 'Matt, let me go to a session of parliament. I'll tell them a thing or two. And why aren't there any girls in parliament?'

'There are, but they don't say anything.'

'Then I'll speak for them all. What an idea—there's some nasty girl in one courtyard and right away they're saying abolish all girls. There are plenty of nasty boys, too. And so does that mean all boys should be abolished? I can't understand how Europeans can think up so many intelligent things and still be so stupid and barbaric.'

Klu Klu drove to parliament with Matt, her heart pounding, not because she was afraid, but because her head was full of ideas.

Everyone stared at Klu Klu, but she sat beside Matt in the royal box as cool as a cucumber.

Felek opened the session. He rang his bell and said: 'The session is now open. Today's agenda: Point one—that every child should have a watch. Point two—that children should not be kissed. Point three—that children should have more pockets. Point four—that girls should be abolished.'

Fifteen delegates had signed up to speak on point one.

One delegate said that children need watches because they have to be in school on time and can't be late. Older children could get along without watches more easily because they knew how to gauge the time.

'If my parents' clock is slow, why should I have to suffer for it?' said the second speaker. 'If I had my own watch, I'd make sure it was right.'

'We don't need watches just for school,' said the third delegate. 'We get yelled at if we're late for dinner or stay out playing too long. But how can they blame us for not knowing the time, when we don't have any watches?'

'Kids need watches for games, too,' said the fourth delegate. 'You can't time races or see who can stand on one leg the longest, without a watch.'

'And we get cheated when we rent boats by the hour. They say the hour's up, and even though they're lying, we have to pay for a whole hour.'

Then Felek rang his bell again. 'Let us put it to a vote. I think the resolution that children need watches will pass unanimously.'

There were, however, nine children who didn't want watches. The journalist ran right over to them and asked why.

'Because we'll wind them too much and break them. Because they're not worth the money. Because you can lose them. Because when you do handstands, they'll slip off and get broken. Because not even all grownups have watches, and so they'll be envious and want to get back at us. Because they're not all that necessary. Because Dad will take my watch away, sell it, and drink up the money.'

Felek rang his bell again. 'The resolution has passed by a majority of the votes, with nine nays.'

But all the delegates were unanimous that not everyone should have the right to kiss them. They did not like sitting on laps and being patted and petted. Some exceptions could be made for parents, but none for aunts. A committee was elected to work out the bill in detail, and then there would be another vote.

On point three of the agenda, it was resolved that girls should have two pockets and boys six.

Klu Klu was outraged. Why should girls have only a third as many pockets—that is, four pockets fewer—than boys? But she did not say anything and waited to see what would happen next.

Felek rang his bell: Now the question of abolishing girls.

And then it started.

'Girls are crybabies. Girls are gossipy. Girls are tattle-tales. Girls are fakers. And so dainty. Girls have butter-fingers. Girls are stuck-up. Girls are touchy. Girls have secrets. Girls scratch.'

The poor girl delegates just sat there with tears in their eyes.

But then Klu Klu's voice rang out from the royal box. 'I would like to speak.'

The room grew quiet.

'In my country, in Africa, the girls are as good as the boys in everything—running, climbing trees, doing somersaults. But I don't understand you people at all. The boys are always quarreling with the girls. They keep them from playing and don't even want to play with them. And I think there are more bad boys than there are bad girls.'

'Ho-ho-ho,' laughed many boys.

Felek rang his bell as a signal that Klu Klu should not be interrupted.

'Boys are rough, boys fight, boys have dirty hands and ears, boys ruin their clothes, boys …'

Now there was more laughter.

Felek rang his bell again.

'Boys rip pages from their books and ruin them. They don't like to study. They make a lot of noise and break windows. They take advantage of girls, who are weak in Europe because of their dresses and long hair …'

'So let them cut off their hair.'

'So let them wear pants.'

Felek rang his bell.

'… girls are weaker and so boys treat them badly. And then they even pretend that it was an accident.'

The place went wild. Some delegates began whistling through their fingers. All the rest were yelling and hollering.

'Look who's telling us what to do.'

'She's black as coal!'

'Monkeys belong in cages.'

'The king's girlfriend!'

'Matt's wife.'

'Matt, Matt, you pussycat.'

'Sing us a song, you yellow canary.'

One delegate jumped up on his chair, shouting so loud his face was red. Felek knew him. It was Antek, a pickpocket, as bad as they come.

'Antek, I swear to God,' shouted Felek, 'I'll knock all your teeth out.'

'Try it. Big Mr. Minister. Baron von Rauch. Felek, the big angel. Remember when you stole the apples from that woman's basket? Baron von Crook.'

Felek threw his inkwell and bell at Antek. The delegates had divided into three groups. One group was hightailing it out of the meeting room, and the other two were fighting.

Matt watched it all, his face white as chalk. The journalist was busily taking notes.

'Calm down, Baron von Rauch. This is nothing so terrible. It's just the factions forming,' said the journalist to Felek.

Felek did calm down, because the delegates had forgotten all about him and were now fighting among themselves.

Klu Klu was itching to lower herself down over the railing of the royal box, grab one of the delegates' chairs, and show those wise guys what African girls knew about fighting. Klu Klu knew that she had started it all and felt sorry for causing Matt so much trouble. But she had no regrets. She had to speak her mind. And what had they said about her? That she was black? Big surprise. That she should be in a cage with the monkeys? She'd already been in one and just let them try to put her back. That she was Matt's girlfriend? She liked that idea. The only problem was that she couldn't jump into the fight, because of that stupid European etiquette.

And those boys, just look how they fought! The clumsy ninnies, the boobs. They had already been fighting for ten minutes, and nobody had won yet. They jumped back and forth like goats, missing half their punches.

And Felek's aim had been off when he threw his ink-well and bell. Klu Klu would have needed only one thing or the other to knock that big shot Antek off his chair.

Then Klu Klu couldn't stand it any more. She hopped onto the railing, sprang through the air to a chandelier, then swung herself over the foreign journalists' desk, making the five boys attacking Antek scatter like pesky flies.

'You want to fight?'

Antek took a swing at her but was soon to regret it. He was hit four times, or rather, only once, because

Klu Klu had hit him with her head, one leg, and both hands all at the same time. Antek fell to the floor with a broken nose, a twisted neck, a numb hand, and three teeth knocked out.

What weak teeth these white boys have, thought Klu Klu.

She dashed over to the minister's table, dipped her handkerchief in a glass of water, and placed it under Antek's nose. 'Don't worry,' she said in a soothing voice, 'your hand's not broken. In Africa, we need only one day to get over a fight like this. You're more delicate here, but you'll feel fine in a week. I'm very sorry about your teeth. African children are so much stronger than you people.'

MATT returned to his palace, his feelings deeply hurt.

He would never ever set foot inside the children's parliament again.

What horrible ingratitude. That's the thanks he gets for all his work and plans, for all the dangerous journeys he made, and for defending his country so heroically.

Make them magicians, give them dolls that reach to the sky—they're so dumb. It's too bad I started the whole thing. What complaints! The roof leaks, the food's no good, there are no games to play at camp. Where's there another country where children have a zoo like ours? Or such fireworks and brass bands? They even have their own newspaper. It wasn't worth it. Tomorrow that very newspaper would inform the whole world that Matt had been called a pussycat and a yellow canary. No, it wasn't worth it.

Matt announced that he would no longer read the letters from the children, nor would there be any audiences after lunch. And there would be no more presents. He'd had it!

Matt telephoned the Prime Minister for advice.

'Please connect me with the Prime Minister's private apartment.'

'Who's speaking?'

'The king.'

'The Prime Minister is not at home,' said the Prime Minister, not realizing that Matt would recognize his voice.

'But I know it's you I'm talking to,' said Matt.

'Ah, it's Your Royal Highness, I beg your pardon. But I can't come to the palace. I'm sick, and just getting into bed. That's why I said I wasn't at home.'

Matt hung up.

'He's lying,' said Matt, pacing his study. 'He doesn't want to come see me because he already knows what happened in parliament. Now no one will respect me any more, people will make fun of me.'

Just then, the footman announced the arrival of Felek and the journalist.

'Send them in!' ordered Matt.

'I have come to ask Your Royal Highness what I should write about today's session of the Proparl for tomorrow's paper. If we write nothing at all, that'll cause rumors and gossip. So we can say that the session was stormy, that Baron von Rauch offered his resignation, which means that he feels offended and no longer wishes to be Prime Minister and will be given a medal by the king.'

'And what will you write about me?'

'Nothing at all. It's not proper to write about such things. But Antek is the most difficult problem. Antek is a delegate, and so he can't be flogged. The delegates can fight among themselves, but the government has no right to punish them, because they have immunity. Besides, Antek already got a good walloping from Klu Klu, and maybe now he'll settle down.'

Matt was so happy that there wasn't going to be any article about Antek's mockery of the king that he was even ready to forgive him.

'Tomorrow's session will begin at twelve.'

'That does not concern me in the least, because I won't be going.'

'That's not good,' said the journalist. 'They might think that Your Royal Highness is afraid.'

'But my feelings have been very hurt,' said Matt, with tears in his eyes.

'A group of delegates will come to beg Your Royal Highness's pardon.'

'Fine,' agreed Matt.

The journalist left, because he had to write his article right away so that it could be printed the next morning.

But Felek stayed.

'I told you a long time ago you should stop being called Matt,' said Felek.

'What of it?' Matt interrupted irritably. 'Now you're Baron von Rauch, but they called you worse names than me.'

'Sure, but I'm just a minister, and you're the king. It's worse when a king is called names.'

Klu Klu did not go to the next session, but Matt had to. At first, he did not like being there at all, but everyone was so quiet and the speeches were so interesting that Matt soon forgot about everything that had happened the day before.

The topics under discussion were red ink and grownups laughing at children.

'Our teachers always correct our homework and tests with red ink, but we have to write in black. Red ink is prettier, and we want to use it, too.'

'Yes,' said one of the girl delegates, 'and they should give us extra paper to protect our books. Book covers can get dirty. And also we should have decals to decorate our exercise books.'

There was a burst of applause when the girl finished speaking. The boys wanted to show that they were not at all angry at the girls and that yesterday's hullabaloo had just been the work of a few bad apples. And a few bad apples out of a couple of hundred delegates weren't all that many.

They spoke for a very long time on the subject of grownups making fun of children.

'If you ask them a question or do something wrong, they either get angry and yell at us or make fun of us. That's not right. Grownups think they know everything, but they don't. My father can't name the bays in Australia or all the rivers in America. And he doesn't know which lake the Nile flows out of.'

'The Nile's not in America, it's in Africa,' said one of the delegates from his seat.

'I know! I just mentioned it as an example. Grownups don't know much about stamps and they don't know how to whistle through their fingers and that's why they say it isn't nice.'

'My uncle can whistle.'

'But not through his fingers.'

'Maybe he can, how do you know?'

'You're a dummy.'

Another quarrel might have started, but the chairman rang his bell and said that delegates could not be called dummies and anyone who did so would be expelled from the hall.

'What does that mean, expelled from the hall?'

'That's a parliamentary expression. In school we'd say thrown out the door.'

And so the delegates were gradually learning how to behave in parliament.

One delegate arrived late, near the end of the session.

'Excuse me for being late,' he said, 'but my mother didn't want to let me come at all, because yesterday I came home with a scratched nose and bruises from the fight.'

'That's against the law. A delegate has immunity, and his parents cannot forbid him to attend parliament. What sort of system would that be? He was elected a delegate, and he has to attend. You can get your nose scratched in school, too, but parents don't forbid you to go to school.'

This was the beginning of the quarrel between the children and the grownups, but only the beginning.

Now I must tell you something which neither Matt nor the delegates knew yet: the foreign newspapers had started writing about the children's parliament. And all the children in other countries had started talking about rights and reforms both in school and at home. And if they were given a bad grade unfairly or if someone grew angry at them, they would say right away: 'That would never have happened if we had our own delegates.'

In Queen Campanelli's little country in the south of Europe, something had made the children angry and they had gone on strike. They knew that the children's flag was supposed to be green. And so they marched beneath a green flag.

The grownups were very angry.

'A fine kettle of fish. We don't have enough trouble with the workers and their red flag, now the kids are starting up. That's all we needed.'

This news made Matt very happy, and there was a long article about it in the children's newspaper, entitled 'The Movement Begins.'

The article said that Queen Campanelli's country had a warm climate and the children there were hot-blooded, which was why they had been the first to demand their rights. It also said:

> It won't be long before all the children in the whole world are marching under the green flag. Children will realize that people shouldn't fight. And there will be peace in the world. People will love each other. And there will be no more wars. Because if

children learn not to fight when they're little, they won't fight when they grow up.

King Matt was the first to say that children should have a green flag. That was King Matt's idea, and so he should be the king of all the children in the world.

Princess Klu Klu is returning to Africa and will explain everything to the native children. That will be good.

Now children will have the same rights as the grownups and be real citizens. Now children will not be obedient out of fear of punishment but because they want a good and peaceful world.

The paper had many other interesting things to say. Matt was very surprised that the sad king had said it was hard to be a reformer, that, more often than not, reformers came to a bad end and it was only after their death that people saw that they had been right and built monuments to them.

But everything's going well for me, thought Matt. I'm not in any danger. Sure, I've had plenty of worries and troubles, but you have to expect that if you're going to run a country.

AT THAT very moment, a group of young people, meaning people over fifteen, had gathered in front of parliament. One of them climbed up a streetlight and shouted: 'They've forgotten all about us. We want to have delegates, too. The grownups have their own parliament, the children have theirs, what's wrong with us? We won't allow those squirts to order us around. If the kids get chocolate, we should get cigarettes. It's not fair.'

The delegates arrived for a session, but the big boys would not let them in.

'Fine delegates you are! You don't even know your multiplication tables yet, and you think "mouses" is the plural of "mouse." '

'And some of them don't even know how to write.'

'They're supposed to govern the country?'

'Down with their government!'

The prefect of police telephoned the palace to say that Matt should stay home because there was trouble brewing. At the same time, he sent out the mounted police, who began to disperse the crowd. But most of the boys began throwing their books and lunch boxes at the police. Some of them even started tearing up the cobblestones from the street. Just then, the prefect of police came out on a balcony and shouted: 'If you don't leave here now, I'll call in the army. And if you throw stones at them, they'll shoot in the air first, and if that doesn't work, they'll open fire on you.'

The boys paid no attention and grew even more furious. They broke in the doors and burst into the hall where parliament met.

'We're not budging until we get the same rights the children have.'

Everyone had lost his head and had no idea what to do next. Then suddenly Matt appeared in the royal box. He had not heeded the prefect of police and had come himself to find out what the trouble was.

'We want a parliament, too, we want delegates, we want rights.' First they shouted, then they started hollering so loud you couldn't make out a word of it.

Matt stood in silence. He was waiting. When they saw that shouting wasn't going to get them anywhere, they began to shush themselves: 'Quiet, enough, stop.'

Finally, someone cried: 'The king wants to speak.' The room grew still.

'Citizens,' said Matt. 'Your demands are just. But you'll be grownups soon and can run for the grownups' parliament. I began with the children because I'm still little myself and I know what children need. You can't do everything all at once. I have too much work as it is. When I turn fifteen, if everything's all set with the children, I'll make reforms for people your age.'

'But we won't need your help, because we'll already be in the grownups' parliament by then.'

Matt saw that he had taken the wrong tack. 'But why pester us? You already have mustaches and smoke cigarettes. Go to the big people's parliament. They should take you in there.'

The older boys, who already had little mustaches, began to think: It's true. What do we need this sissy parliament for? We can be in a real parliament.

And the younger ones were ashamed to admit that they didn't smoke cigarettes yet, and so they said: 'All right.'

They left. But on their way to the grownups' parliament they ran into soldiers with fixed bayonets, who stopped the procession. Some wanted to go back, but there were soldiers behind them, too. So they split up—some went down one street to the right, and others to the left. Then they split up again, but the soldiers attacked them from behind, chasing after them. And when they had split them up into little groups, the police began arresting them.

When Matt learned of this, he was very angry at the prefect of police, because it looked as if the king had deceived the boys. But the prefect explained that there was no other way. And so Matt ordered that a proclamation be posted on the street corners requesting the boys to choose the three smartest among them to come to the palace for an audience with Matt.

That evening, the king was asked to come to a council of ministers.

'Things are bad,' said the Minister of Education. 'The children won't study. They laugh when the teachers tell them to do something. "What will you do to us? We can do whatever we want to. We'll complain to the king. And tell our delegates." The teachers don't know what to do. The older children are completely out of hand. They say: "Brats rule the country while we work like dogs? We're no dummies. Since we don't have our own delegates, we can do without schools, too." The older boys never used to fight with the younger ones, but now they pester them and tease them all the time. "Go on, go complain to your delegates." They pull their ears and hit them. The teachers say they'll wait two more weeks, but they'll quit if things don't quiet down. Two have already left. One opened a soda-water stand, and the other one started a button factory.'

'Most of the grownups are very dissatisfied,' said the Minister of Internal Affairs. Yesterday, in a café, a man said that the children have gotten swelled heads, think they can do whatever they want to, and make so much noise it can drive you crazy. They jump on the sofas, they play soccer in the house, they roam the streets without permission, and their clothes are so torn that soon they'll be walking around half-naked, like savages. The man said other things as well, but I can't repeat them. I ordered him arrested for lèse-majesté.'

'Now I know what to do,' said Matt. 'Everyone who goes to school will be considered an office worker. They'll keep on doing their reading, writing, and arithmetic at school. School will be their office. Children should be paid for the work they do. And so we'll pay them. What difference does it make whether we give them chocolate, skates, dolls, or money? And the children will know they have to work or else they won't receive their salary.'

'We can try it,' agreed the ministers.

Matt had totally forgotten that the country was now ruled by parliament, not by him, and he ordered that the proclamation be written and posted on every street corner.

Early the next morning, the journalist came rushing in, mad as a hornet, and said: 'If Your Royal Highness is going to plaster the latest news all over the city, what do we need newspapers for?'

Then Felek, who had followed the journalist in, said: 'What's the point of parliament if Your Royal Highness is going to make new laws himself?'

'Yes,' agreed the journalist, 'Baron von Rauch is right. The king can say what he wants, but the final decision rests with the delegates. And they might even have a better idea.'

Matt could see that he had been in too much of a hurry. But what should be done now?

'Your Royal Highness should telephone instructions that, for the time being, chocolate will continue to be distributed. Otherwise, there'll be a revolution. And today we will discuss this issue in parliament.'

Matt had a premonition of trouble, and trouble there was. The delegates wanted the problem examined by a subcommittee. But Matt objected. 'If it goes to a subcommittee, that means a long wait. But the teachers said that they'd only wait two weeks for things to change before walking out.'

The journalist went over to Felek and whispered something in his ear. Felek grinned and asked for the floor when Matt was finished.

'Delegates, gentlemen,' said Felek. 'I used to go to school and I know what goes on there. One year I was sent to the cloakroom seventy times, had to stand in the corner a hundred and five times, and was kicked out of school one hundred and twelve times, and all for no reason! And do you think that school was anything special? Forget it. I went to six different schools, and it was the same everywhere. Grownups don't go to school, and so they don't know how unfair everything is there. If the teachers can't wait and really don't want to teach children, we can make a law that they have to teach grownups. And when the grownups see how lousy school is, they won't always be after us to do our homework. And when the teachers find out that they can't boss grownups around, they'll stop crabbing about us.'

Then out came everybody's complaints about teachers and school. One delegate had been kept back unfairly, one had made only two mistakes and had still gotten a D, one was late to school because of a bad foot and he still had to stand in the corner, and one hadn't been able to memorize a poem because his little brother had torn out the page, but the teacher said that was just an excuse.

When the delegates were tired and hungry, Felek put the proposal to a vote. 'The subcommittee will consider how to make things fair in school, and also if the children are to be paid like office workers. In the meantime, the grownups will attend school. All those in agreement, raise your right hand.'

A couple of delegates wanted to voice objections, but the majority had already raised their hands, and Felek said: 'Parliament has passed the resolution.'

WORDS cannot describe what went on in Matt's country when people learned of the decision passed by the children's parliament.

'This is anarchy!' said some people angrily. 'Who are they giving orders to? We have our own parliament, and we don't have to submit to them. Their parliament decides what the children are to do, and they have no right to interfere in our affairs.'

'All right, say we do go to school, then who'll work?' others asked.

'Let the children get a taste of work. They'll see it's not as easy as they think.'

'Who knows?' said those with calmer heads. 'It might even be a good idea. When the children realize how much knowledge work requires, they'll have more respect for us.'

The people who were out of work were the happiest of all.

'Matt is a wise king. We were about to start a revolution, but he came up with a good idea. Our bones ache from digging coal, and now we'll be sitting on comfortable benches while learning interesting things. But how much will we be paid?'

A law was passed that people would be paid the same for schoolwork as for regular work, because work was work. And another law was passed saying the children would go to work and the grownups would go to school.

There was tremendous confusion, because most of the boys only wanted to be firemen or drive a truck and the girls wanted to work in toy stores and pastry shops. There were the usual stupid ideas: one boy wanted to be a hangman, one boy wanted to be an Indian, and one boy wanted to be a lunatic.

'But we all can't be firemen and work in toy stores!'

'I don't care about that. I just want to do what I want.'

There were many family quarrels when the children handed their parents their textbooks and workbooks.

'You got your books all dirty and now the teachers will yell at us for being messy,' said one mother.

'You lost your pencil and now I don't have anything to write with and the teacher will be mad,' said one father.

'You were late with breakfast, so write me a note saying that's why I'm tardy,' said one grandmother.

But the teachers were very happy. Now they'd get a little rest, because grownups were calmer than children.

'They'll set a good example for the children,' said the teachers.

Of course there were some people who had a good laugh at the whole thing, and some who thought it interesting and different.

But everyone said it wouldn't last long.

The city looked strange with the grownups walking to school carrying books and the children going to the offices, factories, and stores. Some grownups were grumpy or ashamed, but others didn't mind at all.

'So we're children again. That's not so bad either.'

Some of them even ran into old classmates they'd once sat next to in school. They talked about their old teachers, the games they used to play, and the mischief they'd made.

'You remember our old Latin teacher?' said one man, who was now an industrial engineer.

'Do you remember that fight we had once, what was it over?'

'Sure I do. I bought a jackknife and you said it was made out of iron, not steel.'

'And we were sent to the cloakroom.'

A doctor and a lawyer got so carried away with stories about the old days that they completely forgot they were no longer boys and started chasing each other and knocking people off the sidewalks; a passing teacher told them that was no way to behave in public.

But some grownups were very angry. A fat woman who owned a restaurant was on her way to school in an absolute fury, when a mechanic recognized her.

'Look, there goes that big fat cow. She's always cheating us at her restaurant. She waters your vodka and charges you the price of a whole herring for one slice. You know what, let's trip her. If we're going to be children again, we might as well do it right.'

He put his foot in front of her. The fat woman almost fell on her face. Her books went flying.

'You bad boys!' she yelled.

'It was an accident.'

'You just wait, I'll tell the teacher you weren't letting people walk down the street in peace.'

The children, however, were very calm and dignified and by nine o'clock were at work in the offices and stores.

All the grownups were in school. The older people sat in the back to be nearer the stove. They figured on catching a few winks during class.

And so the grownups did their reading, writing, and arithmetic. Everything went pretty well. The teachers tested them to see how much they had forgotten. The teachers only got angry at the grownups a few times for not paying attention. It was hard for them to pay attention, because they were all thinking about what was happening at home and in the factories and stores.

The girls were working as hard as they could to make their first dinner a delicious one. But not all of them knew how to cook.

'You know what, let's serve jam instead of soup.'

And so they went to the store to buy some jam.

'Oh, it's too expensive. Let's buy the jam somewhere else.'

Some children bargained to show they were smart shoppers, and some salesmen wanted to brag that they had the best prices in town, and so business went well.

'Ten more oranges, please.'

'And a pound of raisins.'

'And some Swiss cheese. But make sure it's fresh, or I'll bring it back.'

'I have nothing but the best cheese, and my oranges have nice thin skin.'

'Fine, how much will that be?'

The salesmen would try to add it all up, then give up and ask: 'How much money do you have?'

'Twenty.'

'That's not enough for all this stuff.'

'I'll bring the rest later.'

'Well, all right.'

'But please give me my change.'

'How can you be so stupid! First, you don't give me enough money, and then you want change.'

It has to be admitted that the children weren't always polite to one another in the stores and offices, and often said things like 'You're dumb!' 'You're lying!' 'Get out of here!' 'No means no.' 'Watch it!' 'What do you want now?' 'Scram!' and so on.

They also said things like 'You just wait until Mama comes home from school.'

Or 'I'm telling my dad everything as soon as school's over.'

The street kids caused the most trouble—they'd run into a store, stuff their pockets, and refuse to pay.

There was a sort of police force. Boys stood on the street corners, but they still weren't sure what they were supposed to do.

'What kind of policeman are you, anyway! Some bad kids ran into my store, grabbed a handful of dried plums, and then ran out without paying,' said one salesgirl.

'Which way did they run?'

'How should I know?'

'Well, if you don't know, how can I help you?'

'You're the policeman, you should be watching.'

'Sure. You have one store and you can't keep an eye on it, and I have fifty stores to keep an eye on.'

'You're a jerk.'

'If you're going to call me names, don't call me the next time you're in trouble.'

The policeman left the store, stumbling on his sword.

'Listen to her. She wants me to catch the thief, but she doesn't even know which way he went. This is a lousy job. All you do is stand around like a dope. And that stingy salesgirl didn't even offer me an apple. I don't want to be a policeman any more, and that's final. Let people do whatever they want. I can go back to school if they don't like the way I'm doing my job.'

When the grownups came home from school, the children opened the door for them and asked: 'Did you hand in your composition, Mommy?'

'Did you do your homework, Daddy?'

'Who'd you sit next to, Gramma?'

'What row are you in?'

After work, some children stopped by the school to walk their mother or father home.

'Well, what did you do at the office?' the father would ask.

'Nothing much. I sat at my desk, then I watched a funeral go by out the window. I tried to smoke a cigarette, but it tasted terrible. They put some papers on my desk and I signed them all. Then three men came to see me. They must have been speaking French or English, and I told them I couldn't understand what they were talking about. Then it was teatime, but there was no tea, so I ate some sugar. I called up some of my classmates to find out what they were doing, but the telephones are all messed up. I talked to one friend who was working at the post office. He said there were a lot of letters with foreign stamps there.'

Dinner had turned out well in some homes but had been burned to a crisp in others. And some children hadn't even been able to light the stove, which meant that now their mothers had to make dinner in a hurry.

'I have to rush,' said one mother, 'because I have a lot of homework for tomorrow. Our teacher said grownups have to do more homework than children. But that's not fair. The teachers in the other schools aren't giving such big assignments.'

'And did anyone have to stand in the corner?'

The mother was a little embarrassed. 'Yes.'

'For what?'

'There were two women in the back row who knew each other from before. They had shared a summer house or something. They chatted during the whole lesson. The teacher told them to stop twice, but they kept right on chatting. And finally the teacher made them stand in the corner.'

'Did they cry?'

'One laughed, but the other one had tears in her eyes.'

'Did the boys pick on you?'

'A little.'

'That's just how it was for us,' said the children gleefully.

MATT was sitting in his study reading the newspaper, which gave an accurate report on the first day. The article admitted that things were far from running smoothly, that the telephones were working very badly and the letters weren't being sorted properly at the post office. A train had been derailed, but nobody knew how many people had been hurt because the telegraph system wasn't working. Patience was needed; the children didn't know how things worked yet. Every reform needs time. There's never been a reform that didn't jolt the economy.

Another article said that a subcommittee was working out the details of the law concerning the schools in such a way that teachers, children, and parents would all be satisfied.

Suddenly Klu Klu came running in. She clapped her hands and jumped for joy. 'Guess what just happened.'

'Well, what?' asked Matt.

'One thousand African children just arrived.'

Matt had forgotten that he had wired King Bum Drum to send one hundred children. But a parrot or some other bird must have tapped the wire with its beak, which made the telegraph tap out an extra zero. And so it turned out that Matt had invited a thousand children, not a hundred.

Matt was upset by the news, but Klu Klu was happy as could be. 'That's even better. The sooner more children start studying, the sooner we can build a new Africa.'

Klu Klu set right to work. She had all the children line up in the royal gardens. She chose ten she knew to be reliable and put each of them in charge of one hundred children. And they in turn chose a leader for each group of ten. Every leader of ten was given a room in the summer palace, while the ten main leaders lived in Matt's winter palace. Klu Klu told them what the rules were in Europe. They passed on this information to the other leaders, who then explained things to their groups of ten.

The same method would be used for their schooling.

'Where are they going to sleep?'

'For now, they can sleep on the floor. After all, they're still uncivilized, so what do they care?'

'But what are they going to eat?' asked Matt. 'The cooks are all in school.'

'They can eat raw meat for now. After all, they're still uncivilized, so what do they care?'

Klu Klu hated to waste time and gave the first class right after lunch. She explained everything so clearly that in four hours the leaders had already learned quite a bit and could start teaching their own groups.

Everything seemed to be going well, until a messenger on horseback galloped up to the palace to report that, by accident, the children had opened the wolf cage at the zoo and let all the wolves out. The people in the city were too terrified to leave their houses.

'Even my horse was afraid, and I had to whip him hard,' said the messenger.

'But how did the wolves get out?'

'It wasn't the children's fault,' said the messenger. 'The zookeepers left for school without telling the kids who took their places about the switches that open the cages. And so they threw a switch by accident.'

'How many wolves got out?'

'Twelve. One of them is very bad. Catching him won't be easy.'

'And where are the wolves now?'

'Nobody knows, they ran off in all directions. People say that they've seen them running down the streets. But you can't believe them, because they're so frightened they think every dog's a wolf. There are even rumors that all the animals have escaped from their cages. One woman swore that she was chased by a tiger, a hippopotamus, and two cobras.'

As soon as Klu Klu found out, she asked what wolves were like, because there were none in Africa and she'd never seen one. She asked Matt a million questions.

'Do they roar? Do they slink around before they attack, or do they jump right at you? Do they use their teeth or their claws? Will they attack you even if they're not hungry? Are they brave or cowardly? Do they have good hearing, smell, sight?'

Matt was ashamed that he knew so little about wolves, but he told her what he could.

'I think,' said Klu Klu, 'that they're hiding in the park near the zoo. I'll go there with my group leaders and fix this situation in two minutes. Too bad the lions and tigers didn't escape. That would have made for better hunting.'

Matt, Klu Klu, and the ten group leaders set off for the zoo. People stood at their windows and watched. There wasn't a single person on the street. The stores were closed up tight. The city looked deserted.

Matt was ashamed that his people were so cowardly. When they reached the zoo, the group leaders began playing their drums and flutes as loud as they could. But they could not spot any wolves in the bushes or trees.

'Halt!' cried Klu Klu. 'Ready with your bows. Something's moving over there.'

Klu Klu dashed forward, grabbed hold of a branch, and pulled herself up into the tree, a great big wolf snapping at her heels. Standing on its hind legs, the wolf scratched the trunk with its front claws. It howled, and all the other wolves answered it with howls.

'It's the leader,' cried Klu Klu. 'They won't be any problem without him. Go around the bushes and drive them out.'

They did what Klu Klu said. Frightened by all the noise, the wolves began to run away. The group leaders shot their smallest arrows at them and banged their drums loudly. They came at the wolves from the right and the left. And five minutes later, all eleven wolves were back in their cage.

They locked the cage right away. Now the twelfth wolf saw that he was all alone and bounded away.

Klu Klu hopped down from the tree. 'Hurry,' she cried. 'Don't let him escape from the park.'

But it was too late. The crazed wolf had fled into the city. And now the people really did see a wolf running through the streets, chased by Klu Klu and ten black children. Matt was bringing up the rear. He couldn't keep up with those African children. Sweaty and tired, he could barely stand on his feet. Just then, a kind old woman invited him into her apartment and gave him some milk and rolls.

'King Matt,' she said, 'you are a good king. I'm eighty years old and I've seen all sorts of kings. Some were better than others. But there's never been one like you. You didn't forget about us old people. You're sending us to school and you're kind enough to pay us to study. I have a son who lives far away, in another country. He writes to me twice a year. I save his letters, but I can't read them. But I don't want strangers to read them to me, because there might be something secret in them and maybe they'd trick me and not tell me what the letters really said. But now I'll be able to find out for myself. The teacher said that if I really try I'll be able to write to him myself in two months. That will make my son so happy.'

Matt finished his milk, kissed the old woman's hand, thanked her, and left.

Meanwhile, the wolf had jumped through an open manhole into a sewer. Klu Klu was about to crawl in after it.

'Stop! I won't allow it,' cried Matt. 'It's dark down there. You'll either suffocate or that wolf will tear you to pieces.'

But Klu Klu wouldn't be stopped. She put a hunting knife between her teeth and climbed down into the sewer. Now even the African children were afraid, because there was nothing more dangerous than fighting a wild animal in the dark.

Trying to decide what to do, Matt suddenly remembered that he had a flashlight with him. And then, without even stopping to think, he lowered himself into the sewer. Where could they be in such a narrow pipe? But this wasn't the main pipe. Up ahead, he could see a river of water, mud, and filth. The stench was so bad it made Matt gag.

'Klu Klu,' called Matt, his voice echoing back from every direction, for the sewers ran under the entire city. Matt didn't know whether Klu Klu had answered or not. He kept turning his flashlight off to keep the batteries from going dead. Just then, up to his knees in water, Matt heard a terrible racket in one of the tunnels.

He turned on his flashlight and saw Klu Klu and the wolf. Klu Klu was stabbing the wolf in the throat with her knife, but then the wolf grabbed her hand in its teeth. Klu Klu quickly switched the knife from that hand to the other and began stabbing the wolf again. The wolf let go of her hand, lowered its head, and was about to sink its teeth into her stomach. If it tore open her stomach, that would be the end of Klu Klu. His revolver in one hand, Matt rushed at the wolf, shining his flashlight right into the wolf's eyes. Blinded by the light, the wolf bared its teeth and snarled. Matt shot the wolf right through the eye.

Klu Klu had fainted. Matt began to drag her out, but he was afraid that she would sink in the muck. He could barely stand on his feet himself. Things might have taken a bad turn, but, up above, the group leaders had not been wasting time. Klu Klu had ordered them to stay put, but how long could they just stand there like a bunch of ninnies? And so they had crawled down into the sewer and noticed the light right away. First they carried out Klu Klu, then Matt, and, last, the dead wolf.

'MATT, what have you done?' said the sad king. 'Matt, come to your senses, you're in great danger. It's a shame, you had a chance but you wasted it. I came here to warn you, but I'm afraid it's too late. I would have been here a week ago, but your trains are useless since the children took over the railroads. I had to travel from the border in farm wagons. Maybe that was for the best, because I passed through villages and little towns and I know what the people are saying about you. Things are bad, Matt, take my word.'

The sad king had left his own country in the utmost secrecy and had come to help Matt.

'But what happened that's so bad?' asked Matt in a worried voice.

'A lot. But you're being deceived, the wool's being pulled over your eyes, and so you don't know what's going on.'

'I know everything,' said Matt, taking offense. 'I read the paper every day. The children are gradually getting the hang of things, the subcommittee is working. And reforms aren't easy—there are always some rough spots. I know it's been bumpy.'

'Listen, Matt, you only read one paper, your own. And it's full of lies. Here, read some other papers.'

The sad king laid a roll of newspapers tied with string on Matt's desk.

Matt slowly unrolled the newspapers. He read only the headlines, that's all it took to see what was going on. And what Matt read made his head reel.

KING MATT HAS GONE MAD

PRIME MINISTER IS THIEF

BLACK DEVILS RULE

KING TO MARRY AFRICAN

SPY ESCAPES FROM PRISON

NEWSPAPER BOY FELEK NOW BARON

TWO FORTRESSES BLOWN UP

COUNTRY WITHOUT CANNONS OR GUNPOWDER

WAR IMMINENT

MINISTERS SHIPPING THEIR JEWELS OUT OF THE COUNTRY

DOWN WITH THE TYRANT KING

'It's these papers,' cried Matt, 'that are full of lies! What does this mean—black devils rule? The black children came here to study. And they've been more than helpful. When the wolves escaped from the zoo, they risked their lives to drive them back into their cage. Klu Klu almost lost a hand. We have cannons and we have gunpowder. I know that Felek was once a newspaper boy, but he was never a thief, and I'm not a tyrant.'

'Matt, don't be angry, it won't do any good. I'm telling you—things are bad. If you like, we can go into town and you can see for yourself.'

Matt disguised himself as an ordinary boy, and the sad king wore ordinary clothes, too.

They came to the same barracks Matt had slipped past with Felek the night he ran away from the palace to go off to war. He had been so happy then, a child who knew nothing at all. Now he knew everything and had nothing to look forward to.

An old soldier was sitting by the barracks smoking his pipe.

'What's the good word?' asked Matt.

'Things are bad. The children are running the show now. They keep shooting off twenty-one-gun salutes and wrecking the cannons. The army's a shambles.' The old soldier broke into tears.

They walked past a factory. A worker was sitting outside with a book on his knees, memorizing poetry for school.

'How are things in the factory?'

'Go inside and have a look. Anyone who wants to can go in now.'

They went in. There were papers strewn everywhere in the payroll office, the main boiler had burst, all the machines were idle. A couple of boys were wandering around the factory.

'What are you doing here?'

'Well, they sent five hundred of us over here to work. But the other boys said "We're nobody's fools," and they took off. About thirty of us stayed. We don't know what to do, everything's busted. The rest of the guys left, but we're sweeping up a little. Our parents are in school and it's boring to just sit around at home. Besides, it doesn't feel right to take money you didn't earn.'

Half the stores on the street were closed, even though everyone knew that the wolves were back in their cage.

They went into a store. There was a nice girl at the counter.

'Why are so many stores closed?' asked Matt.

'Because everything's been stolen. There's no police, no soldiers. Hoodlums are roaming the streets and robbing stores in broad daylight. The store owners brought all their stuff home for safekeeping.'

Next they went to the train station. A train was lying on its side in the middle of the yard.

'What happened?'

'The switchman went off to play soccer and the station-master went fishing. The engineer didn't know where the emergency brake was. A hundred people were killed.'

Matt bit his lip to keep from bursting into tears.

There was a hospital near the train station. The children were supposed to take care of the patients. If they didn't have too much homework, the doctors would run in for half an hour or so. But that didn't help much. The patients were groaning and dying. The children were crying, because they were afraid and didn't know how to help the patients.

'Well, Matt, should we go back to the palace?'

'No, I have to go to the newspaper office and have a talk with that journalist,' said Matt calmly, though it was clear that he was seething within.

'I can't go there with you,' said the sad king. 'I might be recognized.'

'I won't be long,' said Matt, and he set off quickly.

The sad king watched him go, shook his head, and returned to the palace.

Now Matt wasn't walking, he ran. Fists clenched, he could feel the blood of King Henryk the Hasty rising in him.

'Just you wait, you crook, you liar, you cheat, you'll answer to me for everything.'

Matt burst into the journalist's office. The journalist was at his desk, and Felek was lying on the couch, smoking a cigar.

'Aha, so you're here, too!' shouted Matt. 'All the better, since you're both involved. What have you done to my country?'

'Would Your Royal Highness like to sit down and rest?' asked the journalist in his soft, pleasant voice.

Matt shuddered. Now he was convinced that the journalist was a spy. His heart had told him that long ago, but only now was he certain.

'Take this, you spy!' cried Matt, firing the revolver that had never left his side since the war, but in a lightning move the journalist grabbed Matt's hand and the bullet struck the ceiling.

'Children shouldn't play with guns,' said the journalist with a smile, squeezing Matt's hand so hard the bones started to crunch. Matt's hand opened. The journalist took the revolver and locked it in his desk.

'Now we can discuss things calmly. And so what is it that Your Royal Highness has against me? Didn't I defend Your

Royal Highness in my newspaper, didn't I try to keep things peaceful, offer explanations, and praise Klu Klu? Is that why Your Royal Highness calls me a spy and wants to shoot me?'

'And whose idea was it to make that stupid law about sending grownups to school?'

'How am I to blame for that? The children voted in that law themselves.'

'Why didn't you say anything about our fortresses being blown up?'

'The Minister of War was supposed to report that to you. I couldn't write about it in the paper, it's a military secret.'

'But why did you ask me so many questions about the fire in the old king's forest?'

'A journalist has to ask questions about everything. Then he chooses what he thinks should go in his paper. Your Royal Highness read my paper every day. Was there anything bad in it?'

'Everything was very good, too good,' said Matt, laughing bitterly.

The journalist looked Matt right in the eye and asked: 'Does Your Royal Highness still say I'm a spy?'

'I say you are!' cried Felek, leaping up from the sofa.

The journalist turned pale, glanced furiously at Felek, and was out the door before the two boys realized what was happening.

'See you soon, you snot-nosed brats,' he shouted, and dashed down the stairs.

A car screeched to a stop in front of the building.

'Stop him, grab him!' Felek shouted through the window.

But it was too late. The car had already disappeared around the corner. Besides, who could have stopped him? Not the few passersby and children standing around to see what the fuss was about.

Matt was still stunned by it all. Felek threw himself at Matt's feet and wept.

'Have me hung, my king, it's all my fault,' said Felek between sobs. 'What a miserable wretch I am! What have I done?'

'HOLD on, Felek, we'll talk about that later. What's done is done. The main thing is to be calm and careful. We can't think about the past. We have to think about the future and what has to be done now.'

Felek still wanted to confess everything, but Matt didn't want to lose a second.

'Listen, Felek, the telephones are out of order. You're the only one I can count on now. Do you know where the ministers live?'

'Of course I do. They all live in different parts of town. But that doesn't matter. I've got good legs. I was a newspaper boy for two years. You want them summoned to the palace?'

'Immediately.' Matt glanced at his watch. 'How long will you need?'

'A half an hour.'

'Fine. They are to be in my throne room in two hours. If anyone says he's sick, remind him that the blood of Henryk the Hasty flows in my veins.'

'They'll come, all right!' cried Felek.

He took off his boots and his elegant coat with his medal on it. Felek smeared his pants, hands, and face with printer's ink, then dashed off barefoot to summon the ministers. Matt set off at a run for the palace, because he wanted to talk with the sad king again before meeting with his ministers.

'Where's that man who was here this morning?' said Matt, panting, as soon as Klu Klu opened the door.

'He's gone. He left a letter on your desk.'

Matt ran into his office with a sinking feeling. He grabbed the letter and read it:

Dear Matt, my friend,

What I feared the most has now happened. I have to leave you. Dear Matt, if I didn't know you so well, I would have proposed that you come with me to my country, but I knew you wouldn't agree. I'll be taking the northern highway, and if you wish, you could catch up with me on horseback in two hours. I will stop at the inn and I may wait a little while. But if I don't, remember that I am your friend. Trust me even when you think that I have betrayed you.

> Whatever I do will be for your own good. One thing I beg of you—my coming here must be our secret. No one, but no one, can know about this. This letter must be burned at once! I feel sorry for you, you poor child, an orphan all alone in the world. I would be so happy to spare you even a tenth part of the misfortunes awaiting you. But maybe you'll come with me. This letter absolutely must be burned.

Matt read the letter through quickly, lit a candle, and held the edge of the paper to the flame. The paper began to smolder, burst into flame, and curled into a blackened scroll. The flame singed Matt's fingers, but he paid no attention to the pain.

My soul is suffering more than my fingers, he thought.

On the wall across from Matt's desk hung portraits of his father and mother.

'Poor orphan, all alone,' Matt said with a sigh, gazing at the portraits of his dead parents.

He could sigh but could not allow himself to weep. In a short while he would be sitting on his throne, and he could not attend the meeting with eyes red from crying.

Klu Klu slipped quietly into the room and waited meekly. Her presence irritated Matt at first, but after a moment he asked her quite gently: 'What do you want, Klu Klu?'

'The king is hiding his worries from Klu Klu. The king doesn't want to trust wild Klu Klu with his secrets, but Klu Klu knows and Klu Klu will not let the king down.'

Klu Klu said this very solemnly, with both of her hands raised, just as Bum Drum had once sworn his allegiance to Matt.

'And just what do you know, Klu Klu?' asked Matt, very moved.

'The white kings envied Matt for having so much gold. They want to conquer Matt and kill him. The sad king feels sorry for Matt, but he is weak and afraid of the powerful white kings.'

'Quiet, Klu Klu.'

'Klu Klu will be quiet as the grave, but Klu Klu recognized the sad king. That burnt letter might betray Matt, but Klu Klu never would!'

'Quiet, Klu Klu, not another word!' cried Matt, throwing the ashes of the burnt letter to the floor and stomping them with his feet.

'Klu Klu swears she won't say another word.'

It was time for this conversation to end, because the footmen, who had just returned from school, burst into Matt's study.

Matt turned red with anger.

'What's the meaning of this!' he shouted. 'Since when have the royal footmen dared enter the royal study shouting and hollering? Didn't you have enough time to shout and play in school?'

The master of ceremonies blushed up to his ears. 'Your Royal Highness, I beg your forgiveness for them. But these poor souls never had a chance to play when they were children. First, they were apprentice footmen or scullions; now they're footmen. They've had to be quiet and obedient all their lives. And so now they're running wild.'

'All right, then, all right. Prepare the throne room. There'll be a meeting in half an hour.'

'But I've got so much homework for tomorrow,' moaned one footman.

'I've got to draw a map.'

'I have six assignments and a whole page of—'

'You won't be going to school tomorrow!' Matt interrupted them in a threatening voice.

The footmen bowed and quietly left the room. But a fight almost broke out in the doorway, because one footman shoved another one, who fell and banged his chin against the door handle.

Felek came running in, dirty and sweaty, his pants ripped and torn.

'It's all arranged. They'll all be here.' And then Felek began telling Matt the whole story.

'What the newspaper said was true. I stole money and took bribes. When I took your place at an audience, I didn't give out all the packages to the children. If I liked something, I kept it for myself. If someone gave me money or presents, I'd give him one of the better packages. I had a few helpers, including Antek, who came every day and took something. But I was never a spy. The journalist told me what to do. He told me to take the name Baron and demand a medal. He pretended to be my friend. Then one day he told me we must forge a document saying that Matt was retiring all the ministers, depriving the grownups of all their rights, and transferring power to the children. I wouldn't do it. Then the journalist put on his hat and said: 'If you don't, I'll go to the king and tell him that you're stealing packages and taking bribes.' That scared me silly. I couldn't see how he knew all that, but I figured it was part of his job. But now I know he was a spy. And there's more. There was another forged document, some sort of proclamation to all the children of the world.'

Matt put his hands behind his back and paced the office for a long time.

'You have done a lot of bad things, Felek. But I forgive you.'

'What? You forgive me? If Your Royal Highness really forgives me, I know what I should do.'

'What?' asked Matt.

'I'll tell my father everything. Then he'll give me such a beating I'll never forget what I've done as long as I live.'

'Don't do that, Felek. What good is that? There are better ways of paying for what you did. The country's in trouble. I need people I can count on. That means you, Felek.'

'The Minister of War's car has arrived,' announced the marshal of the court.

Matt put on his crown—and what a heavy crown it was that day—and entered the throne room.

'Mr. Minister of War, tell me everything you know. But be quick and don't beat around the bush, because I know a lot myself already.'

'I can report to Your Royal Highness that we have three fortresses left out of five, four hundred cannons left out of a thousand, and two hundred thousand serviceable rifles. We had enough ammunition for three months, now we have enough for ten days.'

'What about boots, knapsacks, and bread?'

'Our supplies are intact, except that all the marmalade's been eaten up.'

'Is your information accurate?'

'One hundred percent.'

'Do you think there will be a war soon?'

'Politics is not my department.'

'Can the damaged cannons and rifles be repaired quickly?'

'Some of them were badly damaged, but some can be repaired, if the factories go back to work.'

Matt remembered the factory he had been in, and felt his head sink under the weight of his crown, heavier now than ever.

'How is the troops' morale, Mr. Minister?'

'The soldiers and the officers are grumbling. It offends them to have to go to civilian schools. When I received the letter of dismissal—'

'The letter was a forgery. I knew nothing about it.'

The Minister of War frowned. 'When I received that forged letter, a delegation of soldiers came to see me, demanding to be sent to military schools. So I gave them a tongue-lashing: You'll march to civilian schools if those are your orders, and you'll march through fire and hell itself if those are your orders.'

'Would they forgive me if I put things back the way they were?'

The Minister of War drew his saber. 'Your Royal Highness, you can count on us, from me down to the lowliest private. We'll march shoulder to shoulder with our hero and king leading us. We'll defend our country and our honor as soldiers.'

'That's good, that's very good.'

All's not lost yet, thought Matt.

THE ministers were late and quite out of breath, because they were not used to going anywhere on foot. Out of habit, the marshal of the court announced that the ministers' cars had arrived, but in fact their cars had been ruined by their children, and their chauffeurs were busy doing homework.

Matt told them what had happened and that it was all the work of the journalist-spy. Now they had to find a way out of the trouble.

They immediately instructed the newspaper to announce that the children had to go back to school tomorrow; if anyone heard the news late, he still had to go even if he was tardy. The grownups could wait till the noon break, but then they had to return to their old jobs. The unemployed would continue to receive pay for another month, and then, if they wished, they could go to Bum Drum's country to build houses, schools, and hospitals. Both parliaments would be closed temporarily. The grownups' parliament would be opened first, and then the question of youths over fifteen years of age would be considered. When the subcommittee had worked out the regulations, the children's parliament would be reopened as well, except that now the children would state their desires and then the grownups' parliament would either approve or reject them. The children would not be able to give orders to grownups. Only children who were well behaved and doing well in school would be able to vote for delegates.

Matt and all the ministers signed the proclamation.

Matt wrote a second proclamation to the army, in which he recalled their victory in the last war.

'Our two most important fortresses have been blown up. And so let the heroic heart of every soldier be our fortress against anyone who would attack our land,' concluded the proclamation, which was signed by Matt and the Minister of War.

The Minister of Commerce asked the storekeepers to get everything back in order and reopen their stores. That would make the city look less dreary and dirty.

The Minister of Education promised the children that their parliament would reopen soon if they worked diligently in school.

The prefect of police guaranteed that, first thing tomorrow, the police would be back on duty.

'There's no more we can do right now,' said the Prime Minister. 'We have to wait until the telegraph and postal systems are working to find out what's been happening in the rest of the country and the world.'

'But what could have happened?' cried Matt in alarm, because everything seemed to be going too well. But perhaps the sad king had only been trying to frighten him.

'We don't know. We don't know anything.'

Everything was fine the next day. After the first class of the day, when the newspaper was read aloud, the teachers said farewell to their pupils and the grownups left for home. It took a little time for them to give the children back their schoolbooks and papers, but by twelve o'clock things were back to normal. And it must be said that everyone was happy—the grownups, the children, and the teachers.

The teachers did not admit this to the children, but the grownups had given them a lot of problems, too. There were quite a few troublemakers among those under thirty: they quarreled, laughed, and made noise during class. The older grownups were bored; they kept saying that their seats weren't comfortable, that they had headaches, that the room was stuffy and the ink was no good. The oldest ones slept, or paid no attention, and didn't mind when the teachers yelled at them, because many of them were deaf. The younger grownups were always playing tricks on the older ones, who kept complaining to the teachers. And the teachers really were used to having children in school and were glad when things went back to normal.

The office workers pretended to be angry because the children had left things a mess, but they also saw the good side of it—if some important paper was ever missing, they could always blame it on the children. Because there are different sorts of officials: those who keep their papers in order, and those who do not.

Things were worse in the factories, but the unemployed workers were glad to lend a hand, hoping that when the foremen saw how well they worked, they might keep them on.

There were a few minor disturbances, but the police were well rested and set to work first thing in the morning. The crooks were lying low, because they had stolen plenty and eaten until they were stuffed, and now they were afraid their crimes would be brought to light. And some of them, the ones who weren't real crooks, even returned what they had taken.

When the royal automobile drove around the city late that day, Matt saw little trace of yesterday's chaos.

Matt was waiting for news, which was bound to come sometime that evening.

Meanwhile, Klu Klu had resumed her classes with the group leaders. Matt came to one class, and he was surprised at how quickly the African children were learning. But Klu Klu explained that she had chosen the smartest and hardest-working ones to be group leaders and the others would not learn as quickly as they did. Poor Klu Klu had no idea what a sad end would soon come to her lessons.

As usual, the Prime Minister was the first to arrive. The Minister of War had been the first to arrive the day before, because he was used to traveling by foot.

The Prime Minister was carrying a portfolio of papers under his arm, and he looked sad and worried.

'How are things, Mr. Minister?'

'Things are bad,' he said, sighing. 'But we might have expected it. Maybe it's even better this way.'

'So what's going on? Be quick about it.'

'War!'

Matt shuddered.

When all the ministers arrived, the meeting began.

The old king had renounced his throne and given the crown to his son. The son had declared war on Matt and immediately set off with his army for Matt's capital.

'Has he crossed the border?'

'Two days ago. He's thirty miles inside the country.'

They began reading the telegrams and letters, which took a long time. Matt closed his weary eyes; he listened closely, but did not say a word.

Maybe it's even better this way, he thought.

The Minister of War took the floor. 'I don't know what route the enemy has chosen yet, but he's probably marching on the two fortresses that were blown up. If he advances quickly, he can reach the capital in five days. If not, we can expect him here in ten days.'

'What, aren't we going out to meet him?' cried Matt suddenly.

'Impossible. The people will have to defend themselves. We'll send out a couple of small detachments, but it's a waste of men and rifles. My opinion is—let them come. The main battle will take place on the field right outside the capital. Either we win or ...'

He didn't finish his sentence.

'Is there any chance the other two kings might help us?' interrupted the Minister of Foreign Affairs.

'There's no time for that,' cut in the Minister of War. 'Besides, that's not my department.'

The Minister of Foreign Affairs spoke for a long time about what had to be done so the other two kings would come out against Matt's enemy.

'We can certainly count on the sad king. But he doesn't like going to war and doesn't have many soldiers. He won't be any help. He didn't take part in the last war, either. He'll do what the king who's the friend of the Oriental kings does. Matt left him all the Oriental kings, and so he has no reason to fight us. But who knows? Maybe he wants some of the African kings back.'

Then the Prime Minister spoke: 'Gentlemen, you may not agree with me, but please don't get angry. Here is my advice: send a note to the enemy, saying we don't want war and asking him to state clearly what he wants. I think he only wants money. Why else would he have yielded us a seaport and sold us ten ships so cheaply? Because he wanted Bum Drum to send us gold. We have plenty of money. Why not give him half?'

Matt said nothing. He clenched his fists and remained silent.

'Mr. Prime Minister,' said the Minister of Finance. 'I don't think he'll agree. Why take half the gold when you can take it all? Why should he stop fighting when he's sure he can win?'

Now Matt clenched his fists until his fingernails dug into his flesh. He was waiting.

'I think we have to send him a note,' said the Minister of War. 'If he answers it, we can reply to his note, but that's not my department. But I do know that this will take a few days, or a couple of days, or even just one day. Every hour is precious. In the meantime, we could be repairing fifty or a hundred cannons and a couple of thousand rifles.'

'But what if he agrees to take half the gold and cease hostilities?' asked Matt in a soft and very pleasant voice that sounded strange and not like him at all.

There was a moment of silence. Everyone looked at the Minister of War, who turned pale, then red, then pale again before sputtering out: 'Then we agree, too.'

Then he added: 'We can't win this war all by ourselves. And it's too late for help.'

Matt closed his eyes and kept them closed until the end of the meeting. But Matt wasn't sleeping; Matt's lips twitched every time he heard the ministers say: 'We humbly request that the enemy king …' as they composed the note.

When he picked up his pen to sign, Matt asked: 'Can't we write something else instead of "We humbly request"?'

The note was rewritten and the expression 'We humbly request' was changed to 'We desire.'

'We desire to cease hostilities.'

'We desire to settle this quarrel peaceably.'

'We desire to pay the war costs with half our gold.'

It was two o'clock in the morning when Matt signed the note. Without taking off his clothes, he flung himself on his bed, but sleep wouldn't come. And he was still awake at dawn.

'Victory or death,' he kept saying. 'Victory or death.'

THE old king's son was advancing with his entire army toward the two fortresses that had been blown up. Just as the Minister of War had guessed, for that was his department. But the enemy was advancing very slowly, and there the Minister of War had been wrong.

The young king had to be extremely careful; he was moving slowly because he made his army dig trenches whenever they halted. This was the first time he had ever gone to war, and he was afraid of being surrounded. He remembered what his father had done in the last war—first he had let Matt enter the country and then he attacked him from the rear. The young king had to be very careful not to lose this war. Otherwise, everyone would say: 'The old king was better, we want him back.' And so he had to prove that he really was better than his father.

He preferred to move slowly, carefully. And why should he hurry? Matt couldn't wage war, because his soldiers were going to school and the children were ruining the cannons. They had their cunning journalist-spy in Matt's capital making sure there was as much disorder and confusion as possible. Things had worked out wonderfully well—the children had done a better job ruining the railroads and telegraph system than any saboteur could have. It would take some time for Matt to find out that a war had started, and even then, he wouldn't be able to field many troops.

And with those thoughts in mind, the old king's son saw no reason to hurry. His soldiers should save their strength for the battle outside Matt's capital. He knew there would have to be at least one big battle.

His troops marched on and on without meeting any resistance. The citizens of Matt's country saw that no one was coming to defend them, which made them angry at Matt. And so they didn't fight either. Some of them even greeted the enemy as saviors, saying: 'Send the children back to school, Matt's day is done ...'

Then suddenly someone appeared waving a white flag.

'Aha, so Matt's found out about the war.'

The young king read Matt's letter and began to laugh. 'Oho-ho, your Matt is so generous, he'll give me half his gold. What a present, ho-ho-ho, who wouldn't be tempted?'

'What answer shall I bring my king? If half our gold isn't enough, we can give you more. But I would like an answer, please.'

'All right, then, tell King Matt that you don't negotiate with children, you give them a good thrashing. And don't bring me any more letters, or we might take you prisoner. Off with you, and be quick about it!'

The young king threw Matt's letter to the ground and trampled it underfoot.

'Your Royal Highness, international law requires that a king's letter be answered in writing.'

'Fine, then, I'll write to him.'

The young king picked up Matt's letter, now crumpled and dirty, and he wrote but three words on it: 'I'm no fool!'

Meanwhile, news of the war and Matt's letter had spread through the capital and everyone was impatiently awaiting the answer.

The young king's reply made everyone furious.

'That conceited little squirt. We'll show him.'

The city began preparing to defend itself.

'We'll show him yet.'

Everyone was on Matt's side. People forgot their grudges and their grievances and saw only the good in him. Now all the newspapers, and not just one, were writing about Matt the Reformer, Matt the Hero.

The factories were working day and night. The troops drilled in the streets and on the squares. Everyone kept repeating Matt's words: 'Victory or death!'

Every day, there was fresh news and fresh rumors, some bad, some good.

The enemy is approaching the capital.

The sad king has promised to help Matt.

Bum Drum has sent all his soldiers.

Each time Klu Klu brought her thousand students into the city, the people would be seized by such fervor they would throw flowers at her and carry her on their shoulders.

Meanwhile, the enemy was indeed approaching.

And then one day the great battle began.

The people in the city heard the sound of guns. In the evening, they climbed up on their roofs and said they saw artillery fire—though they really hadn't.

On the second day of the battle, the guns sounded fainter. Everyone said that meant that Matt was winning and was driving the enemy away from the capital.

The third day was quiet.

The enemy must be far away now.

But then news arrived from the battlefield that the enemy had indeed withdrawn three miles but had not been smashed. The enemy had simply moved back to the trenches he had dug earlier just to be on the safe side.

Matt could have won the battle, but he did not have enough cannons and powder. The enemy had not been prepared to meet such stiff resistance, but Matt had to be very sparing with his powder so as not to be left without any at all. It was a shame, but what else could he do?

Meanwhile, the journalist-spy had gone to see the young king, who attacked him furiously. 'Why did you tell me that Matt had no cannons or powder! You useless fool! If I hadn't been careful, I could have lost the war.'

Only then did the spy tell him what had happened—Matt had uncovered him, fired a shot at him; he had barely escaped with his life and had spent a week hiding in a cellar. He said that someone must have betrayed them, for Matt had gone out into the city and seen the terrible chaos for himself. He told the young king about Felek and everything else.

'Matt's not in a good situation. He doesn't have much powder and cannon. But it's easier to defend than to attack. And besides, he's in his capital; everything he needs is right at hand. And we have to ship everything in from far away. We can't win it alone. The friend of the Oriental kings has to come to our aid.'

'Maybe he will, maybe he won't. He doesn't like me very much. And besides, if he helps us, we'll have to split with him.'

'That's how it goes.'

But maybe it would be smarter to take half the gold and make peace, thought the young king.

But you have to finish what you start. And so the spy was sent to the capital of the king who was the friend of the Oriental kings, to try to persuade him to attack Matt.

But the king didn't want to.

'Matt hasn't done me any harm.'

But the spy kept at it.

'You should join us against Matt because Matt will lose the war anyway. After all, the young king is already at Matt's capital. He's got that far by himself and he can go the rest of the way alone. But what does that mean? That means he gets everything for himself. The young king doesn't need help, he simply wants to share the spoils so the other kings won't be envious of him.'

'First, I want to confer with the sad king. Either we'll both join you or neither of us will.'

'When can I expect an answer?'

'In three days.'

'Fine.'

And so the friend of the Oriental kings wrote to the sad king asking what he wanted to do. He received an immediate reply saying that the sad king was seriously ill and could not answer the letter. Then came a letter from Matt asking for his help, saying that he had been unfairly attacked.

'You can see for yourself what the young king is like: he pretended to be my friend by giving me a seaport as a present and selling me ships. But now he's blown up two of my fortresses and he took advantage of the children's ruining the telephones and telegraph to attack me. I asked him what his grievances were and told him I would pay him half my gold if he hadn't really meant the seaport as a present. But he spouted a lot of nonsense and then wrote me saying: 'I'm no fool.' Is that right?'

Matt wrote a similar letter, but one more heartfelt, to the sad king.

The sad king was not ill at all. When leaving his country in secret to see Matt, he had ordered his doctor to say he was ill and to allow no one into his bedroom.

Every morning, the doctor would go into the empty bedroom and pretend to examine the king. Then he would bring in all sorts of medicine and food; the medicine he poured down the sink, the food he ate himself.

But when the sad king finally returned from his journey and was really back in his bed, he looked so exhausted that everyone believed he'd been ill. Because it's hard traveling in a country where there's a war on, especially if you have to conceal your identity.

As soon as the sad king went to his office and read both letters, he said: 'Prepare the royal train for me. I am going to see the king who is the friend of the Oriental kings.'

The sad king hoped he could persuade the other king to ally himself with Matt, but he didn't know what a cunning trick the spy had up his sleeve.

'OH, so Matt didn't do you any harm!' said the spy, hissing with fury as he left the king who was the friend of the Oriental kings. 'I have three days. I have to do something to make him angry at Matt. Then he'll sing a different tune.' In his pocket the spy had a document with Felek's signature and a forgery of Matt's. This document was supposed to be a manifesto addressed to all the children of the world.

CHILDREN!

I, Matt the First, appeal for your help in carrying out my reforms. I want a world where children won't have to obey the grownups, where they can do whatever they feel like. We're always hearing "You can't do this, that's not nice, that's not polite." It's not fair. Why can grownups do everything and we can't do anything? They're always mad at us and yelling at us and punishing us. They even hit us. I want children to have the same rights as grownups. I am a king and I know history well. In the old days, peasants, workers, women, and blacks had no rights. Now they all have rights. The children are the only ones with none!

I have already given the children in my country their rights. The children in Queen Campanelli's country have begun an uprising. Start your own revolution and demand your rights. If your kings don't agree, overthrow them and elect me your king. I want to be the king of all the children in the world—white, yellow, and black. I will give you freedom. So help me make my world revolution!

SIGNED,
KING MATT
MINISTER BARON VON RAUCH

The journalist went to a printer and paid him to print up thousands of copies of the manifesto and to hand them out all over the city. He smeared a few copies with mud, then dried them off, crumpled them up, and put them in his pocket.

The two kings were conferring, and had just about decided to join with Matt, when in walked the journalist to say: 'Look what Matt's up to. He's inciting the children to revolt, he wants to become king of the world. Here are three leaflets I found on the street. I'm sorry they're a bit dirty.'

The two kings read the leaflets and grew very concerned.

'There's no choice. We have to side against Matt. Now he's interfering with our children. They're not his subjects, and neither are the Oriental children. That's very bad.'

The sad king had tears in his eyes.

What has Matt gone and done now? he thought. Why did he write that manifesto?

But there was no way out of it.

Maybe it will even be better for Matt if I declare war on him, too, thought the sad king. As things stand now, they won't show him any pity when they win, and maybe I could be of some help to Matt afterwards.

At first, Matt refused to believe that the other two kings were advancing on him, too.

So, he thought, even the sad king has betrayed me. Well, that's how it goes. In the last war, I showed them Matt in victory, and this time I'll show them Matt in death.

The entire city went out with shovels and began to dig trenches and build ramparts. They dug three lines of trenches—one fifteen miles from the city, one ten, and one five.

'We will withdraw step by step.'

When the young king learned that the two other armies were on their way with help, he began the battle himself, because he wanted to be the first to set foot in the capital. He was counting on a quick victory and took the first line of trenches without much trouble. But the second line of defense was stronger, the ramparts higher, the trenches wider, and the barbed wire thicker.

It was then that the other two armies arrived. And now it was three armies that struck at Matt's men.

The battle lasted the entire day. The enemy suffered heavy losses, and Matt was still holding tight.

'Maybe we should make peace?' said the sad king hesitantly, but the others attacked him at once.

'No, we have to teach that brat a lesson.'

And once again, the battle raged from morning on.

'Aha, they're shooting less now,' said the enemy happily.

And indeed Matt's troops were firing fewer rounds that day, because they had received orders not to waste a single bullet.

'What now?' asked Matt.

'I think,' said the Prime Minister, 'that we have to try to sue for peace again. How can we fight a war without ammunition?'

As the leader of the African detachment, Klu Klu was also at the military council. Her detachment had not been in the battle yet, because it had no weapons. The African children only knew how to use bows and arrows. At first, they couldn't find the right kind of wood for making their bows and arrows. Then they finally did, but still had to make everything from scratch. Now everything was ready.

'Here's my advice,' said Klu Klu. 'Withdraw tonight to the third line of defense. Meanwhile, send someone over to the enemy camp to say that Bum Drum has sent Matt soldiers and wild animals. Tomorrow morning, we'll let the lions and tigers out of their cages and shoot arrows at the enemy. That'll give them a good scare, and then we can talk about making peace.'

'But wouldn't that be cheating?' asked Matt worriedly.

'No, that's called military strategy,' said the Minister of Justice.

Everyone agreed to Klu Klu's plan.

Felek disguised himself as an enemy soldier and crawled to the enemy camp on his belly. Once inside, he began talking with some soldiers and casually mentioned the lions and Bum Drum's soldiers.

But they didn't believe a word of it and laughed at him. 'You dope, you must have dreamed it.'

But still, those soldiers repeated the story.

Later, Felek was stopped by a soldier who said: 'You heard the news?'

'No, what?' asked Felek.

'Bum Drum's sent soldiers and lions to help Matt.'

'Nonsense,' said Felek.

'No, it's not. You can hear the wild animals roaring.'

'Let them roar, what do I care,' said Felek.

'You'll care when a lion's tearing you to pieces.'

'I'm not scared of any lion.'

'What a bigmouth! You against a lion. Look at you—you don't even look like a real soldier.'

Felek walked to another part of the camp. There the soldiers were saying that Bum Drum had sent Matt an entire ship full of poisonous snakes. Now Felek no longer said anything but just listened or laughed in disbelief. But the soldiers shouted at him, told him not to laugh, and said that he'd be better off praying before his stupid laughter got him into trouble.

The soldiers had fallen for it!

After a few days in battle, the soldiers had grown tired and edgy. They were far from home and had been told that it would be an easy battle, that Matt had no gunpowder and wouldn't put up any defense, but they had seen that it wasn't going to be so easy. And now they were so tired, lonely, and angry that they'd believe any nonsense.

Felek crawled back and told Matt how well Klu Klu's idea was working. Matt could feel new courage rising in him. 'I've been lucky before, maybe I'll be lucky this time, too.'

That night, Matt's soldiers left their trenches without making a sound and moved closer to the city. The soldiers brought up the cages with the lions and tigers. Five hundred of the African children stayed near the cages. The other five hundred spread out among the other units in groups of ten so the enemy would see them everywhere.

This was the plan: The next morning, the enemy would see that their fire wasn't being returned and rush to attack. They would find the trenches empty. They'd start rejoicing and cheering. The capital was close by and soon they'd be looting, eating, drinking, and carousing. Then suddenly the Africans would start beating their drums and howling; they'd let the wild animals loose and shoot arrows at their heels to drive them toward the enemy. Panic, disorder, confusion. Then Matt would lead his cavalry into the attack, followed by the infantry.

It would be a terrible battle, but that would only help teach them a lesson once and for all.

'It has to work. A person who's taken by surprise when he's feeling good gets the daylights scared out of him.'

Two other things: Matt's soldiers left plenty of vodka, beer, and wine in the trenches. And hay, paper, and wood were piled by the cages to be set on fire and enrage the animals when the doors were opened.

This would also keep the lions from attacking Matt's own men.

Some people even thought a few snakes should be let out.

'Better forget the snakes,' said Klu Klu. 'They're very moody and finicky. But you can count on the lions.'

BUT the enemy had a plan, too.

'Listen,' said the young king. 'We have to be in Matt's capital tomorrow. Otherwise, we might be in trouble. We're far from home. We have to ship all our supplies in by train, but Matt's at home. It's easier to fight outside a city that's yours, where everything's right at hand. But civilians panic easily. And our job is to help make them even more panicky. Tomorrow morning, our airplanes will start bombing the city, and the civilians will force Matt to surrender. We must make it impossible for our troops to withdraw. We'll position machine guns in the rear, and if they try to retreat, we'll open fire on them.'

'What, open fire on our own troops?'

'We have to be in Matt's capital tomorrow, or I'm in trouble,' repeated the young king. 'And any soldier who tries to flee the battlefield is our enemy and not one of us.'

The soldiers were informed that the general attack and final battle would come tomorrow.

'There are three of us, and Matt's all alone,' read the order of the day. 'Matt is low on cannons and powder. There's a revolution in his capital. His soldiers don't want to fight any more. They're hungry and worn out. Tomorrow we occupy Matt's capital and take him prisoner.'

The planes were fueled up and loaded with bombs for their takeoff at dawn.

Machine guns were positioned behind the troops.

'What for?' asked the soldiers.

'Machine guns are for defense, not for attack,' said the officers.

Still, the soldiers didn't like the idea.

No one slept that night, either in Matt's camp or his enemies'.

Some soldiers cleaned their rifles, others wrote letters home, saying farewell to their loved ones.

There was total silence, except for the crackle of the campfires. But the soldiers could hear their hearts pounding all the louder in that silence.

Dawn.

The sky was still gray when the enemy cannons began firing at Matt's empty trenches. Each time a big gun went off, Matt's soldiers laughed.

'Waste your ammo and waste it good,' said the soldiers, laughing.

Matt stood on a rise, staring at the battlefield through binoculars.

'Here they come!'

Some of the enemy soldiers were running, some crawling cautiously. They kept pouring out of their trenches, first fearful, then braver. Some of them were encouraged by the silence in Matt's trenches, but others found it disturbing.

Suddenly, twenty airplanes rose into the sky, heading straight for Matt's capital. Unfortunately, Matt had only five planes. The children liked the airplanes best of all, which meant that they had ruined nearly all of them.

A furious air battle began. The enemy lost six planes, and all Matt's planes either were shot down or had to make forced landings.

The battle had begun as predicted.

The enemy occupied the first lines of defense with cries of triumph. 'Aha, they ran away. They were scared. They have no cannons. They ran away in such a hurry they didn't even have time to take their vodka with them.'

Some of the soldiers began uncorking the flasks. 'Let's give it a try.'

They drank the vodka, started enjoying themselves, and were ready to call it a day.

'What's the big rush? This is a good place.'

But the young king repeated stubbornly: 'We must be in Matt's capital today.'

The cannons and machine guns were brought up.

'Attack!'

The soldiers were a little tipsy, and reluctant to attack. But orders were orders. Might as well get it over with. So they went out into the open and charged Matt's last line of defense.

Then suddenly the cannons roared, the machine guns began chattering. Bullets and—strangest of all—arrows began raining down on them.

Suddenly, a savage cry arose from Matt's camp, followed by the sound of fifes and drums.

And then suddenly they saw African soldiers in the trenches. They looked small, but maybe that was because they were still pretty far away. There weren't many of them, but the enemy soldiers were seeing double and their ears were ringing.

Then lions and tigers, infuriated by the shooting and the fires, began bounding straight at the attacking enemy. Strange as it may seem, it's more frightening to see one man torn apart by a lion than a hundred killed by bullets. As if a lion's claws were worse than a steel bullet.

Now there was utter confusion. Some soldiers flung their rifles to the ground and ran like madmen right into the barbed wire. Others turned and ran and were fired on by their own machine guns. And thinking they were caught in cross fire, they either fell to the ground or raised their arms to surrender.

The enemy cavalry, which was to support the attack, now came full force at the riflemen, trampling and wounding them.

Smoke, dust, chaos. No one could see anything any more, no one had any idea what was happening. It went on like that for an hour, then another hour.

Later, when historians described this battle, they each wrote a different version of the events, but they all agreed that there'd never been anything like it before.

'Oh,' said the Minister of War, almost in tears, 'if only we had enough ammunition for another two hours!'

But they didn't, and that was that.

'Cavalry, charge!' cried Matt, leaping onto his beautiful white horse.

They had one last hope—to take advantage of the panic, charge the enemy and seize his supplies, then drive him away from the city before he learned that Bum Drum had not come to Matt's aid and that a few African children and two dozen wild animals from the zoo had brought Matt the victory.

No sooner had Matt mounted his horse than he glanced back at the city—and was stunned.

No, it couldn't be. It was some terrible mistake. He must be seeing things.

But, unfortunately, he wasn't.

White flags were fluttering from all the city's towers. The capital was surrendering.

Messengers were already speeding to the city with orders to tear down those white rags and shoot all cowards and traitors. But, unfortunately, it was too late.

The enemy had already spotted those symbols of disgrace and surrender. At first, the enemy soldiers were dumbfounded, but that didn't last long.

In battle, a single glass of vodka can make a soldier drunk, but it only takes one bullet whistling by his head to sober him up.

In battle, fear can change to hope in an instant, despair to fury.

The enemy soldiers rubbed their eyes. Were they dreaming or awake? Matt's cannons were silent, the ground was littered with bullet-riddled lions and tigers. And the white flags meant that the city was surrendering.

The young king understood what had happened and cried: 'Charge!'

First the officers, then the soldiers caught up the cry.

Matt saw what was happening, but there was nothing he could do now.

The enemy was forming ranks and picking up the rifles that had been flung aside. The white flags were disappearing, but it was too late now.

The enemy advanced and reached the barbed wire, which they began cutting with clippers.

'Your Royal Highness,' said an old general, his voice trembling.

Matt knew what he was about to say. Matt jumped down from his horse and, pale as a ghost, shouted: 'Follow me to die with honor!'

There weren't many people willing to follow Matt, just Felek, Antek, Klu Klu, and a few dozen soldiers.

'Where are we going?' they asked.

'The lion house. It's empty now, and solid. We'll defend ourselves there like lions, like kings.'

'There won't be room for everyone there.'

'All the better,' whispered Matt.

There were five cars nearby. They got in, grabbing whatever weapons and ammunition they could find.

After they had pulled away, Matt glanced back, and saw a white flag flying over his camp.

Matt felt that fate was mocking him: he had ordered those banners of shame and surrender torn down in his capital. But now it wasn't the old people, the women and children, terrified by a few dozen bombs, but his army which had thrown itself on the enemy's mercy.

'It's a good thing I'm not there with them now,' said Matt. 'Don't cry, Klu Klu, we'll die a beautiful death. And then people will stop saying that kings only declare wars but don't die fighting like soldiers.'

To die a hero's death was Matt's only desire. Then suddenly he wondered: What kind of funeral will my enemies give me?

BUT even Matt's last wish was not to come true. Instead of one minute of suffering, cruel fate had hours of humiliation and pain and years of painful punishment in store for him.

The army had surrendered. In all Matt's kingdom there was only one place still free, the building where the lions had been kept.

The enemy tried to storm the building, but the attack failed. A negotiator was sent in, carrying the customary white flag for protection. But as soon as he approached the building, he received two mortal wounds—Matt fired a bullet that shattered his skull, and Klu Klu's arrow pierced his heart.

'He killed the negotiator!'

'He's trampled on international law!'

'It's a crime!'

'It's unheard of.'

'The capital must be severely punished for the king's crime.'

But the capital had already renounced Matt, saying: 'Matt is no longer our king.'

While the enemy planes were bombing the capital, the wealthy and prominent citizens held a meeting.

'We've had enough of that wild kid's tyranny. If he wins this time, too, it'll be even worse than if he lost. There's no telling what crazy new idea he'll come up with next. Him and that Felek of his.'

Some people stood up for Matt.

'All the same, he's done a lot of good, too. His mistakes came from a lack of experience. But he has an open mind and he'll put his lessons to good use.'

Matt's supporters might have won the day, but just then a bomb fell so close by that it shattered all the windows in the room where they were meeting.

'Raise the white flags,' cried someone in fear.

No one had the courage to speak out against this low treachery. And we know what happened next.

The shameful flags of surrender were raised and a document was drawn up saying that the city renounced Matt and would not be responsible for his folly.

‘Let’s put an end to this comedy,’ cried the young king. ‘We have conquered all Matt’s country. Are we going to be stopped by that henhouse?’ The young king turned to a general of the artillery and said: ‘Set a cannon here and fire twice on either side of that building. If that stubborn Matt doesn’t come crawling out, destroy that nasty little wolf cub’s den with three rounds.’

‘Yes, sir,’ said the general of the artillery.

But just then the sad king’s sonorous voice rang out: ‘One moment, Your Royal Highness. Please don’t forget that there are three armies here, and three kings.’

The young king bit his lip and said: ‘It’s true there are three of us. But we have different rights. I was the first to declare war and I took the brunt of the battle.’

‘And Your Royal Highness’s men were also the first to flee the battlefield.’

‘But I stopped them.’

‘Because Your Royal Highness knew that we’d come to your aid if you were in any danger.’

The young king did not answer. It was all true. The battle had cost him dearly: half his troops were killed or wounded and unfit for battle. And so now he had to be careful lest his two allies turn into enemies.

‘So, what do you suggest?’ he asked reluctantly.

‘There’s no need for us to hurry. Matt can’t do us any harm from inside that building. We can surround it with soldiers. And maybe hunger will force Matt to surrender. But, meanwhile, let's calmly discuss what's to be done with him after we take him prisoner.'

'I think he should be taken out and shot.'

'And I think,' the sad king said grandly, 'that history would never forgive us if we harmed one hair on that poor, brave child's head.'

'History will be fair,' cried the young king furiously. 'If someone is to blame for so many deaths and so much bloodshed, then he isn't a child—he's a criminal.'

The third king, the friend of the Oriental kings, did not say a word. Even as the other two kings quarreled, they were aware that his would be the deciding vote. He was a sly king.

Why provoke the African kings who are Matt's friends, he thought to himself. 'There's no need to kill Matt. We can put him on a desert island instead. That way, everyone will be happy.'

And so they drew up the following agreement.

Point one. Matt must be taken prisoner alive.

Point two. Matt will be exiled to a desert island.

There was a quarrel over point three, because the sad king wanted Matt to have the right to take ten people of his own choosing with him to keep him company, but the young king would not agree.

‘Only three officers and thirty soldiers can go with Matt, one officer and ten soldiers from each of the victorious kings.’

They argued on for two days, then finally they each yielded a little.

‘All right, then,’ said the young king, ‘ten friends may join him, but only after a year. And Matt is to be told that he’s been sentenced to death, and only at the last minute will we grant him a reprieve. It is absolutely essential that Matt’s people see him weep and plead, that this foolish nation which allowed itself to be led around by the nose realize once and for all that Matt is no hero but a fresh, cowardly brat. Otherwise, in a couple of years, the nation might rebel and demand that Matt be returned. Matt will be older then and even more dangerous than he is now.’

‘Don’t waste time arguing,’ said the king who was the friend of the Oriental kings. ‘Matt could die of hunger in the meantime and you would have been quarreling over nothing.’

The sad king gave in. Two points were added to the agreement.

Point three. Matt will be court-martialed and sentenced to death. Only at the last moment will the three kings grant him a reprieve.

Point four. Matt will spend the first year of captivity alone and under guard. After one year, he will be allowed to choose ten visitors, assuming that they're willing.

They moved on to other points. How many cities and how much money each king would take. They decided that the capital would remain a free city. And so on and so forth.

Then the kings were informed that someone was demanding to be allowed into the meeting on a very important matter.

The man was a chemist who had invented a sleeping gas. If this gas was released anywhere near Matt, who was already weak from hunger, he would fall asleep at once and could be tied up and put in chains.

'My gas can be tried out on animals,' said the chemist.

A cylinder containing the gas was brought at once and placed a few hundred yards from the royal stables. A valve was opened, and out streamed a liquid that evaporated immediately, covering the stables with a smoky cloud. Five minutes later, they went into the stables and found all the horses asleep. Unaware of the experiment, a stable boy was lying on a bed of straw, so sound asleep that, though they shook him and shot their guns off by his ear, he did not blink an eye. The stable boy and the horses only woke up an hour later.

The experiment had been a smashing success. And so it was decided to put an end to the siege that very day.

Matt was lying on a straw mat on the floor near the wall. He tapped lightly on the wall. Maybe somebody would answer? He tapped once, then once again, but no one answered.

Where was Klu Klu, what had happened to Felek? What was going on in the capital?

A key rattled in the iron door and in came two enemy soldiers. One stood by the door, the other placed a cup of milk and a roll by Matt. Matt was about to knock the cup over and spill the milk, but then he decided that made no sense. It was tough, but he had lost the war.

He sat up, and barely able to move because of his chains, he reached out for the cup. The soldiers stood and watched.

Matt ate the roll and said: 'Your kings are awfully stingy. One roll, that's a little on the cheap side. I fed your kings better when they were my guests. And when the old king was my prisoner, I treated him better than this. Now there are three kings to feed me, and all I get is one little cup of milk and one roll.'

And Matt laughed merrily.

The soldiers did not say a word, because they had been strictly forbidden to engage in conversation with the prisoner. But they reported everything immediately to the warden, who telephoned for further instructions.

An hour later, Matt was brought three more rolls and three more cups of milk.

'Oh, that's too much. I don't want to insult my benefactors. There are three of them, so I'll take one roll from each—please take the extra one back.'

After eating, Matt fell asleep. He slept for a very long time and would have slept even longer, but he was awakened a little before midnight.

'Ex-King Matt the Reformer will be tried by a court-martial at twelve o'clock,' said the military prosecutor, reading from a paper with the seals of the three kings on it. 'Please rise.'

'Please tell the court to have my chains removed. They're heavy and hurt my legs.'

The chains were not hurting Matt and were even too loose. But Matt didn't want to look ridiculous in court, encumbered with chains meant for grownup prisoners.

Matt won his point: the heavy irons were replaced by light, elegant gold chains.

His head held high, his step light, Matt entered the prison dining hall, where, not that long ago, he had dictated terms to his ministers after he'd had them thrown in prison.

He looked all around curiously.

The highest-ranking generals in the three kings' armies sat at a long table. The kings themselves were seated on the left side of the room, civilians wearing dress coats and white gloves on the right. Who could they be? They kept turning their heads away so Matt couldn't see them.

The indictment read as follows:

1. King Matt issued a manifesto to all children calling on them to revolt and not obey grownups.
2. King Matt wanted to cause world revolution so that he could become king of the world.
3. Matt shot a negotiator who was approaching him with a white flag. Since by then Matt was no longer even a king, he will be tried as an ordinary criminal. The penalty for this crime is death by hanging or a firing squad.

What did Matt have to say to this?

'It's not true that I issued that manifesto. And it's not true that I was no longer a king when I shot the negotiator. And no one can know whether or not I wanted to become king of the entire world, only I know that.'

'All right, then. Gentlemen, please read your statement,' said the chairman of the court to the men wearing dress coats and white gloves.

They rose reluctantly, and one of them, white as the paper in his trembling hands, read: 'We held a meeting in the capital during the battle, while bombs were demolishing our city. One bomb even blew out all the windows in the very room where we were conferring. We, the residents of the capital, wishing to save our wives and children, decided that we no longer wanted Matt as our king. And so we deprived him of his throne and crown. That was very unpleasant, but we could not take any more. We hung out the white flags as a sign that we did not want war and that it was not our king who was at war, but only Matt, who would have to answer for everything himself. We are not to blame.'

'Sign here, please,' said the chairman of the court, handing Matt a pen.

Matt took the pen, thought for a moment, and then wrote at the bottom of the document: 'I do not agree with this statement by a bunch of traitors and cowards who have sold out their country. I am and will always remain King Matt the First.'

Then, in a resounding voice, Matt read aloud what he had just written.

'Judges, generals, gentlemen,' Matt addressed his enemies. 'I demand to be called King Matt, because that is who I am and who I will be all my life and even after my death. If this is not to be a trial but a crime committed against a vanquished king, then you are disgracing yourselves both as men and as soldiers. You can say what you like, but I will not answer.'

The generals left the room to confer. Matt whistled a soldier's song to himself until they returned.

'Do you admit that you issued a manifesto to the children of the world?' asked the chairman of the court.

No answer.

'Does Your Royal Highness admit that he issued a manifesto to the children of the world?' asked the general.

'I do not. I never issued that manifesto.'

'Summon the witness,' ordered the judge.

The journalist-spy entered the chamber. Matt didn't even wince.

'The witness will testify,' said the judge.

'I can testify that Matt wanted to become king of all the children in the world,' said the journalist.

'Is that true?' asked the judge.

'It is,' answered Matt. 'I did want to. And I probably would have succeeded. But the signature on the manifesto was forged. That spy forged my signature. But the truth is, I did want to be king of all the children.'

The judges examined Matt's signature. They shook their heads—they could see the signature wasn't Matt's but pretended they weren't sure.

But now that no longer mattered. For, after all, Matt had admitted everything himself.

The prosecutor spoke for a long time.

'Matt must be sentenced to death, for otherwise there will be no peace in the world.'

'Do you want somebody to say something in your defense, Matt?'

No answer.

'Does Your Royal Highness wish to have someone speak in your defense?' repeated the chairman.

'There's no need for that,' answered Matt. 'It's late now, why waste time? Better we all get some sleep.'

Matt spoke in a cheerful voice, giving no sign of what he felt in his heart. He had decided to be proud to the end.

The judges left the room as if they were going to deliberate, but returned almost at once with the verdict. 'Death by firing squad.'

'Please sign this,' said the chairman.

No answer.

'I request Your Royal Highness's signature certifying that the trial was held in accordance with the law.'

Matt signed.

Then one of the men wearing dress coats and gloves suddenly threw himself to the floor, flung his arms around Matt's legs, and cried out in tears: 'Oh, my beloved king, forgive me for betraying you. Only now do I see what we've done. If it hadn't been for our cowardice, you'd have conquered them and it would be you sitting in judgment on them.'

The soldiers had to drag the man away from Matt. What was the good of it; his regrets had come too late.

'I wish you a good night, judges, gentlemen,' said Matt, and he left the room calmly and with dignity, like a true king.

Twenty soldiers with their sabers bared accompanied him down the corridor and across the courtyard to his cell.

Matt lay down on his straw mattress and pretended to sleep.

A priest came to the cell, but he felt too sorry for Matt to wake him up. He recited the prayer for people condemned to death, and then left.

Matt still pretended to be asleep. And what he thought and felt that night is Matt's secret.

Matt was led through the city.

He walked down the middle of the street, still bound in golden chains. The streets were lined with soldiers, and behind them the people of the capital.

It was a beautiful day. The sun was shining. Everyone had come out to see their king one last time. Many people had tears in their eyes. But Matt did not see those tears, though that would have made it easier for him to go to his death.

Those who loved Matt said not a word, because they were afraid to express their love and respect for him in the presence of the enemy. Besides, what could they shout? They were used to shouting 'Long live the king!' But how could they shout that now, when the king was going to his death?

But some bums shouted, and shouted loudly. The young king had ordered that they be given vodka and wine from Matt's royal cellar.

'Oooo,' they shouted. 'There goes the king, the little king. He's so little, little King Matt, you're crying. Come here and we'll wipe your nose.'

Matt lifted his head so that everyone could see that his eyes were dry, even though he was frowning. He was looking at the sky, the sun.

He paid no attention to what was going on around him. He had other things on his mind.

What had happened to Klu Klu? Where was Felek? Why had the sad king betrayed him? What would happen to his country? Would he see his father and mother again when the bullets took his life?

The city behind him now, he was tied to a post on the square near a freshly dug grave. But he was still calm and composed when the firing squad loaded their rifles and aimed them at him.

And he was just as calm when, at the last moment, he heard his reprieve: 'Death sentence commuted to exile on a desert island.'

A car pulled up and took Matt back to prison. In one week's time, he would be banished to the desert island.

I'll tell you what happened to Matt on that desert island just as soon as I find out.

KING MATT THE FIRST

The Backstory

Discover the life story of the brave author and find out why Esmé Raji Codell loves this book

VINTAGE CLASSICS

Who's Who in *King Matt the First*

Matt: the hero of our story. Matt is just a little boy when his father dies leaving him alone in the world. Learning to handle his ministers, his subjects and the foreign kings will test Matt's fairness, strength and resolve to their limits.

The Doctor: one of the few consistent people in Matt's life. The Doctor is there when Matt's father dies, he helps him in getting permission to go for walks outside the palace grounds and he advises him on the health of children, which leads to Matt's decision to build summer camps for all the young people in his kingdom.

Felek: Matt's fun but rather unreliable friend. Felek is the boy who helps Matt escape from the palace and go to war. He later becomes the Prime Minister of Children.

Irenka: the little girl that Matt meets in the park. The one thing Irenka would like more than anything is a doll so big it reaches the ceiling. Matt becomes determined to grant her wish.

The Prime Minister: the minister who hatches a plan to create a porcelain doll of Matt so that no one will know he has run off to war. Matt has a tempestuous relationship with him, as he does with all his many ministers and advisers.

Helenka and Stash: Matt's friends.

The sad king: the youngest of Matt's neighbouring kings. He is the only one to have given over his rule to a democratically elected parliament. He helps to teach Matt that the job of a king is to make his subjects happy, but that it can be a very hard thing to do.

The journalist: a man who makes a friendly approach to Matt, offering to report royal reforms and news in his newspaper. The journalist turns out to be a spy, out to deceive Matt, and his actions bring about the downfall of the kingdom.

Bum Drum: one of the African kings, a cannibal and a brave and noble person. He promises Matt large quantities of gold and wild animals for his zoo. He ends up being one of Matt's most important allies.

Klu Klu: Bum Drum's daughter. She is a brilliantly fast, bright and fearless girl who comes to be a great friend of Matt's. She is very scornful of the way that European girls are treated, as inferior to the boys.

A message from the children's author, Esmé Raji Codell

What makes this children's book one of the greatest of all time?

First comes the question of what makes a great children's book, period. It must have humor, adventure, excitement, friendship (romance is optional, and only in small doses). The main character must be one that comes to life on every page, and one that the reader mourns the loss of upon closing the cover. It must have mischief and naughtiness, but placate adults with a lesson or two so that the child may read in peace. Any profanity ought to be hidden in the middle, further along than most grownups are likely to read. If it has the effrontery to lack pictures, it must compensate with lots of lively conversation. The bad must be punished and the good rewarded; enemies are those who misunderstand children. Wishes should be granted, unless they are too greedy. There should be animals. And sweets. And days off from school. And some absence of parents.

These are elements intrinsic to the popular works of J. K. Rowling *(Harry Potter and the Sorcerer's Stone)*, Roald Dahl *(Charlie and the Chocolate Factory)*, and Louis Sachar

(Holes). The other common factor is the overriding idea of the child as a hero, one who can succeed against great odds. In this canon is *King Matt the First*. Conceived for the reading and listening pleasure of orphans by a pediatrician who also happened to be one heck of a writer, *King Matt the First* endured a turbulent era to enjoy a celebrated status among children in Poland comparable to J. M. Barrie's *Peter Pan*.

I came across this book in the mid-1980s when I was working in the children's department of a bookstore. As a bookseller, when I looked at a shelf, I didn't see just books, I saw presents. I saw a row of gifts that authors were trying to give: their world view, their stories, wishes, warnings—the very best of themselves, wrapped up in words.

But.

It's one thing for a writer to give a gift to a child; it's another for that gift to be received. Some gifts are like scratchy sweaters or lipstick kisses and are received as such. But every now and then there comes a bike, a beautiful shining bike of a book, the book that makes children shout 'Thank you!' without prompting, and at the same time allows them to ride away from you as fast as they can go.

The plain, brown binding of my first copy of *King Matt* gave no indication, really, of this bike of a book; in fact, it seemed to be trying to disguise itself as a book for grownups. But the words made clear its true audience, words so deftly written by Janusz Korczak, pseudonym of the renowned and sometimes controversial Polish pediatrician Henryk Goldszmit. He introduced progressive orphanages into Poland and directed two of them before being interned at the Warsaw ghetto, where he ran one. His love and concern for all children was evident in the more than twenty books he authored, his treatise *How to Love a Child* among the most popular. Dubbed 'the Karl Marx of Children,' he worked indefatigably to defend children's rights in juvenile courts, and as 'the Old Doctor,' a popular radio personality of the times, he was able to dispense his message of compassion and respect for children to a wider audience. Like the hero of *King Matt the First*, he founded the first national children's newspaper and ran his orphanages with the help of a children's parliament. Indeed, *King Matt the First* appears to be the most graceful and lasting manifestation of Korczak's visionary assessment of the rich moral life and potential of children.

King Matt the First recounts the adventures of a boy who, after the death of his father, is left with the overwhelming task of ruling a country. Determined not to be a mere figurehead, he struggles to navigate through the guile and ambiguity of his advisers in order to implement his reforms. And what reforms they are! Summer camps in the forests, on mountains, and at seashores so that poor children might enjoy nature! Schools outfitted with seesaws and carousels! The building of a zoo with a menagerie that is the envy of the world! Korczak could have succeeded through his plot fixtures alone: unforgettable is the gift of the biggest doll in the world given to the fire chief's daughter, and fabled are the days during King Matt's reign when the children got to run the kingdom while the adults toiled in school. Any child delights in such extravagances, and in this way Korczak spoils all children like a generous old uncle who comes bearing armloads of lollipops. But at the heart of this story is a child who is wholly alone, dealing, in turns, with conflicts that academics will recognize as Erikson's stages of psychosocial development: the need for autonomy and rebellion against overprotection; the playacting of an adult role in order to determine where initiative is acceptable and what actions are not allowed; the pleasure of industriousness and the desire to persevere; and ultimately, the resolution of an identity, built on outcomes of previous crises and relationships with others. The boy who begins the story merely wearing a crown ends it as a true king, a visionary

leader who has built his place in history not only through accolades but by failure and painful loss, a boy whose fate is determined not only by his choices, but by the choices of those who surround him. The ending of *King Matt the First* is jolting, like waking from a dream at the scariest part only to find that by some miracle you are still intact.

The fate of King Matt is particularly poignant when juxtaposed with the fate of the author and the children who inspired him, who were not afforded a miracle. On August 6, 1942, Korczak and the two hundred children in his orphanage followed behind the green flag, their symbol of children's freedom, to the train station, where the group was taken to the gas chambers at Treblinka. Korczak had several opportunities to escape, but he refused: 'You do not leave a sick child in the night, and you do not leave children at a time like this.' While he could not offer rescue, he could offer comfort, and so, like a true father, he stayed with them to the very last of all of their breaths.

I imagine that Korczak had a sense of what was in store for them. How do you prepare children for such a world that would kill them? By imagining a better one. Korczak knew that the power of story is a path to utopia. If his vision of a better world would not be realized for his children, then maybe it could for children of another generation. I think the legacy of *King Matt* is not only in the surviving of the manuscript, but in the sharing of it, as Korczak did by reading it aloud to his charges. To read this book aloud to a child is to celebrate a message of great hope. If there is a miracle, it is that within all the rubble and ruin of war, a story survived, with words that click along like the spokes of a fleeing bicycle. Each word in the story, though disguised, is the same word over and over: Live! Live! Live for the children who didn't get to live. Live as if the world were your kingdom.

Generations later, I was working as a schoolteacher, many countries and an ocean away from where this book was written. I read this book aloud to children who had the luxury of waking up from bad dreams. I soon discovered that *King Matt the First* asks a lot of its reader in a modern context. When I first read this book to children who were predominantly African-American, I waited for them to explode with righteous indignation. I withered at the prospect of explaining to thirty-some expectant faces that the author probably included things such as African cannibals eating salted flesh because he was sitting in a room full of two hundred kids and wanted to say something that made them go 'Eeeeeewwww.'

But I didn't have to explain it, because the children didn't identify with it, and created their own chorus of 'Eeeeeewwww' just as kids might have half a century ago. It's clear that King Matt is, in fact, partial to the Africans, and that they are more trustworthy and adept than their white counterparts in his kingdom. Klu Klu, the heroine of the story, has her own moments where she doesn't think much of the white people, referring to them on occasion as 'barbaric,' mirroring the white people's flip appraisal of her as 'savage.' Generally, I think characters throughout the book are prejudiced and suspicious of one another, which sounds pretty realistic to me and, evidently, to my young listeners as well. These prejudices stood in the way of progress in the kingdom, which the children recognized immediately as the unfortunate case in real life. I wonder, though, if I had been reading to a group of predominantly Caucasian American children today whose economic or geographical demographic might still segregate them from people of color, I might have been inclined to abridge the book simply to avoid introducing unnecessary negative stereotypes to an audience that doesn't have enough multicultural exposure to counter them. Or maybe I would have taken a deep breath and read it uncensored, putting it into context. I don't know. Even though I consider *King Matt* a masterpiece of world literature, I don't see the book as untouchable. The general rule I have found when it comes to all children's books is that adults should read a book to themselves before sharing it with children. This makes it easier to determine what is best to discuss based on individual values.

Another key to sharing this book is to expect the best from young listeners. I had underestimated the children in their ability to see the universal qualities of the book; I came away with a renewed admiration for Korczak's bravery not only as a human being but as a writer and as an advocate of children. I thought the book was flawed because it says incorrect things. A book for children in which people never say incorrect things is equally flawed in its dishonesty. In this, *King Matt* is controversial.

The last great gift of *King Matt* is candor. Outspoken, impetuous, and inventive, King Matt and his friends Felek and Klu Klu are Everykid, the children who ask 'Why?' and, as often, 'Why not?' But unlike Everykid, King Matt is in a position to demand the answers. This book is a portrait of a child's attempts to give his best gifts to the world. It teaches grownups not only what children's literature can be, but what children can be.

Long may the green flag wave!

How well do you know *King Matt the First*? Take this quiz to find out . . .

(Turn to the back for answers – no cheating!)

1) How does Matt attempt to prevent Felek's father from punishing him for entering the royal gardens?

2) Who introduces Matt to the idea of a parliament and democracy?

3) What do Matt and Helenka quarrel about whilst on holiday?

4) Why does Matt decide to travel to Africa the first time?

5) Who attempts to poison Matt whilst he is on his travels?

6) Why does Matt find Bum Drum lying on a pyre on his second visit to Africa?

7) How does Klu Klu get to Matt's kingdom?

8) Why do European girls have trouble running and climbing, according to Klu Klu?

9) What misguided law does the children's parliament pass that leaves Matt's country virtually in ruins?

10) What disaster takes place when the children accidentally open one of the cages at the zoo?

Who was Janusz Korczak?

Janusz Korczak's real name was Henryk Goldszmit and he was born in either 1878 or 1879. He was a Jew who grew up and lived for most of his life in Warsaw, the capital of Poland. He had an interesting life, doing lots of different things, but mostly he was a doctor, a writer and a director of orphanages in Warsaw.

Henryk's orphanages were not like most orphanages. The first one he set up was especially for Jewish children and it had its own court, parliament and newspaper. Three years later the First World War began and Henryk had to go to war to work as a doctor. Afterwards, he helped to set up a second orphanage in Warsaw for Christian children. Life was not easy in Poland at that time – there was not enough food to eat and money was scarce. But Henryk fought to protect and care for his orphans and spent a lot of time petitioning rich people to help him. Every summer the children from both orphanages would go to a summer camp to get away from life in the city for a while.

In 1939 the Second World War broke out. German troops invaded Poland and although two days later Britain declared war, it was too late for Poland – the Nazis had control of

Warsaw. Henryk was defiant in the face of the Nazis. He refused to wear the 'Jewish star' on his clothes and instead had a large flag made. On the rare occasions that he and his orphans were allowed to leave the orphanage, Henryk led a procession of the children and they flew the orphans' flag. Even though none of them wore the obligatory star on their clothes, no Nazis bothered them. Many people offered Henryk their help to escape Poland but he always refused – he would not leave his children.

In 1942 German soldiers came to collect the children of Henryk's Jewish orphanage to transport them to Treblinka extermination camp. Once again, Henryk was offered the chance to escape but he refused. The children were dressed in their best clothes and each carried a favourite book or toy. So that they wouldn't be afraid, Henryk had told them they were going to the countryside.

An eyewitness wrote in her diary about the day the children were taken away:

> Dr. Janusz Korczak's children's home is empty now. A few days ago we all stood at the window and watched the Germans surround the houses. Rows of children, holding each other by their little hands, began

> to walk out of the doorway. There were tiny tots of two or three years among them, while the oldest ones were perhaps thirteen. Each child carried a little bundle in his hand.

(extract from *The Diary of Mary Berg: Growing Up in the Warsaw Ghetto*)

Henryk and his children were never heard from again. Today, in Warsaw, there is a sculpture of Henryk leading his children to the trains. *King Matt the First* is still a very well-known book in Poland and its author is remembered as a great champion of the rights of children.

What inspired Korczak to write *King Matt the First*?

Korczak lived in a tumultuous time. *King Matt* was first published in 1923, in between the First and Second World Wars. He believed in the rights of children and their need for respect and love – themes we can clearly see in the story of King Matt. But he was also keen to question the political ideas and events of his day. Here are a few of the topics that Korczak explored in writing *King Matt the First . . .*

Monarchy: At the start of the story, Matt's country is an absolute monarchy. This means that whoever has inherited the title of king or queen has total power to do whatever he or she pleases. As we see in the book, the weight of tradition and legal processes sometimes serve to keep the king's wishes in check … but only so far. When Matt's ministers try to block him he says: 'Enough. I won't have it, and that's that. I am the king, and I'm going to stay the king.' When they start citing laws to prevent him from doing what he wants he has all his ministers arrested. That is absolute power.

Of course, in real-life situations, child monarchs generally have an adult in charge to take care of the country until they become old enough to rule.

Democracy: During the story, Matt takes the bold decision to give away his power to a democratically elected parliament. At the time that Korczak was writing, the world was a politically turbulent place with monarchies, democracies and dictatorships jostling for position. Poland had abolished its monarchy in 1910. *King Matt* gives an idea of the different sorts of political systems. It helps us to make up our own mind about what might be the best way to govern a country. What do you think of what the sad king says about his democracy?

> It's beautiful, but what does that matter when there are still wars, still poor people, still unhappy people? I ordered that great parliament building built. And nothing changed. Everything's still the same.

War: King Matt is not afraid of going to war at the beginning of the story but he gets a nasty shock when he sees the reality of war for ordinary people. Korczak's story explores whether war is ever worth its costs, and we find out a bit about the logistics of war – the importance of seaports, fortresses, guns, ships, trains, even soldier's boots. We also learn about reparations – money that the winning country can demand from the losing country after a war. Matt decides not to demand reparations, a decision he later comes to regret when the security of his country is threatened. After both the First and Second World Wars, Poland demanded reparations from Germany.

Diplomacy: Matt achieves a diplomatic success when he invites the other kings to his country and puts on a grand firework display. As the Prime Minister says:

> Your Royal Highness has done a great thing without even intending to. Not all conquering is done by going to war. In war, you fight and win and take what you want. But this is a diplomatic victory, which means getting what you need by bargaining, not war. Now we have a seaport, and that is the important thing.

Cultural diversity: You might have noticed how a lot of references to African people in the book are very outdated. Despite its dated language and ideas, *King Matt* is unusual for its positive view of people of all different ethnicities. For example, Klu Klu is Matt's great friend (and potential love interest) and the fact she is African has no impact on

their relationship. Korczak lived in a time when people were much more wary of different races, ethnicities and religions. Korczak himself, as a Jew, was discriminated against, and, as we know, died in an extermination camp. *King Matt* is a story that was meant to challenge European views about people of different races and beliefs. It also challenges the idea (common in the 1920s) that girls are less strong and capable than boys.

Answers to the *King Matt the First* quiz – how did you do?

1) He names Felek the official Royal Court Favourite.

2) The sad king who plays the violin.

3) A mushroom, and who was the first to see it.

4) To get hold of some of the finest animals for his zoo.

5) The cannibal witch doctor.

6) The legend says that in order to make his people give up cannibalism King Bum Drum has to die by either fire or poison – he has chosen fire.

7) She hides herself in a crate with two monkeys.

8) Because they have long hair and wear long dresses.

9) The children will go to work and the adults will go back to school.

10) Twelve wolves are released and run amok through the city.

Visit www.worldofstories.co.uk